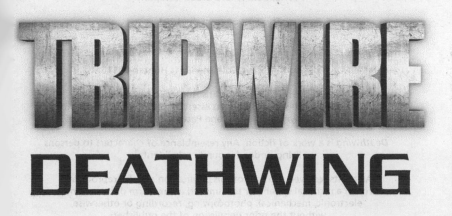

DEATHWING

BY STEVE COLE

AND

CHRIS HUNTER
BOMB-DISPOSAL EXPERT

CORGI BOOKS

TRIPWIRE: DEATHWING
A CORGI BOOK 978 0 552 57339 9
Published in Great Britain by Corgi Books,
an imprint of Random House Children's Books
A Random House Group Company

This edition published 2011

1 3 5 7 9 10 8 6 4 2

The Random House Group Limited supports The Forest Stewardship
Council® (FSC®), the leading international forest-certification organisation.
Our books carrying the FSC label are printed on FSC®-certified paper.
FSC is the only forest-certification scheme supported by the leading
environmental organisations, including Greenpeace. Our
paper procurement policy can be found at
www.randomhouse.co.uk/environment

MIX
Paper from
responsible sources
FSC® C018072

Set in 11/14pt Frutiger by Falcon Oast Graphic Art Ltd.

Corgi Books are published by Random House Children's Books,
61–63 Uxbridge Road, London W5 5SA

www.kidsatrandomhouse.co.uk
www.totallyrandombooks.co.uk
www.randomhouse.co.uk

Addresses for companies within The Random House Group Limited can be
found at: www.randomhouse.co.uk/offices.htm

THE RANDOM HOUSE GROUP Limited Reg. No. 954009

A CIP catalogue record for this book is available from the British Library.

Printed and bound in Great Britain by Clays Ltd, St Ives plc

…at c… …k like a bad day at the o…ce. If som… …le to prevent a major atrocity then I'll take … …ne chin. Every time.'

'And if the good guy… …e too?'

'Everyone is expendable. You know that. Minos and ATLAS can lose battles. What matters is the war.'

Look out for

by Steve Cole and Chris Hunter

'Utterly chilling, edge-of-the-seat stuff'
The Bookbag

'A terrific page-turner of a novel . . . fast paced, littered
with casualties and always enthralling . . . The bomb-
disposal scenes will have you sweating along with Felix'
Writeaway

Also available by Steve Cole:
Z. Rex
Z. Raptor

Also available by Chris Hunter for adult readers:
Eight Lives Down
Extreme Risk

Thanks to Jason Loborik for help
preparing the manuscript.

And thanks also to M. G. Harris
for Mexican guidance.

The Minos Chapter is a wing of the Anti-Terrorist Logistic Assessment Service. Its recruits, drawn from the armed forces of 15 countries, are rigorously trained in a wide range of specialist skills.

Their mission? To turn terrorist tactics back on the terrorists themselves.

All Minos recruits are teenagers.

All of them operate in top secret.

MINOS OPERATOR PROFILE

FILE: CLASSIFIED
Name: Felix James Smith
Operator Passcode: 1179
Operator Status: Active

Operator Role: Entering battlespaces where the disabling and removal of improvised explosive devices is key

Additional training: Tactics, firearms, physical fitness, advanced driving, covert entry techniques, military freefall parachuting, scuba and closed-circuit diving, boat handling and vehicle hotwiring

Age: 15

Additional information: Father, Aiden Christopher Smith, former ATLAS bomb-disposal operative. Killed in Day Zero attack

FILE: CLASSIFIED
Name: Bradley Nathan Rivers
Operator Passcode: 0965
Operator Status: Active

Operator Role: Undercover and covert surveillance duties. Computer 'hacktivist' and electronic security specialist

Additional training: Tactics, firearms, computer programming, advanced 'hack-and-crack' decryption techniques

Age: 15

Additional information: Of US origin (born: New Jersey). Completed ten months of year-long Minos contract

CLASSIFIED INFORMATION

FILE: CLASSIFIED

Name: Classified (Known Alias: 'The Girl')

Operator Passcode: ATLAS resource number 4286

Operator Status: Active

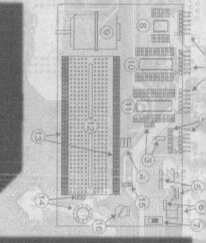

Operator Role: Provide constant support for field operators – co-ordinating operations and data retrieval

Additional training: Strategy, high-speed high-volume data retrieval, tracking skills, high-level computer hacking

Age: 15

Additional information: White female of Eastern European origin. Assigned to ATLAS's shadowy 'tera-head' department; further info restricted

CLASSIFIED INFORMATION

FILE: CLASSIFIED
Name: Hannah Marie Geffen
Operator Passcode: 7205
Operator Status: Active

Operator Role: Undercover and covert surveillance and observation duties. Specialist linguist

Additional training: Foreign languages and cultures, undercover surveillance, tactics, firearms, covert entry techniques

Age: 15 (can pass as an older teenager)

Additional information: Of South African origin

DEATHWING

COUNTDOWN COMMENCING: 28 . . .

This is crazy, thought Felix Smith. *I've dedicated my life to stopping terrorist bomb-makers – and here I am, about to set the explosives myself.*

Cool wind rustled the vegetation that hid him as he took his night-vision goggles and looked down at his target – a newly built laboratory complex in Azcapotzalco, on the northern outskirts of Mexico City. The research due to start at this *Tecnoparque* was described as 'cutting edge', and certainly the clean, angular lines of the buildings looked sharp enough to slice, despite the graininess of his viewfinder. The technology park had taken years to build and cost untold millions.

And now Felix was here to destroy it in seconds – for free.

It was a warm night, but Felix still shivered as he

reached into his backpack to check his gear. The air was wild with the trill of cicadas and other night-time insects; and he feared the cacophony would mask the approach of any security guards who might have spotted him.

Relax, he thought. *You've done your homework. You're good to go.*

For other fifteen-year-olds, homework might be writing essays or solving algebra. For Felix it meant camping out here for two days and nights, observing the comings and goings, and absorbing the feel of the pattern of life. The lab was still a week away from its official opening, but the entire complex was busy with workmen and maintenance crews rushing to finish on time. Trucks came and went, delivering vast banks of machinery and equipment; white-coated technicians swarmed out of fresh-painted receptions and took the stuff away for installation.

But by dusk each night, the complex fell silent, deserted save for a small security team based in a control room away from the main building.

Felix checked his watch. Two a.m.

Time to strike.

He pulled the hood of his dark top over his head, grabbed his pack and picked his way stealthily down the bone-dry hillside towards the laboratory grounds. The path he took was straight, but his thoughts were dancing in circles. Later this week, a lorry-load of primates bred for medical experiments was due to arrive. They would be kept caged in a special facility until scientists were ready to use them in tests. Felix hated the idea of living creatures being used in that way. But he didn't like the idea of using bombs to effect change, either.

Then again, what you think's not important, Felix reflected. At the end of the day he was a boy soldier, an operative of ATLAS – the Anti-Terrorist Logistic Assessment Service – and orders were orders. His mission was to infiltrate the Crusaders for Animal Freedom; a gang of militant extremists who'd killed and maimed dozens with their acts of 'justice for the beast'. *And if trashing this place is what's needed to get into their inner circle, then that's what you do*, he reminded himself. *End of.*

Twenty metres from the chainlink fence that ringed the complex perimeter, Felix crouched down behind a clump of bushes, surveying the grounds beyond. He could see a wireless CCTV camera on a high pole, its gleaming eye staring balefully down.

'Now, let's see what *you're* seeing,' Felix murmured, pulling a handheld camera monitor from his pack. It allowed him to pick up the camera's wireless signal – and sure enough, he could discern the fence and bushes now just as the mechanical lens saw them.

Quickly he reached inside his pack again and felt for a small black box – his Electronic Counter-Measures jammer. The ECM was a genuine life-saver; so many improvised explosive devices were detonated long-range by mobile-phone signals, but this unassuming box jammed transmission, thwarting the bomber. And it would do the same for the video signal from the CCTV camera.

As Felix switched it on, he saw the image on his camera monitor flicker and freeze. He burst forward and sprinted for the fence, smoothly pocketing the monitor before pulling out a pair of wire-cutters. Within moments he was flat on his belly, working the snips upwards through the links at the base of the fence until he had a gap big enough to wriggle through.

Heart slamming itself around his ribcage, he scrambled up the other side, pushed the two sides of the slit-open fence back together and ran over to crouch beneath the camera pole. Then he stowed the snips in his pack and switched off the jammer. On his monitor the image once again flickered, then resumed its dull show of fence and bushes. No alarms. No sound of rushing footsteps.

Security are none the wiser, Felix decided. *Let's keep it that way.*

He moved quietly through the grounds, his mind flashing back to the final days of his intensive training with the Minos Chapter – the shadowy wing of ATLAS that fast-tracked underage operatives for deployment in the war on terror. *Ultimately, the success of any covert op relies on sixty per cent tactics, thirty per cent accurate intelligence and ten per cent luck.*

As of now, I'm relying on luck alone.

When the main lab came into sight at last, Felix felt a swell of relief – a ground-floor window had been left ajar. He'd reasoned that ventilation would be needed in a freshly painted room, and in fact similar open windows graced every storey on the block.

Don't get cocky. That's when you screw up.

Felix fished out a pencil torch and ran over to the window to study the lab's interior. At once he saw a Passive InfraRed Detector mounted on the far wall. Its pyroelectric motion sensors would detect his body heat the moment he climbed inside and trigger the alarm in the security control room – at least it would if it weren't for the ECM jammer. That ought to defeat all PIRs in the immediate area. Felix switched on the little black box, took a deep breath and then pulled himself through the window.

He landed softly, swallowed hard and kept down low on the spotless tiles. The stench of fresh paint was like nails up his nostrils. He did his best to ignore it as he slowly explored the lab, which was full of weird and wonderful equipment. A large fume cupboard stood against one wall – he recognized it from chemistry lessons at school, just as he recognized the little black gas-taps built into the benches and the small kitchen in the corner. He moved through into a sterile white passage studded with grey wooden doors. Steadying his breath, he checked each of them in turn, listening constantly for approaching guards. If he got caught and landed his butt in jail . . .

Only Black Ops spooks at the highest level knew of the Minos Chapter's existence. That was the whole point. Using 'child soldiers' in the war against terror was a hard call for any government to defend, and as a tactic it was only valid if the enemy remained ignorant. If the bomb-emplacers realized that the homeless teen loitering in the park was secretly recording their plans and conversations . . . If the terrorist paymaster guessed that the punk kid burglar they'd surprised in their flat had been actually lifting fingerprints or planting listening devices . . .

If Minos was ever exposed, its young agents would be placed in deadly danger and a dozen governments would face the mother of all shit-storms from press and public. Small wonder then that any president or prime minister would deny all knowledge of the Chapter and leave its agents to sink or swim.

Felix knew he was on his own.

Finally he found what he'd been searching for – a door marked MAINTENANCE STORE at the end of the passageway. He opened it and flinched from the acrid smell of bleach. It was a good-sized room lined with crowded shelves. *An Aladdin's cave for cleaners*, he thought, *and for any bomb-maker worth his salt.*

Time to get creative.

Felix began scouring the shelves for anything he could use to make an IED – Improvised Explosive Device. He knew you could make a bomb from pretty much anything – if you knew what you were doing. He scanned the list of ingredients on every single container, searching mental databanks for names and formulas that might signal success.

Eventually Felix left the store with a bottle of paint remover and a plastic carton of vile-smelling disinfectant. *Now all I need is acid*, he thought, and jogged lightly back to the lab he'd explored earlier. He soon found the refrigerated space below the fume cabinet was neatly lined with etched-glass bottles full of colourless liquids. He selected hydrochloric acid, put it beside the paint cleaner and disinfectant, and blew out a long breath.

He had all he needed to make MEKP – methyl ethyl ketone peroxide, a super-powerful liquid explosive. It was extremely dangerous to handle, but that same sensitivity made it disturbingly easy to detonate. Gingerly Felix unscrewed the lid of the paint remover and carefully poured an amount into a 500ml glass beaker. He decanted some disinfectant into another then put both into the fridge beneath the fume cabinet to cool.

It chafed at Felix's nerves having to stay here even longer, but success depended on doing things right. As he waited, he drew a deep breath and wiped the sweat from his eyes. After a few minutes he took out the chilled beakers and cautiously added the paint remover to the disinfectant before slowly stirring it.

Now for the really fun part.

Delicately, Felix opened the bottle of hydrochloric acid and added it to his concoction, drop by drop. He prayed the mixture wouldn't get too hot. If it rose above five degrees, what was left of the lab would be redecorated in shades of claret.

The mixture separated into two layers; a thick oily layer on the top, and a white, thinner liquid beneath. The oily part was the MEKP, and Felix quickly poured it off into another glass beaker.

We're in business.

Felix carefully lifted the beaker of MEKP and walked slowly towards the small kitchen area he'd passed before – what he needed now was a kettle to bring events to the boil. He put the beaker down gently, poured a little water into the kettle and then lowered the glass vessel inside before snapping the lid firmly shut. Then he ran back into the main lab and started turning on gas taps. A steady hissing insinuated itself into the air. Almost at once, the smell of gas started to dizzy his head.

'Time to get out of here,' Felix murmured. He took a last look round at the pristine lab, crossed back to the kitchen and flicked the switch on the kettle. Then he grabbed his pack, pulled his hood back over his head and ran back to the open window and swung himself out. He heard the first stirrings of the boiling kettle add to the snake-like chorus behind him. It would force the MEKP's temperature well beyond safety and his homemade explosive would detonate, in turn igniting the gas-rich air and then . . .

Keeping his head down, Felix sprinted away across the dark grounds. Within moments he'd set off the alarms he'd so carefully avoided on his way in. They shrieked at the night like frightened animals, but it didn't matter – secrecy was no longer his priority. He knew he'd seem little more than a faceless blur on CCTV; all that mattered now was distance.

Don't sweat it, Security, thought Felix, flying over the short grass, bracing himself as best he could. *I don't reckon you'll even have time to leave your control room before—*

All thoughts shattered as a blinding, searing flash froze the night sky. Felix felt his eardrums pop as a devastating shockwave smashed him to the ground. He turned and stared as a cyclone of fire and shrapnel, flying glass and debris roared into the air. Distorted metal roof panels spiralled skywards and rubble rained down, tearing chunks from the pristine lawns as they landed.

And then there was only the idiot clamour of the surviving alarms, muffled in his ringing ears. He saw the twisted shadow of the lab complex behind him, shrouded in acrid-smelling smoke and dust.

Job done, thought Felix in a daze, catching high, excited shouts in Spanish from somewhere beyond the choking smoke-cloud. Snatching up his pack, he resumed his run for the split in the fence, legs trembling and ego singing, a mess of emotions as he chased after safety, running into the darkness.

COUNTDOWN CONTINUES:
...27...

It took some time, but Felix managed to calm his head-long flight, pacing himself for the long slog ahead. In his black joggers and Converses he hoped he looked more like someone in training than a criminal on the run. He pulled out his iPhone and quickly texted the only contact in his book:

Did it.

Then he ran on, through spray-painted canyons floored with cracked asphalt, choked with trash and traffic. The air stank of spice, garbage and diesel. The few working streetlamps gave light enough to hint at the dangers lurking in vacant lots and derelict buildings, no more. Glancing up he saw the crescent moon shine like a perfect fingernail through the canopy of cables strung between buildings and telegraph poles.

Felix quickened his pace. He knew from his premission briefing that Mexico City was one of the world's danger capitals, a megacity that trailed only Seoul and Tokyo for the sheer numbers crammed into its colossal urban sprawl. Hundreds of murders and kidnappings happened all over, every day. You could quite easily disappear and never be seen again.

His phone chimed and buzzed in his pocket. Felix slowed down, pulled it out, read the message.

Just heard reports. Wow! Come to 4a Dr Juan Ignacio St. Colonia Doctores. Use password. X

'Gotcha,' Felix murmured.

Things were moving. He didn't know where the hell *Colonia Doctores* was, but after two nights in a crummy hostel in Obrera, anything would be a step up.

Suddenly he heard a catcall from up ahead. A few kids around his own age, shabbier even than the corner they stood on, were gesturing through a cloud of smoke and neon. As they started towards him, Felix swore inwardly. They'd obviously spotted his iPhone and decided that three against one was decent enough odds. He quickly glanced in the other direction, wondering if he could outrun them and lose himself in one of the myriad dingy alleyways that snaked off from the deserted street. *Can't afford trouble. Can't waste any time.* If he missed his assignation, all his efforts on this task, all the weeks off-grid – undercover, or 'going grey' as the spooks called it – would count for nothing.

Too late.

The eldest-looking kid ran ahead of the others, lashing out wildly with his fist. Skidding to a stop, Felix easily deflected the lazy blow with his wrist and countered with a lightning-fast punch to his attacker's face. Crying out, the kid stopped dead, held up one hand to his bloodied nose, his free arm swatting the air aimlessly. *You started this*, thought Felix, *now I've got to finish it, fast*. He grabbed the flailing fist, swung the boy round and sent him sprawling headfirst into a crumbling wall. Then he squared up to the other two kids. Their faces had visibly blanched, even in the feeble half-light of the street.

'Still wanna mess?' Felix snarled.

As he started towards them, the boys turned and scuttled back to their corner as though nothing had happened, leaving their friend groaning on the ground. Felix glanced quickly around the murky street, praying the encounter hadn't drawn any undue attention.

He sprinted off again. *Like anyone around here would care anyway*.

As he ran, his fingers strayed to the tiny pendant he wore around his neck in the shape of a stylized M – it contained his miniaturized tracker, a device that sent his precise location to an ultra-secure Minos satellite.

I need to find my way to Doctores, fast.

Felix paused on a scruffy, near-deserted boulevard. The night's cover was creeping away as the first hints of dawn greyed the streets, leaving him exposed. He looked all around. A beggar was trudging slowly along the pavement, collecting trash with his bare hands. An old woman was opening a grubby food stall, ready for the early morning shift-workers. No visible threats.

Time for a shortcut.

Ignoring the iPhone, he pulled another, cheaper phone from his rucksack. *'Smartphones are minicomputers that keep a hidden log of anything you do,'* his spook instructors had taught him. *'If you need to call in, use only pay-as-you-go mobiles – do not register them and bin them after one use.'*

In moments Felix was dialling the number of the teraheads – ATLAS's smart and shadowy support staff, named for the terabytes of data they retained and reeled out on cue. He knew they'd be keeping constant track of his movements, ready to advise or provide situation updates. And one of them in particular . . .

'State your name and passcode.'

Result – straight through to the Girl.

'Felix Smith, one-one-seven-nine,' he murmured. 'How're you doing?'

'You've been running like the wind.' Her voice was clipped and east European. 'Were you pursued?'

Felix savoured the trace of concern. He had only met the Girl once but for some reason her dark eyes and black bobbed hair had become key fixtures of his daydream landscape. 'Negative,' he breathed, as the beggar meandered past. 'No pursuit. I need to know, was . . . was anyone hurt?'

'No casualties reported,' the Girl said. 'Your explosion caused a chain reaction that wrote off a neighbouring building, but luckily it was empty.'

Felix felt his heart thump a little steadier. 'Thank God.'

'It's good you got out of Azcapotzalco as quickly as you did,' she went on. 'The whole place is swarming with police now. Have you received instructions from the CAF for your post-task rendezvous?'

'An address in Doctores. Four-a, Doctor Juan Ignacio Street.'

'That neighbourhood's a dump, well off the tourist track. I'd better guide you. More discreet than you checking a map book.' The Girl paused, and her voice seemed to grow a fraction frostier. 'Can't keep Chessa waiting, can we?'

Felix frowned. Chessa Lopez had provided his way into the core of the CAF cell – a sixteen-year-old Latina whose older sister was tight with the pressure group's founder, Gregor Manton. 'I could almost believe you were jealous.'

'Jealous of you spending weeks undercover in the skuzziest parts of Colorado, getting to know terrorist roaches?'

'Chessa's not so bad. She's got some pretty militant views, but that's 'cos her big sister's fed them to her all her life. Shifted from care home to care home, "the two of us against the world" . . .' Felix paused, aware of the Girl's silence and that his tongue had run away with him a little. 'I mean, she's crazy, of course,' he backtracked quickly. 'But, you know . . . she's had it tough.'

'Shall we get on?' the Girl said briskly. 'You want to head west along Avenue Luis Yuren. It should be just across the road from you.'

'I see it.' Felix started walking, glad to change the subject. 'Nice graffiti on the walls. What does *Hoy es un buen dìa para morir* mean?'

'"Today is a good day to die",' the Girl said drily. 'You'd better get running again. You've another twelve kilometres to cover.'

'Won't I look suspicious? Won't the police be after me?'

'We're monitoring their radios. I'll guide you along a route that avoids patrol cars and all CCTV cameras. As far as the authorities are concerned, you'll have vanished like a ghost.'

How reassuring, thought Felix, setting off again at a fast jog. The exotic-sounding place names – Huitzilihuitl, Xochiquetzal, De Los Misterios – tripped off the Girl's tongue while Felix dodged the traffic at huge intersections and raced down quiet, eerie streets lined with dried palms and dusty windows. Dense, sticky smells of taco and tamale rose from lonely stands with hand-daubed signs and plastic tarps for roofs. Felix felt a sharp pang of hunger, but he decided that would-be animal activists didn't show up for group meetings with their breath stinking of spicy beef. His stomach grumbled but his feet kept bumping him along.

The seamier neighbourhoods began to dominate, with their low-rise office blocks and rent-by-the-hour hotels. Heavy bars and shutters shielded most shops, apartments and parking garages. Felix began to feel the entire city was a sprawling prison with rows of bare, spindly trees looming over him like twisted jailers.

'You're only a couple of kilometres from Doctores now,' the Girl advised. 'At the roundabout, take the fourth exit onto Paseo de la Reforma. Then you want to hang first left – it'll bring you to Juan Ignacio Street.'

'Got it.'

'Now, wipe the call register and dispose of this phone,' the Girl said curtly. 'I'll advise Zane you're en route to the CAF rendezvous. He's staying in Milpa Alta to the south of Mexico City, and wants your report as soon as you can safely get away.'

Felix pictured his unorthodox handler – the big, black, bluff and brilliant Zane Samuel – and wasn't sure whether to feel glad or intimidated. 'How do I contact him?'

'You don't. When you can, head for the health spa at the Villanueva Hotel in Tecaxtitla. It's about thirty-five kilometres away from Doctores – the distance will give you ample opportunity to lose any tails. We'll track your movements through your pendant so Zane will know when to meet you at the pool.'

'Some people you really don't want to see in Speedos,' Felix quipped. But he knew the rationale – it was straight out of the good spook's handbook. *If you're off-grid and want a conversation face to face, meet your contact in a public swimming baths. The noise and echoes make it pretty much impossible for your voice to be recorded.* 'Thanks for your help. I'm glad we talked.' He paused. 'I've been feeling kind of cut off from Minos. It's good to be reminded who I really am. I just wish I knew a bit more about who *you* are. I mean, surely you could at least tell me your name?'

'You don't give your laptop a name, do you?' she said

simply. 'Anonymity is standard procedure. I'm a resource to you, Felix. And you are a user to me. You're clear on that?'

'Whatever you say.' Felix felt a prickle of hurt pride. 'I mean, you'd know. You're the tera-head.'

'Yes, I am.' She sounded husky and resigned. 'Good luck, Felix. Out.'

The phone went silent. Felix dropped it down the nearest drain with a sudden pang of self-pity. In a city of twenty-two million he felt horribly alone. But then, ever since his dad died, hadn't it always been that way? His mum had her own life in Australia, and he'd walked out on his loathsome old aunt in London to enlist. He had no other family, and Minos didn't like you making too many friends. Relationships weakened your resolve. Care could leave you compromised.

All you could do was just get on with the job.

'Soon I'll have the CAF for company,' he muttered, jogging off again. 'And that's where my problems *really* start.'

By the time Felix had threaded his way through the streets of Doctores, the sun was up and hovering low over the horizon, its disc distorted by the smog-haze shrouding the city. His clothes were wet with sweat and he was feeling the burn from his exertions. *Getting out of shape*, he realized. *Got to sort that when all this is over . . . How optimistic am I?*

Now Felix looked across the busy street at the shabby apartment block where Chessa was presumably waiting.

He supposed a group like the CAF wouldn't blow cause-money on decent accommodation. But who else would be waiting with her? Zane had briefed Felix that the CAF had money-laundering links to a big Mexican car-theft ring – 'chop shops', where stolen cars were stripped for spares and sold abroad to Africa or South America – a racket that in turn was linked to the largest and best-organized terrorist group in existence: Orpheus.

Orpheus had emerged dominant among the ragtag of twenty-first-century terror cells. It had absorbed some and worked together with others to create a kind of covert supergroup dedicated to the overthrow of the old political order – and the removal of Western 'interference' in the affairs of other countries. Since Day Zero – the destruction of Heathrow Airport, along with thousands of lives, over two years ago – their targets had proliferated and their terror tactics grown more audacious.

The subsequent struggle to subdue Orpheus by any means necessary had birthed the Minos Chapter – and brought him here.

He tried to think himself into character – *Felix Smith, misguided teen idealist hitting back at the society that failed him*. He prayed that his 'legend' – the details of his cover story set up by Minos head-sheds – was watertight; by now, the CAF chiefs must surely have analysed it to death. And if they suspected he was fake, a spy trying to infiltrate their organization . . .

Who'll cry over one more murder in Mexico City?

Felix crossed the street quickly through a gap in the

traffic then climbed the steps to the building's front door. He rang the buzzer for apartment 4a.

A deep Spanish voice hissed through the intercom. '¿Quién es?'

'Uh . . . It's Felix. Felix Smith.' He straightened, put more swagger in his voice as he delivered the code phrase Chessa had given him. 'Justice for the beast.'

The door buzzed open to reveal a dark and dingy hallway.

Hoy es un buen día para morir, thought Felix, and went inside.

hallway.

... **26** ...

The hallway was all stink and shadows. A cloud of flies
swooped and buzzed at the new arrival like tiny gossips.
Felix swatted them away and jogged up bare, protesting
steps. Threadbare drapes were still pulled shut against the
morning sunshine; it was cooler in here and he found his
sweat-soaked clothes now clung uncomfortably.

A man was waiting in an open doorway on the fourth
floor – tall and lean in baggy jeans that sagged around his
hips exposing black boxers, and a sleeveless T-shirt that
showed his arms, displaying muscles and tattoos in equal
measure. His head was shaved, adding emphasis to the
thick brows that squared his eyelids in an arrogant glower.
It was almost a caricature of the classic *cholo* look –
Mexican gangster style.

Languidly the man called back through the doorway
in a heavy Spanish accent. 'Hey, *Fresa*. Your date showed.'

'Felix?' Chessa's voice, high and demure with an

American twang, cut through the heavy air. 'Send him in, Beni.'

Beni stepped aside like a belligerent bouncer to let Felix inside, followed him in and then closed the door behind him. The dark apartment reeked of spice and cigarette smoke; Cuban music played from a radio in the small, filthy kitchen, losing a battle of noise with the blare of the TV from another room. A tall, skinny girl with dyed red hair and olive skin flitted out from one of the doorways. Her pierced navel glinted out from between a blue crop top and skinny jeans.

Felix smiled at her. 'Hey, Chessa.'

'Hey, yourself.' Though Chessa was sixteen, her wide dark eyes shone with a child's delight. 'The news channels are all over what you did. Unbelievable!'

Felix shrugged and smiled back. 'I told you I'd sort it.'

'You must want in with the CAF real bad,' said Beni, eyeing Felix closely. 'Or maybe you really want inside the *Fresa*, yes?'

'You're disgusting, Beni.' Chessa's cheeks reddened. 'Don't you have a truck to go organize?'

'And two cars to go with it.' Beni shrugged. 'It's all right. *El Piraña*'s got his generals on it.'

'El who?' Felix wondered.

'That's me. The piranha.' He grinned, revealing a mouth of broken yellow teeth. 'I see the unwary, I bite.'

What comic book did you get that from? thought Felix. 'Wow, OK . . . I'll remember that.'

'You better, *cabrón*.' With a low belch Beni sauntered

into a gloomy room dominated by a large bed and closed the door behind him.

'Nice guy.' Felix raised an eyebrow. 'What's with the "Fresa" stuff?'

Chessa rolled her eyes. 'Stupid slang. Well, it's Spanish for strawberry, but . . . He's basically calling me a stuck-up bitch 'cos I won't go into his room with him. He's like, "I'm the piranha, the king of the chop-shops, these streets are mine, these rooms are mine, you could be mine too." And I'm like, "No way, cheese-ass . . . My sister's tight with Gregor Manton – you screw with me, you get the CAF's boss coming down on you . . ."'

So Beni's big in car crime, Felix thought. *Must run the ring with links to Orpheus.* He nodded at Chessa as she chattered on, describing her long night spent waiting and fending off Beni's advances. *Zane was right to make her my target*, he thought. *A loose mouth – the perfect way to learn more about the CAF.*

If the inner circle accepts me.

'Anyway, why am I telling you this?' Chessa's smile was wide and lopsided. 'You did it, Felix! The whole lab trashed. Justice for the beast! Manton's going to be so pleased with you . . .'

Let's hope so.

Her perfect brow furrowed suddenly, as she pulled a phone from her back pocket. 'He said he'd be here by now,' she mused, checking the time. 'Must have got held up.'

'He?'

'Manton.'

Somehow, Felix hadn't expected to meet the man himself so soon. 'I, er . . . I thought you were just hiding me till the heat died down and we could get back to Colorado,' he said, as nonchalantly as he could.

Smiling, she shook her head and tugged Felix into a living room sparsely furnished in mismatched styles. A pair of dining chairs formed a makeshift stand for an oversized TV in one corner, its vast screen a grainy wash of colour. Felix saw an aerial view of a smoking stack of debris, cops crawling all over it, the live pictures streaming from the cockpit of a local news copter. He didn't recognize the scrolling Spanish text, but he recognized his handiwork well enough.

'Just look at that!' Chessa threw her skinny arms around him, laughing, excited. Felix hugged her back, a little heavy-hearted, then broke off the embrace. A key part of his task had been to get Chessa's trust – a useful intelligence asset – and exploit it. But over the last few weeks he'd come to realize he really did like her. She'd flown here from Manton's base somewhere in Colorado to keep tabs on Felix because her passport was clean; she had no proven involvement with extremist groups. Being able to travel freely made her an asset to the CAF – and Felix's own cover story had been designed to maximize his own desirability.

But now his talents had been tested and his achievement was on display, would Manton take him into his confidence? He guessed he'd find out pretty soon.

'You must be stoked after doing that.' Chessa smiled

up at him. 'I mean, oh my God! One-man wrecking crew! Are you stoked?'

'I was stoked enough to run sixteen kilometres to get here.' Felix sank into a worn-out armchair. 'Now I'm kind of running on empty.'

'You want a drink? Smoke?'

'Just some water. Please.'

Chessa grinned. 'I got a bottle. Coming right up.'

As she left the room, Felix heard the muffled sound of the buzzer downstairs. He felt a chill shiver through him. *Here we go, then*.

'Beni,' Chessa yelled from the kitchen. Felix thumbed the remote and turned off the TV so he could hear. 'Beni – that must be Manton – let him in, huh?'

Beni emerged from his room and ambled towards the main door. He flicked the intercom switch and muttered a few words into it, but Felix could barely make out the crackled response with the kitchen radio still blaring away.

As Chessa came running back in, Felix heard heavy footsteps on the stairs, followed by a tall, looming figure at the half-open door.

'Hey, amigo.' Beni shook hands with the man, inclined his head respectfully. 'Glad you could show.'

'Greg!' called Chessa. 'Good to see you. How're you doing?'

'Hello, Chessa.' The voice sounded American but was hardened with a Germanic edge; thin and reedy, it didn't seem to fit such a large man. 'I'm doing good.'

So this is him, Felix thought, gripped by a strange

calm as he rose from his chair. *The big man. The way into the CAF.*

Or the way out of everything.

Manton strode into the room, stopping a couple of metres away from Felix. Gregor Manton was an arresting sight, a big, gaunt bear of a man in his thirties with close-cropped red hair. His hawkish features were peppered with moles, as though little black seeds were sprouting from the freckled flesh. Behind horn-rimmed glasses his intense blue eyes betrayed not only intelligence but a fanatical fervour. In his crumpled linen suit, he almost managed to exude an air of respectability – except of course that Felix knew he was wanted internationally for the murder of five people linked to animal experiments, not to mention killing the wife and child of a university dean in a botched car bombing. As mastermind of the CAF he was also wanted on several counts of blackmail, extortion, criminal threatening and assault.

All that and he says, 'I'm doing good.' But Felix knew Manton believed absolutely that his behaviour was justified; the people he targeted sanctioned the torture and murder of animals. If innocents sometimes got in the way, it was regrettable but effective propaganda. The law was slow to listen to appeals, but acts of terror spoke loud and clear.

Manton's piercing eyes were fixed on Felix. 'So this is our new boy wonder?' His voice was casual but assured. 'Please, take a seat, Felix, you must be tired out.' He gestured to a tatty armchair. 'Turn it round to face me.'

Felix did as he was told while Manton sat down

himself on a stool and gave Beni a pointed look. 'I'd like you to stay for this conversation. As we discussed.'

Beni grimaced, gave the briefest of nods, and moved past Felix towards the sofa as if to sit down. Then suddenly he darted sideways; by the time Felix clocked the hunting knife in the tattooed hand it was at his throat. Beni smiled through sharp, nicotine-stained teeth. 'Nothing personal.'

Felix held absolutely still, fear scattering hard through his thoughts. *He knows. Manton knows I'm a fake.* He felt the pressure of the blade at his Adam's apple as he swallowed hard. If it broke the skin it could slice through an artery. Game over.

'Beni?' Chessa's face was caught between shock and bewilderment. 'What are you doing?'

'He's following my instructions,' said Manton mildly, regarding Felix with a mix of suspicion and intrigue. 'You did a good job, Felix. What did you use for explosives?'

'I . . .' Felix took a deep calming breath. *If Manton really wanted you dead, he'd have had killed you on sight. He must just be suspicious. You've got to convince him.* 'I cooked up a jar of MEKP inside the lab. It's an organic peroxide.'

'You improvised an explosive device that powerful?'

'I was aiming to impress,' Felix reminded him.

Manton's cold blue eyes narrowed a little. 'I've been looking into your history. A colourful affair, wouldn't you say?'

'I guess.' A moment's doubt pricked him harder than

the knifepoint. If ATLAS had left any chinks in his off-grid armour, he was dead.

'So, Felix,' Manton went on. 'Your dad was an ATO, a bomb-disposal expert?'

'An Ammunition Technical Officer,' Felix agreed, steeling himself; a part of his legend was a hatred for authority, his father included. 'And, God, didn't we all know about it – Aiden Smith, superman! He was so determined I was going to grow up just like him, a credit to society, the big hero . . . I was brought up making and defusing all kinds of IEDs.'

Manton nodded. 'Your father was killed on Day Zero, yes?'

'Yeah. He was defusing a bomb beneath Heathrow.' Felix felt sick at the all-too-real memories. *God, I miss you, Dad.* 'It was actually a come-on – Orpheus planted a whole load of dummy IEDs in the local area to make sure as many ATOs as possible were taken out in the main impact.'

Manton displayed no emotion. 'So . . . you must hate Orpheus?'

'No.' Felix felt sweat prickling against the cold blade at his neck. 'I can see where they're coming from.' He heard the spook's sonorous voice in his head: *You must try to believe the lies you're telling – picture yourself in the life you've embroidered and then recount what you see . . .* 'Force is the only way to make people listen.'

'But they killed your father.'

Felix looked Manton in the eyes. 'My dad was an asshole. He made out he was in bomb disposal to save lives but the only thing he cared about was the rush.' *I'm so sorry, Dad.* 'He just wanted me to toe the line. *His line.'*

'So then, why did you follow in his footsteps and join the army?'

"Cos they dropped the joining-up age to fourteen in the UK after Day Zero – and I couldn't wait to ditch school.'

Manton steepled his fingers. 'I understand you were discharged from the army after eight months for blowing up the officers' mess.'

'That's right.' *The hell it is – I was actually fast-tracked onto the Minos operators' advanced training course.* 'I'd had enough of being told what to do by murdering hypocrites. I watched them demonstrate gas weapons on a cage full of dogs.'

'Scum,' Chessa muttered. 'Eating animals is bad enough, but *that* . . .'

'We had to watch them die in agony. Beagles, they were . . .' Felix trailed off. The incident was pure fiction, but he had pictured it in his head so often it seemed almost real. 'I had to teach the officers the error of their ways. *Boom.* They didn't like it.'

Manton's expression softened just a little. 'I don't suppose they did. What happened then?'

Felix took another deep breath, and the litany of falsehoods went on. He recounted how he'd been caught by CCTV footage and booted out of the army. No education, zero prospects. Manton listened in stony silence as Felix conjured the perfect image of a disaffected teenager with time on his hands and hate in his heart.

'This one time, I tried to set free some dogs from the local pound.' Felix knew Manton had done much the same as a boy – Zane had figured that if the CAF's leader recognized something of his young self in Felix it might help him buy the whole legend. 'They were healthy dogs. They were going to be put down, and no one seemed to care . . . But I screwed up. Set off an alarm, almost got caught. I knew I needed to train myself properly if I was ever going to make a difference to something.'

Manton appeared unmoved. 'And you thought moving to your uncle's place in Colorado would achieve that?'

'Didn't have much choice,' said Felix. 'My mum moved to Australia years back, left me with an aunt who hated my guts. She didn't want me in the house.' *That's true, anyway.* 'When she found I was making bombs in my bedroom, she freaked. It was either call the police and make a scandal, or send me to live with my uncle in the States. But he was cool with that.' *Mainly because he's a GI5 spook in deep cover who's been off-grid for nine years.* Felix pushed reality aside again. 'He runs a metal-works. Has his own workshop.'

'Which you used to build *better* home-made bombs,' Manton concluded.

'We know he did, Greg,' Chessa said, eyes still glued to Beni's knife. "Cos Jeff found that one he left at the state zoo—'

'That's *enough*, Chessa.' Manton's voice stayed quiet but the emphasis indicated his displeasure.

Felix feigned surprised indignation at this revelation. Zane had received intelligence that the CAF were targeting the Springs County Zoo on that night, so Felix had been sure to plant a faulty bomb there first, knowing full well that Manton's men would discover it.

'You were careless,' Manton went on coldly. 'We traced the components you used straight to your uncle's workshop. We watched him – and he led us to *you*.'

Of course I was 'careless' – you had to find me so I could get involved in your business. But Felix pushed away those thoughts. It was Oscar time. 'Wait a second. Chessa . . .' He looked at her with all the hurt he could muster. 'Is that why you came up to me at that café? Why you spent so many days hanging with me? You pretended to like me so you could check me out – for him?'

'I . . . I'm sorry, Felix.' Chessa looked upset, but Felix ignored a tug of guilt. 'Greg needed to know more about you. And you and me, we're, like, near enough the same age and so—'

'I get it. Don't worry.' He glared at Manton. 'Chessa said that if I proved myself I could join up. Well, I've hauled my butt to Mexico, stayed in a hostel for two nights and trashed that lab for you. I wasn't expecting interrogation at knifepoint as a reward.'

Manton leaned forward menacingly. 'And I wasn't expecting an explosives expert to fall into my lap at exactly the time I need one. Particularly one so young and capable.'

'He's not much younger than me,' Chessa said quietly. 'I'm capable, aren't I?'

'You're Coral's sister. You're committed.' Manton's gaze didn't waver from Felix. 'But this one . . .'

'I think it's just luck his bomb went off,' hissed Beni. Leering, he pressed the blade harder against Felix's flesh. 'Dumb luck.'

Manton respects strength and commitment. It's time to assert myself here. Felix closed his eyes, tried to centre himself – then flashed his left hand up and twisted hard on Beni's wrist. The *cholo* gasped and dropped the knife. In a blur of movement, Felix caught the knife by the hilt with his free hand, pushed up from the armchair, pivoted round on his left foot and kicked Beni in the guts with the right. The big man staggered backwards and slammed against the wall.

Manton sprang to his feet and Beni started forward. Felix raised the knife in warning, then hesitated. *Can't seem too slick, too trained.* He turned and tossed the blade behind the TV. 'If we keep this up, someone's going to get hurt.'

Beni swore in Spanish and lunged at Felix, who raised his arms to defend himself. But there was no need. Manton grabbed Beni and hauled him back. 'All right. Leave the fool alone.'

'But he just attacked me,' Beni protested.

Manton's look was withering. 'I was talking to Felix.'

Felix felt a thrill of triumph but did his best to act unbothered. 'I'm sorry if I've come at a bad time for the CAF. If you don't want to use me, then fine. I'll keep going on my own.' He glanced at Beni. 'But I don't like people trying to push me around.'

Beni snorted. Then, lip still curled, he slouched out of the room.

Manton moved closer and Felix felt almost transfixed by the intensity of his gaze. 'So . . . an angry, compassionate young man will do anything to join the crusade against animal cruelty, hmm?'

'That's right.'

'How fortunate that we've found each other at this time.' Manton half smiled. 'With our previous explosives expert . . . unattainable, Coral is on her way here with Deep. They'll clue you in on the next job.'

'You . . .' Felix's pulse quickened. 'You mean I'm in?'

'I think I can help you channel your destructive urges.' Manton's black-scattered face broke into an unexpected grin. 'We must have justice for the beast.'

'Justice for the beast,' Chessa echoed obediently. Her smile was uncertain, fragile. 'What's the job?'

'You'll all be needed. Tonight.'

'So soon?'

'We're working to a timetable,' was all Manton would say. 'And no more improvising this time, Felix. Deep will bring you proper materials to work with.' His smile faded. 'He's a competent deputy; he'll look after you – I don't want to lose another bomb expert quite so soon.'

Chessa frowned. 'Aren't you coming with us?'

'I have other business.' He checked his digital watch. 'A very important meeting.' He strode out of the room to the front door. Then he turned back, his pale eyes narrowing. 'I suggest you get some rest, Felix. Recover your strength. I'm sure Chessa will take care of you . . .'

He closed the door softly behind him. His footsteps receded. A few seconds later the door to the apartment block slammed shut with a bang. Only then did Felix release a long, shaky breath.

He felt Chessa wrap her arms around him.

'You're one of us now! That's, like, so amazing!' Her eyes were agleam. 'I . . . I'm sorry you got hurt, and that I didn't tell you the truth straight away when I met you, but—'

'Forget it.' Felix pulled away from her embrace. 'I'm going out. I could do with some air.'

Chessa's face fell. 'Couldn't you stay?' She fiddled with the hem of her top. 'Beni's mad now, and Greg said you should rest – he won't like it if Coral and Deep come and you're not here.'

'Well, I'm sure you'll tell him all about it just as soon as you can,' Felix retorted. 'That's what you do, isn't it?'

'Wait!' Chessa protested. 'C'mon, Felix . . .'

Ignoring her, he stalked from the room. He had to get out and meet with Zane, and feigning anger with Chessa was the easiest excuse he could think of.

It wasn't only her eyes he felt on him as he left. Glancing back up the stairs, he saw Beni staring sullenly from the darkened apartment, the tip of his lit cigarette a bright warning red.

Just for a moment, it was like staring down the laser sight on an assault rifle. One aiming straight at his head.

. . . 25 . . .

Felix cooled his heels outside Beni's apartment building for a few minutes. He was glad to glimpse Chessa watching from the window; now she wouldn't think he was trying to trail Manton.

I wish someone was, he thought. *What's this meeting he's got that's so important?*

Realizing that if he lingered much longer Chessa might come down after him, Felix hurried off, making his way across the city as erratically as possible.

First he took one of the special green-and-white bikes available as part of the city's fight against pollution. He had been told by the spooks that riding a bicycle was one of the best ways to avoid being followed; it was too fast for anyone on foot to keep up, and too slow for a car to trail without drawing a ton of attention.

A familiar thrill of danger tugged at his chest. *My first time in deep cover and it might finally be paying off.* He cycled over cracked asphalt, passing rows and rows of cars jammed in traffic. He clocked the drivers' faces, and the resignation and frustration there reminded him of his first weeks on this assignment.

Felix had busted his hand badly during his last mission, and there was no way he could be tasked on IED disposal duties for several weeks. So instead, he'd been trained up for this undercover mission. Becoming a real spy had sounded attractive at first – until he'd realized how much boring practical work was involved. How much time he'd have to spend alone, pretending to be someone he wasn't.

He whizzed on, the sun glaring down on him, thinking back to those first weeks in Colorado – getting used to the thinner air, hand slowly healing, mind slowly curdling as he worked dead-end jobs by day and spent each night poring over his legend with his 'uncle' Pete.

Pete was a sound bloke; he'd tried to put Felix at his ease, even though he was clearly worried about taking on someone so green. '*Screw this up, mate, and we could both wind up dead—*'

Felix braked hard as a taxi cut him up, narrowly avoiding a collision. 'Roger that, Pete,' he muttered shakily, setting off again. 'I'm doing my best.'

But then there were times when he missed the boredom of those early days off-grid, washing dishes in the diner where Chessa and her sister drank coffee and picked at veggie food. He remembered how his fingers had ached as he'd built that bomb at the zoo for Manton to find, and the electric moment that Chessa had first approached him a few days later. He thought of the way they'd talked and drunk together late at night. He'd been nervous of giving himself away; she'd misread that as shyness in her company, and she'd thought him sweet.

'*I don't bite*,' she'd told him, smiling. '*Not like my sister . . .* she *bites.*'

'Amen to that,' Felix murmured, remembering his first meeting with Coral. Smart and self-educated, she acted more like an overprotective mum to Chessa than a sister – the mum neither of them had ever known. God help the guy who ever tried to come between them.

God help me, thought Felix.

After he had cycled a couple of kilometres south he ditched the bike and caught a Metro train. It was crowded and stifling hot, but at least he could rest a little. Music blared from the backpack of a pirate CD seller as he hawked his merchandise. As the train passed from station to station other would-be salesmen boarded and departed in an endless stream: old men selling superglue and boys with dirty faces peddling warm cans of soda. Felix forced his way off his carriage several times at different stations, only to get back on again a few carriages down. If anyone from the CAF was following him, he wasn't going to make it easy for them.

After a stifling hour on the blue line, Felix got off at a station called Taxqueña and had no problem finding a green and white taxi that would take him to Milpa Alta. The borough was far more rural than downtown Mexico City, the temperature cooler thanks to a higher altitude, and amazing views of mountains and volcanoes made up for the lines of scruffy houses leaning lazily in the morning sunlight.

Felix covered the last kilometre or so on foot, weary but still wary as he entered the air-conditioned reception and made his way to the second-floor spa. Feet aching, he bought a pair of swim shorts from the assistant and helped himself to a beige towel that might once have been white. Then he went through to the pool. It was all but empty, and from the stink of bleach and the cloudy water Felix could guess why. But with a thrill of relief and excitement he saw Zane was there doing lengths, his powerful crawl propelling him through the lanes. Fatigue forgotten, Felix dropped into the shallow end and waited as his handler closed the distance between them.

'Hey,' said Felix simply.

Zane rose up from the water like a dark leviathan and pulled off his nose clip. 'Felix!' He bared his teeth in a wide grin. 'About time you showed. The chlorine in this damn water's stripping my throat.'

'God, sir, I'm glad to see you.'

'Sure you are.' Zane nodded, his eyes searching out Felix's. 'But you're OK, right? You're handling all this just fine.'

'Right.' Felix put on a harder front. 'It's not a problem.'

'You did good last night – and since you made it here, I guess the morning after's gone OK too, huh?'

'Could have been worse.' Felix always felt slightly wrong-footed by the casual nature of Minos debriefs. 'Manton showed.'

'In person?' Zane looked grave as Felix nodded.

'Damn. We knew he was some place in Mexico, but figured he'd vet you long distance.'

'This was kind of personal. He got his pet thug to hold me at knifepoint while he went through my legend.'

Zane was still watching Felix closely. 'Your cover wasn't compromised?'

'It's cool,' Felix insisted. 'I think I impressed him. He wants me to take part in another job tonight. Two CAF types are on their way, Coral and Deep. Coral you know—'

'Chessa's hardcore big sister.' Zane nodded. '"Deep" will be Abudeep Chua, a buddy of Manton's from way back. Former biochemistry student turned radical. He's a Brit wanted by the Met's Counter-Terrorism Command – makes his own tear gas and pepper spray, supplies it to demo activists across Europe to help riots go with a swing.'

'Look forward to meeting him,' joked Felix.

'There are alerts out on the pair of them at every airport, so they can't fly anywhere legit,' Zane went on. 'Instead they've smuggled themselves across the Mexico border. Last night. And it looks likely their transport was arranged for them by Orpheus.'

'So this job must be for Orpheus's benefit as well as the CAF's.' Felix sighed. 'If I wind up helping them to kill innocent people . . .'

'Hey.' Zane's eyes bored into him. 'No one said the water wasn't gonna get deep. You know how it works, Felix – sacrifice one to save a thousand. If you keep in with Manton we have a real chance to find out who he deals with and how high up they are in the Orpheus command structure. Get enough intel to smash them wide open so they can't hurt anybody ever again.' He splashed Felix suddenly and laughed, breaking the spell. 'Manton say anything else?'

'Nothing much. He said he won't be on this job himself – got an appointment.'

'Damn it, I wish I could've organized a tail.'

'I figured it was too risky for me to go after him,' said Felix, relieved when Zane nodded. 'I know he needs a truck – this walking gangster cliché who owns the flat in Doctores is providing it, along with a couple of cars – a guy called Beni, alias *El Piraña*. Runs a stolen auto racket. I figure he must be the one dealing with Orpheus. Maybe he even helped Coral and Deep cross the border.'

'Makes sense. We'll get digging,' Zane assured him. 'Any clues as to the target? What the CAF need this transport for?'

'No. But Manton said Deep and Coral were bringing proper bomb-making gear with them.'

'Figures,' Zane agreed. 'And the target could be another lab. Why else would they want you to prove you can total one like you did last night?'

'I guess I've kind of come to the rescue of the CAF,' mused Felix. 'Just as they lose their own bomb emplacer, I suddenly appear.' He paused. 'That's not a coincidence, is it?'

'We arranged an accident for the dude. The wrong mix of chemicals.' Zane sniffed and screwed up his nose. 'Just like this damned water.'

Felix didn't smile. He was too busy feeling the ice creeping down his spine. 'Did you kill him?'

'He was injured. We think Manton killed the guy himself.' Zane kept his voice low, his tone casual. 'The CAF couldn't take him to hospital, could they? Too many questions. Easier all round if . . .' He mimed a firing gun with his fingers.

'And you knew that would happen?'

'Yeah, and I cried my eyes out over the poor terrorist bastard.' Zane's eyes were dark as coals. 'We're not playing around here, Felix. You know that. Gotta focus on the wider picture. The CAF and Orpheus are both ruthless, both committed – and they got something cooking together, something big. Something that could make Day Zero look like a bad day at the office. If some scum has to die to prevent a major atrocity then I'll take that on the chin. Every time.'

Felix nodded slowly. 'And if the good guys die too?'

'Everyone is expendable. You know that. Minos and ATLAS can lose battles. What matters is the war.' Zane cracked the world's smallest smile. 'That said, this is one battle I aim to win. So stay with me on this one, Felix. And stay well under cover. I got another Minos operator coming at the CAF from another angle, in New York, but it looks like his story's reaching a dead end. We need more info. A lot more. And you gotta do whatever it takes to get it. You hearing me, Felix?'

'I'm hearing you.'

'Then enjoy your swim and then get the hell back to

Doctores.' Zane heaved himself out of the pool. 'Good luck, soldier.'

'Yes, sir.' Felix watched him pad away towards the changing rooms. Then he took a good few deep breaths before throwing himself forward into an aggressive front crawl through the stinking water.

He had a whole lot of nervous energy to burn off.

... 24 ...

Felix arrived back at the flat in Doctores to find that *El Piraña* was out for a 'business lunch' – and that Coral and Deep had already arrived.

Coral he'd met before in Colorado, through Chessa. She was shorter than her sister, with the same deep tan to her skin and dark hair cut in a lopsided bob. She wore glasses, her eyes small and cold behind them like olive stones.

'Where did you go, Felix?' Coral asked as she stood aside to let him in. Her tone suggested curiosity, but her eyes were hard with suspicion. 'If Greg says you're one of us that's enough for me. But you left Chessa all alone with that ape Beni. She was upset.'

'Leave it, Coral.' Still sitting on the couch, Chessa looked embarrassed. 'I told you I'm fine.'

'I know when you're fine, Chess.' Coral looked at her sister critically; her voice was patronizing, her American accent less pronounced than her sister's. 'I know you inside and out, and no way were you fine this morning.'

'That wasn't because of Beni!' She sighed and looked down at her feet. 'I mean . . .'

'Look, I'm sorry,' Felix said, and he meant it. 'Sorry I blew up at you.' He sat down beside her. 'Friends?'

Chessa smiled shyly and nodded. 'I guess.'

'So where *did* you go?' Coral persisted.

'I was on a bit of a high, I needed to come down. So I went for a run. A swim.' Felix slipped off his pack and dumped it on the floor. He'd stopped off in neighbouring Navarte to buy a swimming pool ticket; what the spooks called 'wallet litter'. He had little doubt that Coral or Deep – or Beni, for that matter – would go through his possessions looking for anything incriminating the first chance they got. *Well, let them*, he thought. His false ID and passport were indistinguishable from the real thing. His bank cards were legit. Blockbuster rental card, club memberships, receipts, they were all there in his wallet going back a year, carefully forged by ATLAS pros, apparently confirming his six-month residency in Colorado.

'Felix?' A short Asian man in jeans and a checked shirt came into the room, arm outstretched. His big smile presented a friendly welcome, but his dark eyes weren't joining in. 'My name's Deep. Manton's number two. It's good to hear a London accent.'

'Too right it is.' Felix stood up and shook hands – and, as he did so, glimpsed the handgun tucked into Deep's shoulder holster. 'How was your trip?'

'Like something out of a film!' Deep chuckled. 'Me flying Coral and some slabs of C4 in a crop-spraying plane across *El Camino del Diablo* . . .'

Plastic explosive – guess I really won't be improvising. Felix raised his eyebrows. 'You're a pilot?'

'Handy when you need to avoid customs.' He smiled at Coral. 'What would the CAF do without me, eh?'

Coral deadpanned: 'Get another pilot?'

'Watch it.' Deep mimed shooting her with his fingers, the grin on his face turning sickly. 'Anyhow, I put us down in Coahuila and we travelled the rest of the way buried under straw in the back of a farmer's pick-up. You couldn't make it up . . .'

'Where'd you get the C4?' asked Felix.

'Stole it from a construction site,' said Deep. 'Detonators too.'

'Did the farmer know you were carrying bomb stuff?' Chessa asked, incredulous.

Coral shook her head as if weary. 'He's not a real farmer, duh! He smuggles people for a living. Bribes the border guards.' She snorted. 'Those lackeys are as cheap as their principles.'

'Lucky for us,' Chess murmured.

'Unlucky for their dogs.' Coral shook her head and Felix braced himself for one of her lectures. Almost anything could set her off. But he knew one of the reasons he didn't like to listen was that deep down he felt she was right to care as she did, in the face of so much indifference. He understood where she was coming from. He'd cared enough to risk his life with Minos, and she cared enough to risk hers for the CAF.

'Poor creatures,' she went on. 'Improperly trained, worked too hard and with too many handlers, caged in kennels—'

'Or cross-trained,' Chessa piped up. 'Made to sniff out drugs *and* explosives. Then if they don't perform or make the wrong decision . . .'

'If people want to blow each other up, fine. But putting animals in danger?' Deep leaned back on the sofa, stretching noisily. 'It's sick. Making animals slaves to human neuroses.'

'It *is* slavery,' Coral agreed, and Chessa nodded firmly.

Felix bit his tongue. He'd seen real love between handlers and their dogs, knew so many working dogs who lived with their trainers. He supposed it was like just about anything – good and bad mixed up together. There were no easy answers. Maybe that was why Felix had always found it easier to dodge the question altogether.

Deep pulled an inhaler from his pocket and took a puff. 'There was this bloke in Alabama running a training centre for explosive detection dogs. Post Day Zero he got a massive contract worth millions from the US government. But he didn't train the dogs properly. They went into action but were useless. Hundreds had to be returned. Anyway, the bloke in Alabama got fined, so to mitigate some of his losses he downsized his business and put down his dogs.'

Coral nodded fiercely. 'The world calls *him* a businessman and the person who cares a terrorist.'

She's right, it stinks, thought Felix. *But when caring*

for animals leads to human murder . . . how can that make things right? Even so, he felt under pressure to contribute. 'People just don't get it – when the ones who care can't take the cruelty any more, they have to act. They can't just stand by and do nothing.'

'You said it,' said Deep. 'So get started making those bombs, yeah?'

Coral pulled out a phone. 'I'm going to check up on our friend *"El Piraña"* ' – she used her fingers to make the speech marks around his name as she said it – 'to make sure our transport will be ready by nightfall. Deep, you'll watch our new recruit, won't you? Closely.'

'Yeah, course. It's London boys together, eh, mate?' Again, Deep's smile failed to reach his eyes. 'This is gonna be the job, people. This is the one that's really gonna make a difference.'

Felix felt his guts twist. *That's what I'm afraid of.*

Felix grabbed a few hours' sleep on the couch, then spent the rest of the afternoon turning the living room into a bomb factory. He was preparing breaching charges strong enough to blow open a bank vault. Deep watched him closely as he carefully cut a hole in a small cream-coloured slab of C4 with a ceramic knife and inserted a plain detonator, before securing the assembly with black electrical tape. Chessa was perched on the edge of the sofa, her skinny legs drawn up to her chest, resting her chin on her knees.

'What if that thing goes off by mistake?' she asked plaintively.

'C4 is pretty tough to detonate,' Felix explained. 'Even if you set it on fire it would just burn pretty slowly.'

'I saw that in a film,' said Deep. 'These soldiers in Vietnam used to light lumps of C4 and heat their food over it.'

'But you've put detonators into it,' Chessa persisted.

'These blasting caps need a pyrotechnic fuse,' Felix explained. 'When we get on site I'll put one in and crimp it in place. It'll burn down into the ignition mix, which will detonate the primary explosive – a little mercury fulminate – and *that* in turn will detonate the C4. Until then we're cool – there's so little primary explosive in those dets, you'd have to hit them with a sledgehammer if you wanted them to go off.'

Chessa gave him an impressed smile. 'Sounds like you know what you're doing.'

'Course.' Self-consciously, Felix looked over at Deep. 'Hope you're going to tell Manton how good I am.'

'We all need to know how good you are,' Deep replied. 'I hope you're going to prove it.' He pulled a pale cotton satchel from behind him and placed it carefully on the table. 'There's a stack more C4 in here, some electric blasting caps . . .' He fished into his pocket. 'And a mobile phone.'

Felix looked into Deep's dark eyes. 'You want me to make an RCIED.'

Chessa looked blank. 'Excuse me?'

'Radio-Controlled Improvised Explosive Device,' Felix muttered. What he didn't mention was that he recognized the white camouflage satchel with its heavy-duty straps. This hadn't come from any construction company.

It was a US Army issue canvas bag used to contain assault demolition assemblies. They'd been used by soldiers in Iraq to collapse houses occupied by insurgents, to save clearing them room by room.

How had Deep – or Manton – got hold of them?

Chessa interrupted his thoughts. 'I don't see how a cell phone sets off a bomb.'

'When we phone its number, the receiver triggers a firing pulse into the electrical detonator,' said Felix, his eyes still on Deep. 'You've got enough C4 here to bring down a bridge. What's it for?'

'We need to cover our tracks,' said Deep. 'No one must know what we've taken.'

So that explains why I had to blow up something so big for my initiation test, Felix reflected. 'What *are* we taking?'

Deep regarded him coolly. 'You ask a lot of questions. Don't you, mate?'

Felix shrugged. 'I'm used to relying on myself. If we're going to be a team, I need to know what we're working towards.'

'That's easy,' Chessa said. 'Justice for the beast.'

Felix glanced at her. It seemed that simple statement was enough for Chessa. Like 'Justice for my dad' was enough for him.

He looked down at his handiwork and sighed. *Guess we've both been well trained, Chessa. Haven't we?*

Beni prowled back into the apartment around six, like a big, rangy wolf stalking his territory. He smelled of chilli and petrol, and Coral, following on behind him, did not look impressed. Acknowledging no one, baggy trousers clinging on beneath his hips, he sat down beside the TV. 'Well. We're good to go.'

'Two cars out front,' Coral elaborated. 'Passat and a Phaeton.'

'Both hot?' asked Deep.

'Ringers. False plates and spray jobs.' Beni lit another cigarette. 'Cops will give us no trouble. I'll lead the way in the refrigerated truck.' He winked at Chessa. 'Want to ride with me, *Fresa*?'

'She's coming with me,' Coral said firmly. 'You can drive alone, Beni.'

'Right.' Deep shot her a look. 'Just what I was going to say.'

Coral met his gaze. 'Then I said it for you, didn't I?'

Deep let the point drop and took another scoosh on his inhaler. 'I'll ride with you, Felix.'

'Four of us need two cars?' Felix queried.

Deep nodded. 'We take different routes back after the job. Just in case.'

Beni peered at Felix's handiwork. 'Is that thing really going to go off?'

'Fruit goes off,' said Felix, deliberately trying to get a rise out of him. 'This will detonate when the time is right.'

'I like to put my faith in something more basic. Something I make myself.' Beni pulled a dark bottle from his bag. A sharp chemical smell filled the air.

Chessa sat up straight, face screwed up. 'What the hell?'

'Old-school grenade,' he smirked at his uneasy audience. 'My special take on the Molotov cocktail. Ignites on impact. A few of these helped me take over this patch.'

'For God's sake put it away,' Coral told him.

Deep nodded. 'If you drop that thing in here . . .'

'What do you even need it for?' said Felix, joining the attack.

'I'm always prepared.' Beni pushed out his jaw. 'That's why I'm still alive, you get me? Jeez, you animal-lovers, you're so uptight the whole time . . .' He stalked from the room, but the smell of him hung unpleasantly in the uneasy silence.

'That idiot's a liability,' Coral said quietly.

'We couldn't do this job without him,' Deep murmured.

'*This* job,' Coral agreed. 'But Greg says, never again.'

'I know.' Deep's fingers drummed lightly on his shoulder holster. 'But let's focus on one job at a time, shall we?'

Coral nodded and looked over at Chessa. 'Don't worry about him. I'm here.'

'I know,' Chessa said softly, still glaring hatefully after Beni.

Felix wondered how walls so thin could hold an atmosphere so thick.

... 23 ...

After less than two minutes on the road, Felix realized that night driving in Mexico City was not for the faint-hearted.

This is a nightmare, he thought. Road signs and signals might just as well have been invisible; cars ran red lights, pushed through crowded crossings, took U-turns without warning and generally did their best to total the oncoming traffic. *And I thought things were tough on the road this morning . . .*

'This is why I learned to fly,' Deep muttered. 'Give me a Cessna or a heli over a car any day.'

If he'd been allowed to drive, Felix might have felt happier; at least he'd have some control over his fate. But he was playing the dysfunctional bad-boy animal activist, not the fast-tracked teen spook with the advanced driving test pass already under his belt. So he shut up, held his stomach and let Deep get on with manoeuvring the Phaeton northwards through this traffic war zone.

Beni's big grey lorry at least made an easy target to trail. Coral and Chessa's battered green Passat stuck to it like butter to bread, and Deep fought to keep them both in sight, stopping and starting through the congested streets.

'Coral's good at driving,' Felix remarked.

'Yeah,' Deep agreed, 'at driving people crazy.'

Interesting, thought Felix. 'Uh . . . Have you known her long?'

'I've known her all kinds of ways, mate. Knew her before Manton did.' Deep glanced at Felix. 'It was through me she met him.'

His tone was even, but something in his face suggested . . . what? Deep was a hard man to read. His eyes gave little away, a sense of cold appraisal constantly there; he looked at those around him as a scientist might look at bacteria in a Petri dish, and Felix wondered if he'd always been that way.

Change the subject, he thought. 'Can you tell me where we're going now?'

'Won't mean anything to you,' Deep said tersely. 'San Juan del Rio. About a hundred miles along Federal Highway Fifty-seven.'

'And what do we find there?'

'An easier ride than this, I hope.'

By the time they'd reached the outskirts of the city and picked up Highway 57, the car reeked of sweat despite the air con. The time was edging towards midnight and the traffic thinning out a little. Beni's lorry thundered along, nudging the speed limit. The road was a patchwork of uneven surfaces and the tyres sang in many pitches as they journeyed on, keeping a safe distance behind Coral and Chessa. Felix stared out at the brooding hulks of distant mountains and at far-off townships, their meagre scatterings of light all but lost amid the landscape.

Finally, Beni's lorry slowed and pulled into a lay-by. As Coral and Deep followed suit, Felix felt nerves in his stomach twitch at the prospect of action. The night was oppressively warm as he left the cooled vehicle, wired and alert. The rush and thunder of passing traffic along the main road mingled with the steady thrum of the cicadas.

Coral looked tired as she came over to join Deep. Chessa followed like a shadow, and gave Felix a nervy smile. Deep waited until Beni had jumped down from the truck's cab before briefing his audience in clipped, nononsense tones. 'Our objective is reached by turning left onto the access road one kilometre along from here. Coral, you know what to do, yeah?'

'Chess and I will park fifty metres down that track and carry on to the main gates on foot,' said Coral. 'From there we'll gain access to the security hub.'

'How?' Felix asked bluntly.

Coral pulled a scarf from Chessa's neck to reveal a skimpy top with a plunging neckline. 'Feminine wiles. My pretty little sister will say our car broke down and ask them nicely for help.'

Beni leered down her top. 'They might be wanting to help themselves.'

Chessa grimaced and covered herself up as best she could. Felix reached out to place a reassuring hand on her shoulder – then caught the hard look Coral hurled his way and let it drop.

'Me and Felix will park beside your car. Call once you've disabled the guards.' Deep passed her a small spray can. 'I mixed up something special. Aim for the eyes.' To Felix's alarm he pulled out Ziploc bags with sodden wads of cotton wool inside. 'Once you've blinded them, this should put them to sleep. Make sure you don't inhale – get me?'

'I could put them to sleep easier,' Beni piped up. 'I brought my grenade. Boom.'

'Beni, you will not touch your stupid bloody grenade,' Deep told him coldly. 'Bring in the truck once we've got into the complex. Back up to the gates. We'll load the consignment on board and when we're done, you get the hell away. Drive north on Highway Fifty-seven till you hit a truck stop outside El Pinto. You'll be met there by your contact.'

Beni smiled his crooked smile. 'A man from the Big O.'

'You'll swap vehicles with him,' Deep continued, 'then return to the apartment. We'll hand over the rest of your payment then.'

'Sweet,' cooed Beni.

The Big O is Orpheus, Felix realized, but played dumb. 'I don't get it. Whatever we're stealing . . . isn't it for the CAF?'

Coral gave him a beady look through her glasses and

ignored the question. 'Once the truck is away, Felix, you'll place your bombs.'

'Right.' As before at the flat, Deep gave her a look that might have been resentful. 'We'll retreat a safe distance and destroy the complex, leaving no trace.'

'What about the guards?' asked Chessa. 'They could ID us.'

Beni shook his head. 'In that top they won't be looking at your face, *Fresa*.'

A meaningful look passed between Coral and Deep. 'I've told you not to worry about the guards, Chess. They won't be a problem.'

Felix felt sick as he caught the implications. *Can I let them murder innocent civilians, just to keep my cover . . . ?* He remembered Zane talking at the pool. '*See the bigger picture . . . The CAF and Orpheus . . . they got something cooking together that could make Day Zero look like a bad day at the office . . .*'

I've got to see this through, thought Felix numbly, *whatever the consequences.*

Deep must have mistaken his concern for fear. 'Don't sweat it, Felix,' he said, a touch impatiently. 'You'll be fine if you do as we tell you.'

'Right. Now, let's do this.' Coral muttered the phrase over and over as if to psych herself up. Chessa rearranged the scarf around her neck, looking self-conscious. Felix gave her what he hoped was an encouraging smile as she got back into the Passat and drove away with her sister.

'So now we wait.' Deep took another puff on his

inhaler. As terrorists went, he was way wide of the traditional picture. *That's the problem*, Felix reflected. *The bad guys don't come with labels.*

After a few minutes, Deep suggested to Felix they wait in position. Leaving Beni to strut around his truck smoking roll-ups, Felix sat in nervous silence as Deep steered the Phaeton back onto the highway and to the dark stretch of the access road. The Passat had been parked beside a weathered sign for *Laboratorios del Lupita*, and Deep parked just in front of it.

Felix stared down at his pack full of explosive, wondering for the hundredth time what they would be taking and how much of the lab would still be standing in the morning. *Please let the place be empty* . . .

Almost twenty minutes had crawled by before Deep's phone buzzed into life.

'Finally.' Deep snatched it up and hit answer. 'Coral?'

Her voice sounded through the earpiece. 'Get up here.'

Deep thrust the phone at Felix and started the Phaeton's engine, roaring off along the track. It took a good minute to reach the lab – being set back so far from the road was probably one of the reasons the CAF had targeted it. Huge, high steel gates stood open under floodlights. Deep brought the car skidding to a stop and scrambled out. The security hub was a small white unit just beside the gates. As Felix grabbed his pack and raced towards it he saw Coral and Chessa inside, stooped over three prone security guards, tying their hands with lengths of nylon rope.

'Result!' Deep's smile was genuine now, the skin around his eyes creased with thick wrinkles. 'The stuff worked, then?'

'Like a dream.' Coral turned to him triumphantly. 'They thought we were helpless girls, stranded on the roadside. Said they would take care of us.'

'But *you* took care of them.' Deep put a hand on her shoulder. 'Well done. Knew I could count on you.'

Coral shrank awkwardly from the contact. '*Greg* knew you could count on me.' She turned to her sister. 'All right, Chess?'

'Those poor men.' Chess looked far from all right. 'The spray really hurt them. I'm glad your chloroform knocked them out quickly.'

'Yeah, it does the job.' Deep looked shifty. 'Now, we've gotta go. Where's the keys?'

'Here.' Coral handed him a key fob with a white pass-card she had taken from one of the guards. 'I've disabled the alarms and CCTV feed.'

'Well, let's try to keep things quiet in any case.' Deep snatched the card. 'Felix – with me.'

Felix ran after him as he pelted away towards the complex. Clearly Deep had studied the layout, because he ignored the first two doors they passed in the main building in favour of a separate block. He swiped the pass-card and the door jumped open with an abrasive buzz.

'Get those breaching charges ready,' Deep ordered Felix as motion-sensitive lighting flickered on. The corridor was grey, enlivened by strips of yellow-and-black hazard tape on several doors and warning signs in Spanish that

Felix wished he understood. Deep went on ahead, clearly looking for something in particular.

He found it behind one of the hazard doors. While Felix got busy crimping the fuse into the taped-up wad of the C4, Deep vanished from view.

'In here,' he hissed urgently.

Heart pounding, Felix took the charges and followed Deep into a smart, spartan laboratory. Deep looked agitated, jabbing a finger towards a huge, imposing metal door at the back of the room. It was adorned with more hazard warnings and instructions on critical temperatures. 'We need to open that door. You can sort that, yeah?'

Felix simply nodded. He knew better than to ask questions or make protests right now; Deep was a biochemistry expert, he must have calculated it would be safe to let off an explosion so close to whatever materials lay on the other side. He attached one breaching charge to each of the door's heavy hinges.

'Ready?' Felix looked at Deep, who nodded and ran back outside into the corridor, his fingers in his ears. Felix struck a safety match and lit the fuse before running outside to join Deep, slamming the door shut behind him. A hollow metallic *boom* shook the corridor, and plaster showered down from the ceiling. Felix was still crouched and coughing even as Deep ran back inside the smoke-filled room.

'Come on, then,' he called, 'give us a hand.'

Felix ran inside and found Deep trying to clear jars and boxes from a porter's trolley. The vault room behind the now shattered door was refrigerated, and much of the smoke was actually steam as the cold and warm air mixed.

'Bring that trolley and help me load up.' Deep produced a torch and shone it into the darkness of the vault. Felix tried to make sense of the labels in the frantic sweeps of torchlight – butyl acrylate, methyl-something-or-other . . . it was no use. Deep hefted a large plastic drum off a shelf and Felix manhandled it onto the trolley. More and more containers appeared in front of him, to a soundtrack of thumping and sloshing. Soon the trolley was fully loaded.

'Go get another one,' Deep panted.

No wonder we need a truck, thought Felix. 'What about Chessa and Coral? Can't they help us?'

Deep grunted. 'They're getting hold of something else.'

Soon Felix and Deep had loaded up three trolleys. Deep had to keep breaking off to use his inhaler.

'If you tell me what you need, I can carry on loading while you start taking these out to the lorry,' suggested Felix.

'I know what I'm looking for,' said Deep, 'you don't. Move this lot out to the truck, quick as you can.'

Felix nodded, grabbed a trolley and hauled it out into the corridor, crunching over plaster and debris as he raced for the exit. Before he opened the fire door, he pulled out his phone and took a photograph of some of the container labels. Then he wheeled his load out into the night, muscles straining, breath coming in stubborn puffs. Beni's truck was now parked in the open gateway as Coral had instructed, and Felix headed towards it. He saw *El Piraña*'s glowering face in one of the oversized wing mirrors.

'Give me a hand,' he yelled.

The hand Beni gave him contained only a middle finger, waved at his face.

'Fine, I'll do it myself,' muttered Felix, straining to shift the large tubs of chemicals into the back of the refrigerated truck. As he finished, he gave the trolley a push towards the security hub, cursed loudly as if it had drifted off by accident, then went to reclaim it. He peered in through the window at the fallen security guards. There was no sign of movement. He wasn't even sure if they were breathing.

I've got to see if they're OK . . .

Felix raced back across the forecourt with the trolley, retracing his frantic steps to the cold vault he had blasted open. Deep was still sorting through bottles and jars on the steaming shelves. Three more trolleys had been filled to capacity.

'Take the next one,' Deep ordered. 'Hurry.'

Obediently, Felix manoeuvred it round and out through the doorway. His clothes were drenched with sweat but he tried to keep his head cool, to focus on the situation and what he could do to win a positive result for Minos without blowing his cover into as many bits as the shattered vault. If just one of the security guards would wake up, Felix could help him and his friends escape then pretend he had been overpowered; Chessa and Coral's knot-tying could take the blame. Beni wouldn't notice a thing inside his cab.

But if the men couldn't be revived, would Felix have time to get them clear? If Coral or Deep checked on them, how would he ever explain it away?

He wished Zane were here, or one of the handful of friends he'd made in Minos. He felt horribly alone.

He wheeled the trolley over to the truck and busied himself unloading it. Again he let the trolley drift towards the security hub and chased lightly after it. This time he ducked inside and crouched down low next to one of the guards, checking his pulse.

With a shock he realized the man was dead.

What the hell had Deep's rags been soaked in? The other two were sweating hard, their breathing shallow. Felix tried to move one into a sitting position and cuffed him lightly about the face, hoping he would revive. 'Come on,' he muttered. 'Wake up, wake up . . .'

'What gives, *puto*? You pick fights with men who sleep? The only way you can win, huh?'

Beni was framed in the doorway, a satchel slung over one shoulder.

'I heard this one call out,' Felix said, keeping his voice steady and tone casual. 'Thought I'd better shut him up in case he tried to raise the alarm.'

'That's why you told him to wake up, huh?' Beni sneered and shook his head. 'Maybe beg him to call the cops?'

'Don't be stupid,' Felix stood up and let the guard slip back to the floor. 'Why would I do that?'

'You've been chicken about this whole job. A little kiddie out of his depth.'

Felix tried to laugh off the accusations. 'You don't know what you're talking about.'

'I think maybe I do.' Beni took a threatening step closer. 'You're not the only one round here who can set a bomb. How do you think I took charge of the biggest stolen car ring in Mexico City? By eliminating my competition.' He reached into his satchel and pulled out the murky flask grenade. And he smiled.

. . . 22 . . .

'You tried to make a fool of me.' Beni's lips twitched as he bared his yellow teeth. 'You act the big man in front of Manton and try to make me look small. Yes?'

Felix understood now the real reason for the grenade exhibition back at Doctores – simple showing off to save lost face. 'What're you going to do – torch this lab yourself to show Coral and Deep they don't need me?'

'You think I'm stupid? Some street punk, no education?' Beni pulled a taped-up block from his pocket. '*Now* who's stupid?'

Felix froze. 'How did you get hold of one of my breaching charges?'

'Not yours. *Mine.*' Beni's leer was back on his face. 'You underestimated me. *El Piraña* is a fool, you thought. But who'll look the fool when your CAF friends come back and find you've blown yourself to bits?'

Felix licked his dry lips as Beni held the home-made

grenade up to the breaching charge. *He's going to use it as the primary explosive to ignite the C4.* 'So you get revenge on me and make me look like an amateur,' Felix said hoarsely. 'You think that's going to put you straight with Manton? Reckon he'll just forget you got your ass whumped by a fifteen-year-old kid?'

Beni scowled. 'You took me by surprise.'

As good a cue as any, thought Felix – and he dived forward at Beni. In the single second he was launching through the air he assessed his priorities – *Grab the grenade before Beni can use it. Disable him so he can't hurt me. Find some way to stop him telling Deep and Coral I was helping the guard—*

His head slammed into Beni's chest. The *cholo* swore as he lost his balance and dropped the C4. Felix flashed out an arm and grabbed for the deadly flask even as the two of them went down hard together. His fingers closed on the glass neck but he couldn't wrest it from Beni's grip.

A stream of angry Spanish fired in Felix's ear – then Beni punched him in the side of the head. Felix rolled clear and scrambled to his feet, and like a mirror image Beni did the same.

Except Beni then grabbed a cell phone from the desk and threw it at Felix's face.

As Felix brought up a hand to deflect the missile, Beni roared and charged him, forcing him backwards. The sharp edge of a filing cabinet bit into Felix's spine and he gasped with pain. Beni's features were twisted in a feral snarl, eyes dark and burning, the grenade still clamped in his left hand. He spat in Felix's face and gripped him by the throat.

Felix brought up an arm to break Beni's grip, then butted the *cholo*'s nose. There was a loud crack and a rush of blood fouled Beni's mouth and chin as he staggered backwards, trampling the guards' prone bodies. Felix lunged for the grenade – but Beni pulled a handgun from a shoulder holster beneath his jacket.

Felix felt the world slow around him. *This is it. End of.* 'You underestimated me again.' A grin sat red and ugly on *El Piraña*'s face as he kept Felix covered, his gun arm stretched out in front of him, holding the weapon parallel to the ground like the movie gangsters he clearly idolized. Then slowly he crouched and fumbled for the breaching charge with the same hand that gripped the grenade. 'I can shoot you, *then* blow you apart.' He clasped both grenade and charge to his chest, and straightened. 'There won't be enough of you left for anyone to know it wasn't your own stupid fault . . .'

Felix knew there was no way to disarm Beni safely. He backed slowly away towards the door, racking his brain for a way to win back the advantage.

'No further,' Beni hissed, his finger tightening on the trigger.

Felix stared past him, caught a flash of movement through the glass. 'Someone's coming.'

'Pathetic,' Beni sneered, refusing to turn his head. 'The oldest trick in the—'

The window beside him shattered. A spurt of red leaped from Beni's neck and he staggered sideways, stumbled over the guard's body at his feet, and started to drop.

The grenade and blasting charge fell faster.

'No!' Felix dived out of the hut through the doorway, rolling over and over across the forecourt – tarmac and sky tumbling together as—

The flash of white shone brilliant as the sun even through Felix's tightly shut eyelids. As he reached the cover of the back wheel of the truck, the noise of the blast sucked his ears hollow. A bank of smoke engulfed him and the shockwave set the truck rocking like a ship at sea. Sick with dread he clamped his hands over his head as the firestorm swelled up and out into the night, and prayed the ordeal would end quickly.

Then through his ringing ears he heard a familiar London accent: 'Oh, great. That's wonderful, that is . . . Just bloody wonderful.'

It's Deep. Felix crawled out from behind the truck wheel and saw the man beside his trolley of chemicals, a Glock 179mm in his hand.

Felix staggered over to join him, one arm raised against the intense heat of the inferno now raging inside the security hub.

Deep turned to face him, his eyes wide and angry. 'How'd that happen? Eh?'

'Beni was holding his grenade when you shot him,' he shouted. 'Those security guards . . .'

'I worked out that Beni was holding the grenade, thanks,' Deep yelled. 'I mean, how come he's holding a gun on you?'

Coral came storming up behind him with a shocked-looking Chess – both were carrying large white cardboard boxes. 'What the hell is this?'

'Beni forced me into the hub at gunpoint,' Felix said quickly. 'He wanted to get me back for showing him up in front of Manton. He was going to torch security so you wouldn't find my body, you'd think I'd run out.'

'I couldn't let Beni shoot the kid before he's covered our tracks, Coral, could I?' Deep booted the side of the truck in frustration. 'Manton said we'd have to deal with Beni—'

'*After* Beni had delivered the consignment, not before.' Coral's eyes were daggers in Deep's face. 'We've got a huge truck waiting there and no one to drive it! You've always been trigger-happy—'

'It was meant to be a warning shot, all right?' Deep bawled in her face. 'Now, we don't have time for this.' He rammed the gun back in its holster. 'This place could be crawling with cops any moment, and there's still three more trolleys need loading back inside.'

'Then we'll go get them. Now.' Coral pushed the two boxes she was carrying into Felix's arms; they were surprisingly light. Then she took the one Chessa was carrying and loaded him up further. 'Take these a safe distance behind the gates. Then get your bomb from your car and bring it back to the chemical store.'

'Finishing it off's going to take time,' Felix protested.

'*Just do it!*' Deep screamed in his face as something snapped inside. 'Go and get the bomb! Go!'

A wave of hatred, thicker than the smoke and flames,

tore through Felix as he turned silently and staggered off with the boxes towards the gates. They weighed so little. *What's inside them? What was worth all this?* He dropped them on the ground behind the gates as Coral had instructed; nothing rattled or jangled. He tried to look inside, but they were taped up thickly; any signs of tampering would be spotted in seconds.

Abruptly his state of shock gave way to a rush of nausea that almost overwhelmed him. *Get over it*, he told himself fiercely. *Get over it.* He breathed out hard, then back in deeply, transfixed by the violent whirlwind of flame and smoke rising up into the night. Deep was right, cops would be swarming over the area any minute.

Felix raced back to the Phaeton, its doors still thrown wide open as if in alarm, and pulled the bomb from his holdall in the footwell. *If I deliberately mess up the explosion*, he thought, *ATLAS can do an inventory of all the chemicals missing, work out what the CAF – or Orpheus – might need them for.*

Then he remembered the darkness in Deep's eyes. *'Always been trigger-happy,'* Coral had said . . .

If that bomb fails, I could end up like Beni.

The thoughts flashed through his mind as he worked frantically to finish the RCIED, fingers moving on autopilot. He took four of the eight-ounce sticks of C4 from the bag and quickly taped them together. Then he took out the cell phone and switched it on to check it was working. If he wired up a bomb to a faulty phone he could blow himself to bits and Beni would be granted his wish after all.

Felix caught its start-up chime over the ringing in his ears. So far so good.

He plunged his hands into the bag and pulled out the add-on circuit. The mobile alone hadn't enough juice to fire off a detonator, but by wiring in a specially made circuit with its own power source . . .

In less than fifteen seconds, he'd pulled off the phone's back cover, removed the battery, attached two of the add-on circuit's wires to two of the phone's tiny output connectors, and clunked everything firmly back into position. Instant bomber's delight. All he had to do now was slide the detonator into the explosive and the bomb would be good to go.

But why was he having to do this at all? Experience showed that activists and terrorists alike couldn't wait to take responsibility for a successful hit, so why was Manton so keen on leaving no evidence of their culpability?

You'll figure it out, he told himself, carefully cradling the bomb and running back towards the complex. *And you'll get justice.*

Meantime, focus on staying alive.

Over the hungry roar of the flames Felix heard the clamour of wheels, footfalls and rattling as Coral led the short convoy of loaded trolleys towards the truck. No one spoke, but Deep gestured with his head that Felix should get going. He obeyed and ran into the complex, but instead of going to the chemical store he went deeper into the building, haring down deserted corridors in search of an alternative site. *This place will still be totalled but maybe something of the store will survive, enough to give us some intel.*

When Felix felt he was a fair distance from the ransacked store, he placed the bomb in the middle of a corridor. Then, making sure the detonator was nowhere near the explosive, he switched on the phone again. Once start-up was complete, he took the detonator and slid it into one of the sticks of C4.

We're good to go. The moment he rang that phone, it would send a pulse into the add-on circuit and through that to the electric detonator and then there would be nothing but a shedload of destruction.

Bile rising in his throat, Felix turned and bolted back the way he'd come like an Olympic sprinter. Just as he found his way to the entrance, he ran into Deep.

Oh God, he thought, *please don't ask to see where I put the bomb.*

'All set?' Deep panted.

Felix nodded, praying he didn't look too rattled. 'We're good.'

'Then let's get out of here!' Deep grabbed hold of his arm and pushed him out through the glass and steel door.

The two of them tore across the asphalt, shadows dancing like nameless apparitions in the Halloween light of the fire. Felix saw Chessa was dousing the Phaeton in petrol from a can while Coral pushed it towards the blazing hub. With a hissing *whoosh*, fierce blue flames engulfed the car. Coral snatched the fuel can and lobbed it into the conflagration.

'What're you doing?' panted Felix.

'Coral's going to have to drive the truck,' Chessa said, trembling, 'so we have to dump one of the cars.'

'And torch our forensics before the cops get here.' Deep glowered at Coral as she climbed up into the cab of the lorry. 'I told you, I can drive that thing.'

'Stick to the planes and copters,' Coral told him. 'I drove one of these through the gates of a fur-packing factory in Canada a few years back, I can take it the few kilometres to the drop-off.'

'Whoever meets that truck will be expecting Beni, Coral,' Felix argued. 'When they see you—'

Deep grabbed him roughly by the shoulder. 'Who rattled your chain, newbie? We say how it is – got it?'

Felix nodded quickly and piped down.

Coral hit the ignition and raised her voice over the thick diesel rumble of the engine. 'I'm Greg's girlfriend. If the contact needs to report in, I'll check out.'

'And I'm his number two.' Deep was frantically picking up the cardboard boxes. 'It should be me who does this.'

'You've done enough tonight.' She wrestled the gear lever into reverse. 'Take Chess, Felix and the merchandise to the car and see that this place is blown to hell the second you're all clear.'

As Coral pulled away jerkily, Felix looked down at his iPhone. The number for the mobile wired into the firing cap was set in the memory.

'Come on, then – let's go!' Deep ran down the track after Coral, following the tail-lights as they dwindled into the distance. Once they'd reached the car he hurled the

71

boxes into the boot, opened the driver's door and scrambled inside. Felix jumped into the back and Chessa threw herself after him. Deep turned the key left in the ignition, wrestled the gearstick into reverse and threw the car into a jerky three-point turn so they were facing away from the site. Then he jammed the stick into first and began to ease up on the clutch, the note of the engine rising to a fierce crescendo.

'Do it!' Deep shouted.

Felix pressed CALL, counted seconds in his head and screwed up his eyes. *First last night, now tonight . . . I'm supposed to prevent death and disaster. What am I doing here, what am I going to—*

His helpless thoughts were snatched away by the blinding white violence of the blast. Fear and adrenaline ignited through his blood, as unstoppable as the combustive reaction he'd unleashed. His body was buzzing. His senses felt knife-sharp.

Deep whooped as, wheels spinning, the car rocketed away. Was Chessa screaming or laughing? Felix couldn't tell, his ears were screwed. He gripped her hand as flaming wreckage chased them away from the complex, smoking stone and metal raining down on the scabby tarmac of the federal highway. The moon was lost behind a storm of smoke, rising up from the surrounding hillside like a volcano had gone off.

'You did it!' Deep yelled. 'Son of a bitch, Felix, you really did it!'

'Wow.' There were tears on Chessa's face, but now her gaze seemed as strong and hungry as the flames they were leaving behind. 'You can just *do* that.'

Felix felt himself redden, broke eye contact. He leaned his head back against the cool fabric of the seat, trying to control his breathing, to bury the memory-flashes of death and violence in the buzz of survival.

He knew that, for all this, his mission had barely begun.

Where would he be – and how bloodied – when it reached an end?

... 21 ...

The journey back to Mexico City seemed unbearably long. Felix had been told that Minos Chapter agents were known in some corners of GI5 as the Split-second Squad – a black joke based on their limited life expectancy. Felix had come close to buying it so many times, but he was still here. The danger could be as much of a rush as defusing a bomb. *Try not to seem too used to it though*, he realized. *The CAF think you're strictly amateur.*

He looked at Chessa, so quiet, eyes closed, pretending to be asleep – but the occasional tear still salting her cheek. *Today's radicalized youths become tomorrow's terrorists*; his instructors had banged on at length about that.

He chewed his lip in silence.

'So, Felix.' Deep glanced at him in the rear-view mirror, his cool demeanour reasserted. 'You did good. How're you feeling?'

Felix shrugged his shoulders. 'OK, I guess.'

'That was nice work. I'm impressed.' He looked back at Felix again. 'And that's good news for you.'

Unsure how to respond, Felix said nothing.

'I'm dropping you two at the airport, yeah? You're booked on a flight to Colorado Springs first thing this morning.'

Felix started. 'But I left my passport back at the apartment.'

'And I took it with me, mate.' Deep patted his trouser pocket and flashed a condescending smile. 'Yours too, Chessa.'

Chessa showed no surprise, clearly used to her destiny being decided for her. 'It'll be good to be back home.'

Be good to have one, thought Felix moodily.

'Now, Felix, I've got a question. Sort of hypothetical, but . . . If the only way to deliver a particular IED was to carry it myself – say, in an assault vest – and if my hands were tied so I couldn't free myself . . . how could I get clear of the bomb before it detonates?'

Felix frowned. What was the CAF planning? 'Uh . . . why would you be tied up?'

'Just say I was. Say it needs to be an automatic release thing.'

'Well, you could maybe use a pencil detonator, timed for however long you need.'

'A pencil?'

'It's not a real pencil. It's a brass cartridge with a length of notched lead inside kept separate from a little bit of acid. You crush one end to prime it; the acid eats through the notch in the lead bar, and as the lead snaps it triggers the detonator.'

Deep shook his head. 'And blows me to bits?'

'No, you'd fix it so the det only released a small explosive charge, just enough to break open the harness,' Felix explained. 'Then you could detonate the main explosive remotely once you'd left the area. Of course, if your hands were tied, you wouldn't be able to take off the hostage vest unless your arms were down by your side when it was fastened—'

Deep interrupted. 'Say I needed the bomb to go off straight away.'

Felix shifted uncomfortably in his seat. Where was all this leading? 'I, er . . . I guess that when the first detonator sets off the quick release in the harness, it could light a fuse at the same time—'

'And it's that fuse which sets off the main explosive . . .' Deep nodded. 'We're thinking along the same lines, Felix.'

'We are?'

'We are.' Suddenly a phone rang. Chessa jolted awake. Deep reached for his mobile on the passenger seat. 'It's Coral. She must've made the drop.' He hit answer.

As he did so, Coral's voice burst from the phone's speaker, terse and hushed: 'Deep, I . , . Something is wrong. Men are coming with guns—' The sound of people shouting, unintelligible, broke over her voice. 'Get off me!'

The phone went dead in Deep's hand.

'Oh my God,' breathed Chessa. 'We've got to go help her.'

'Right,' Felix quickly agreed. *I'm for anything that gives me the chance to get more detailed intel on that consignment – especially if there's a chance I can clock someone from Orpheus too.* 'She sounded in big trouble.'

'Nah. She'll be fine,' Deep said, as if trying to convince himself. 'You heard what she said – she's Greg's lady.' He took a big scoosh of his inhaler. 'They're not going to mess with her.'

'They were expecting Beni, like Felix said,' Chessa reminded him, 'not Coral.'

'Chessa, trust me, you do not want to mess with Orpheus people.'

'Like you'd know,' Chess stormed. 'It's Greg who deals with them.'

'I know plenty, love,' Deep snapped. 'I know that for all Manton bangs on about them and us being partners, it's them running the show. They've bought into Manton's idea and they need our expertise to pull it off in the time scale. But if we piss them off . . .' He rubbed the back of his neck. 'It could screw things up for the CAF, for me . . .'

'For you?' Chessa sounded outraged. 'What do you mean, for you?'

Deep shook his head, changed the subject. 'I'm telling you, it'll be all right, yeah?'

'What if Beni had other plans for that consignment?' Felix said slowly. *Play on Deep's paranoia. Threaten the great cause*. 'What if he was going to rip us off, take it for himself, hold it to ransom?'

'You really think . . . ?' Chessa looked appalled. 'Then those guys might not be Orpheus. They could be anyone.'

Deep drove on, brooding for a few moments. Then he slammed both hands down on the steering wheel and twisted hard while stamping on the brakes. The car swung in a screeching U-turn, careered across the humped bank of earth that formed the central reservation and finally tore away in the opposite direction.

Chessa sat up straight. 'We're going after Coral?'

'You noticed.' Deep stepped harder on the accelerator, kept them racing through the darkness. 'And it could be the last thing any of us ever does.'

Yeah. Felix felt that familiar stir of dread and excitement. *Just for a change*.

... 20 ...

There was little traffic to slow them down until they
passed the dirt road to the lab again. The roofs of a dozen
police cars, ambulances and fire engines threw flashes of
blue light up at the night, but couldn't hope to rival the
orange-red of the towering flames above. Felix was glad
when they'd passed by unnoticed.

The digits on the milometer seemed to tick off the
seconds until finally Felix clocked the truck stop ahead, a
barren refuge wedged between the grey stripe of the
road and a sheer cliff face. It seemed quite an open space
for the RV, though Felix supposed that with the police
soon to be combing the surrounding area for
the lab-bombers, immediate access to the main road
would speed up the getaway.

A four-by-four was parked at the truck stop. In the
glare of the Passat headlights a shadowy figure was
visible at the wheel.

'She's there,' said Deep. 'That has to be her, right?'

'I don't see anyone else around,' said Chessa.

'This could be a come on,' Felix offered. 'There could be people waiting for us.'

'An ambush, you mean?' Deep braked sharply. Felix and Chessa were jerked forwards.

'If that really is Coral, she'll see it's us,' said Felix. 'She'll get out of the car.' He swallowed hard. 'Assuming she *can* get out of the car.'

Chessa looked at him, eyes wide and frightened. 'You mean she might be dead?'

Bright yellow lights swept up suddenly behind them and a horn blared as a car had to swing into the middle lane to pass them. Cursing, Deep pulled into the mouth of the lay-by and trained the headlights on the car in front. Through the reflections on the glass of the rear window the figure in the front seat seemed to turn.

'I'm right, that's got to be Coral,' Deep muttered. 'There's no sign of anyone around. So why isn't the silly cow getting out?'

Chessa took a shaky breath. 'If anything happens to her, it'll be down to you—'

'Down to Beni,' Deep retorted. 'Or down to bomb-boy here winding up that stupid son of a—' He thumped the steering wheel in frustration. 'Oh, whatever.' Without another word, he turned off the engine and got out of the car.

Felix undid his seat belt and turned to Chessa. 'I'll go with him. You'd better stay here.'

'Yeah, right,' said Chessa. 'You're younger than me,

don't you *dare* treat me like a kid. That's my sister out there.' She threw open her own door and began to walk cautiously towards the four-by-four.

Felix followed her and Deep just as warily. There was only one explanation that made sense to him.

It was confirmed by Coral just a few seconds later. 'Stay back.' The driver's window was open a little, and her voice came quiet and brittle. 'There's a bomb in the car.'

Both Deep and Chessa went rigid as though playing musical statues. 'There's *what*?' Chessa breathed.

'I don't know what will trigger it. I shouldn't have called you, I'm sorry.' She paused. 'Did you blow up the lab? Did you hide our tracks?'

Felix couldn't believe what he was hearing. *There's devotion to the cause for you. She's asking about the mission even when she's sat on top of a bomb – congrats, Coral, you're a true fanatic.*

'We took care of it,' Deep assured her.

'What happened here?' asked Felix.

'These three men hauled me out of the truck, shouted at me.' Coral was clearly trying to stay calm. 'They weren't expecting me, didn't trust me. They spoke no English, barely spoke any Spanish. I told them I was with the CAF, with Manton. I think maybe they went to check with a superior what to do.'

'That would make sense.' Deep nodded slowly. 'Probably saved your life.'

'But why would they have a car bomb just ready to go?' Felix pointed out.

'I . . . I think they were planning on killing Beni,' Coral

offered. 'It's all I can think of. He laundered money for Orpheus – he was their choice to supply the transport, not ours. When I turned up it threw their plans – I told them he was dead, that was why I'd come instead. They put me in here . . .'

Felix noticed a movement out of the corner of his eye. Deep had his mobile phone to his ear. 'Who are you calling?'

'Manton, who else?' Deep tutted. He waited a few seconds, then cancelled the call impatiently. 'Great. No answer. We're on our own.'

'Keep trying.' Chessa was wiping tears from her face with shaking hands. 'This is, like, a total nightmare. Ever since Greg dreamed up Deathwing *everything*'s a nightmare.'

'That's enough,' Deep hissed at her, eyes flashing.

What's Deathwing? Even in his fear, Felix felt a moment's intrigue. But he forced himself to focus on the task in hand. 'Coral, do you know what kind of bomb it is?'

'They blindfolded me, pushed me in here. I didn't see anything but heard them just outside, felt them doing something to the car . . . They told me to stay. Not to move. Or else, *boom*.'

'Did they all leave in the truck?'

'I told you, I was blindfolded.' The withering note was strong in her voice. 'I've managed to work it loose but my glasses have come off. Haven't seen anyone till you came.'

A huge freight lorry rolled out of the night, rocketing

past them on the carriageway, and the slipstream tugged at the four-by-four, setting it rocking. Deep swore and Chessa gasped.

'You'd better get back to the Passat,' Felix told Deep and Chessa calmly. 'I'm going to sort this.'

Deep frowned, affronted. 'Since when do you give the orders around here?'

'I'll get her out,' Felix insisted.

'Just leave,' Coral shouted. 'If they wanted to kill me they could've done it already.'

Felix shook his head. 'But if this bomb was meant for Beni, they won't have expected him to sit here for ages. Which means they won't have allowed for anything random – like people in another car stopping here, finding you, trying to help you and setting off the bomb. Or one of those lorries passing by so fast their slipstream does the same.'

'Felix is right,' said Chessa. 'Truth is, we don't know *what* those men have gone off to do. That bomb might be on a timer. Or they might decide it's just easier to blow her to bits than waste time finding out who she is.'

'They won't,' Deep insisted. 'We've got a contract. Orpheus needs us if Deathwing's going to work.' He took another couple of puffs from his inhaler. 'And if you screw up getting her out, Felix . . . it could mean all kinds of bad stuff.'

'I won't screw up.' Felix looked Chessa in her teary eyes. 'I promise.'

She glanced away. As he turned and walked slowly towards the four-by-four, he reflected how easy it was to make such promises in situations like these. If he broke the vow, he wouldn't have to worry about any comeback.

He'd already be dead.

But I can't walk from this, Chessa. My best chance of learning what Orpheus and the CAF are planning depends on using you to tap Coral for intelligence. Even if it didn't, I couldn't leave her there to die knowing I did nothing to save her . . .

The order of his priorities shocked Felix for a moment. All this time undercover, isolated, living in constant fear of discovery . . . was he beginning to miss what truly mattered here – saving lives?

No doubts now. You can't afford them.

The sweat was pouring off him and his heart was beating like a drum when he finally reached the vehicle. He froze as a pick-up drove past, closely followed by a car, the drivers heedless of the drama playing out on this darkened truck stop.

As he approached he looked for telltale signs of a secondary device. He found no hidden tripwires next to the car, no disturbed earth that might suggest a pressure plate or trigger of some kind. But now that he was closer he could see blocks of plastic explosive peeping out through the rear window. *The boot must be piled high.*

If the IED detonated now it would frag the car into hundreds of supersonic shards of molten metal. He and Coral would be torn to pieces, and what little remained of their shredded bodies would be vaporized by the napalm fireball that followed.

'Get out of here,' hissed Coral. 'I mean it. I shouldn't

have panicked and called for help. You're putting my life at risk.'

'Orpheus are the ones who did that!' Felix snapped back, flinching as another huge lorry rumbled past and the four-by-four rocked again. 'One good gust of wind could set off this device. Please, keep still in there.' He tried to regulate his breathing and bring his pulse-rate down. 'What *exactly* did the men tell you before they left?'

'I didn't understand much.' She was sounding less composed now. 'They made me put on the seat belt. Said if I tried to get out I'd be blown to pieces.'

'OK. Are the doors locked?'

'Yes. I heard the men walk a long way away, then there was a beep and the doors locked. A key fob.'

'Thanks.' Felix knew now this was almost certainly a victim-operated device, probably attached to the seat-belt-release mechanism. 'Coral, I want you to carefully lean forward and pull on the bonnet-release catch . . .'

'Pop the hood, you mean? Will that be safe?'

'If Orpheus had designed this bomb for Beni it would be rigged to the ignition or something obvious,' he reasoned. 'They wouldn't expect him to open the "hood" as soon as he got inside. Now, can you see the catch?'

'It's dark and I don't even have my glasses.'

'Dumb question. Sorry.' He took a deep breath; he couldn't afford to lose patience with her. 'Can you feel for it? Just whatever you do, don't release that seat belt.'

Felix watched through the tinted glass as she moved forward slowly and groped about down by the floor of the four-by-four. It seemed to take her for ever to find the catch.

When the bonnet suddenly snapped open, Felix's bowels almost did the same.

Trembling with relief, he quickly raised the lid, secured it with the metal prop and studied the engine like a hawk searching for prey. His dad had taught him this little trick of the trade: when you needed to get into a car in a hurry . . .

There.

He frenziedly began unscrewing one of the spark plugs. Once it was free he turned and threw it hard against the ground, smashing it. He bent down and picked up the pieces.

'What are you doing?' Deep called, standing behind his car. 'How much longer you gonna be?'

Felix waved angrily – *Get off my case* – and weighed the largest of the broken pieces of ceramic in his hand. 'Right, turn your head away. I'm breaking the window.'

Ceramic was incredibly hard, and the sharp edge would concentrate the force of impact. He hurled the makeshift missile at the bottom left-hand corner of the driver's window, and the glass shattered instantly.

Coral was revealed, no glasses, a blindfold round her chin, frozen with fear. Felix felt a moment's shock to see her so exposed, so vulnerable – somebody real, in place of a dogma-spouting ice-queen.

Felix eased his head right inside the car and systematically checked out its interior. *Look for absence of the normal, presence of the abnormal.* That phrase from training had become his mantra – and had saved his life.

The first thing he noticed was lights glowing on the dashboard and the hum of the air con. The key was turned in the ignition – and yet the four-by-four had been locked from the outside. Power was getting through to certain systems. Trying to keep calm, he noticed an out-of-place wire leading into the seat-belt connector. *Knew it.* He traced the wire, which vanished under the rear passenger seat – presumably all the way to the explosive in the boot.

But then he noticed something else . . . a length of fishing wire stretching from the underside of Coral's seat and into the door panel. *Bastards.* Not trusting Coral or her story, the bomber had modified his assembly and put a victim-operated IED in there too; a secondary. If he'd opened the door instead of leaning through the window it would have been game over for them both.

Felix shivered. He had two confirmed VO devices. What other surprises might lie in store? 'Right, Coral, I've got no tools and we've got no time.'

'You should've just left the car alone like I told you.' Her eyes were closed, one of them leaking a tear. 'It's not fair. I'm going to die now. We're right on the brink of changing the world and bringing justice for the beast and I'm going to die before I—'

'No one is going to die. Now, listen, I need you to sit tight while I cut through the seat belt, then I'll help you slip out through this window.' He eyed one red light on the dash display with foreboding. 'But first I've got to get something to wedge between your seat and the car's ceiling.'

'Why?'

'There's a pressure sensor in the seat that works with the seat-belt connector. It normally only works when the engine's running, but right now the seat-belt light's on.' Felix licked his lips. 'We can't take the chance that the sensor won't detect the movement when you get up.'

'And that'll set off the bomb?'

'Most likely. I think this rig was only meant to kill Beni when he'd reached wherever he was going, well away from this truck stop.'

'I get it. So the cops called out to the lab wouldn't link the two explosions . . .' Coral trained her small, frightened eyes on his. 'Where the hell did you learn all this stuff?'

'My . . . my dad told me. And I was in the army for a bit, remember?' Felix winced inwardly even as he spoke. Giving two explanations was an elementary cock-up for a professional liar. It was trying too hard, like he was desperate to be believed – and he knew someone like Coral was too smart not to pick up on it. 'Anyway, we need something to trick the sensor into thinking you're still in the seat.' A crafty thought struck him. 'Is . . . is there anything we can use in those boxes you took from the lab?'

'No. Leave them alone.'

'They hardly weigh a thing, what's inside them?'

Coral scowled. 'Little jackets for mice – what else?'

All right, don't tell me then. Guess that was never going to work. Felix looked away towards the open bonnet. *Of course – the metal prop holding it up . . .*

'What are you doing?' Chessa shouted.

Deep shushed her. 'That's not helping.'

Let's hope this can. Felix let his shoulder support the hood and wrestled the pole out from its housing, trying to rock the vehicle as little as possible. With that done, he carefully lowered the bonnet and tried to wedge the end of the prop down between the ceiling and the seat beside Coral's legs; but it was just too short.

'Now what?' she murmured.

Felix looked around desperately and spied a trash-filled litter bin. He ran over, grabbed a couple of squashed cartons and jammed them on top of the pole's sharper end. Then he went back to the four-by-four. Coral held stock-still as he tried to wedge the rod in place.

This time it held.

'Right. I'm going to cut you out of that seat belt.' He unfolded his clasp knife and began frenziedly cutting away at the seat belt. It took only a few seconds to hack through the fabric. Coral released a shaky breath.

'Now it gets tricky,' said Felix. 'On *three*, I want you to get up without knocking the prop and squeeze through the window.'

She grimaced. 'What if I can't—?'

'I'll help you. Try to be quick. Ready?'

Coral nodded nervously.

'OK. One . . . two . . . *three*!'

As Coral rose, Felix reached in, grabbed her under the shoulders and pulled with all his might. She came out through the open window with such force that they both fell to the ground. Coral was making a weird, almost feral whimpering noise; crying, but trying not to.

They scrabbled back onto their feet and Felix grabbed her by the hand. She snatched her fingers away. 'Come on,' he snapped, 'we've got to get clear.'

Together they ran hard, low and fast away from the four-by-four. A gigantic tanker thundered past at crazy speed. *The slipstream*, thought Felix, running faster, dragging Coral with him. *If it rocks the car enough to loosen the prop . . .*

Chessa threw open the door to the Passat and started getting out to greet them, a wide grin on her face.

'Get down!' Felix screamed.

There was a blinding, searing flash as the four-by-four exploded in a whirlwind of fire and shrapnel. The earth-shaking roar rocked the ground beneath their feet. A cloud of flying glass and debris filled the air around them. Distorted metal panels spiralled skywards, while rubble bounced on both sides of the highway. A gearbox landed close to Felix's head, the force of its impact burying it right into the tarmac.

And then there was silence. Sounds collected slowly in Felix's ears – the ragged scrape of his breath, the roar of the flames. Chessa grabbing Coral in a weeping embrace.

'I'm OK, Chess,' she said, voice hoarse and shaky. 'Come on. Get back in the car.'

'We've got to move,' said Deep, coming out from behind the car. 'The cops will be here any minute. Witnesses are rolling up already.'

Felix coughed on smoke. 'No, really. Don't thank me.'

Deep shoved Felix in the chest. 'If you hadn't pissed

off Beni in the first place, tonight would've gone to plan.'

'Easy, Deep.' Coral was staring at Felix, something uncertain in her eyes. 'I guess I'm lucky he knows as much about disabling bombs as he does about making them.'

'He was brilliant,' Chessa said simply.

But Felix felt a shiver of cold despite the heat of the flames. *I came over as too experienced. Took charge too much. Coral's got to be wondering how come.*

'Come on, let's shift!' Deep hissed, swinging himself inside the Passat.

Felix saw that cars were stopping on the other side of the highway, drivers gawping in amazement. Any minute now, people might start filming the scene on their phones, or at the very least remember the green Passat they'd glimpsed through the black diesel fog.

Deep was already gunning the engine. Felix scrambled up, threw himself into the back seat beside Chessa and held on grimly as the car roared away from flames and chaos for the second time that night.

'I hate Deathwing,' Chessa whispered defiantly. 'It's changed everything.'

'No.' Coral, looking tired and drawn, shook her head. 'It's *going* to change everything.'

No one spoke another word the whole way back to Mexico City.

. . . 19 . . .

Felix lay slumped in a chair at Mexico City airport's Terminal One, trying not to look conspicuous. He was wired on caffeine, a sick feeling crowding his stomach. The comedown from a job always floored him, as the adrenaline ebbed away to leave a fifteen-year-old boy, up to his eyes in danger and deceit, wondering if he'd ever get out.

Mexico was abuzz after the spate of explosions. The world's media were flooding in from all over and the cops were out in force. Chessa had listened to the news reports; no one had claimed responsibility for any of the incidents and no one could work out a link between the targets. Some kind of gang feud was being touted as the most likely explanation.

What if we were seen? The nagging voice kept worrying at the back of Felix's mind. *What if the cops are watching the airports, looking out for us?* At first, he hadn't envied Coral and Deep the risk of smuggling themselves back across the US border, but flying officially was proving no less nerve-racking. He and Chessa had checked in and passed security with no problem, but that was no guarantee there weren't police agents waiting for them on the plane.

What would happen to him then?

For the tenth time, Felix told himself to calm down. Pickpockets were known to work this airport, even airside. *Keep up with the furtive glances and you'll wind up attracting the cops' attention for sure.*

He needed something to do. *Call in*, he decided. Chessa was asleep on the chairs opposite – she wouldn't notice him slip away to contact the Girl. She hadn't really seemed to notice much since last night. Like him, she was still wearing the same clothes. Neither of them smelled so good. At least that had got them a bunch of seats to themselves as they waited to board their plane to Denver.

'Chess, I'm going to the bathroom,' he said.

Chessa didn't stir.

Checking there were enough people around to deter *real* pickpockets from targeting her, he strode away through the old, rundown terminal. Shop staff called to him as he passed, trying to entice him into their stores. Keeping his head down, he reached the payphones and quickly dialled the Minos hotline.

He was in luck: the Girl was on duty. As she took his name and passcode she sounded tired.

'Heavy night?' Felix wondered.

'Not as busy as yours,' she returned. 'Four corpses and two explosions? Quite a record.'

'The second explosion was an Orpheus car bomb. Coral Lopez almost went up with it, but I got her out.'

He supposed he was stupid to expect the cool, clipped voice in his ear to give praise or congratulations. It was a given that the work he did was homicidally dangerous. 'Zane is pleased that the fourth corpse at the complex turned out to be Beni and not you.'

'I think the car bomb—'

'—was meant for him, yes. It's the obvious conclusion. So Zane's working with the local police, hauling in members of Beni's car racket to see if they know anything.'

'Whoa,' Felix whistled. 'Doesn't waste much time, does he?'

'We may not *have* much time,' replied the Girl, and Felix knew her well enough to realize she wasn't being melodramatic – just stating a fact. 'We believe Orpheus want to revise and accelerate the timetable for their operation with the CAF.'

Felix asked the obvious question: 'Why?'

She paused a moment. 'According to our intel, Beni was marked for death by Orpheus because their command network suspect there's a double-agent involved in their dealings with the CAF.'

He swallowed uncomfortably. 'And why did they think it was Beni?'

'The CAF's last bomb-maker was killed following an "accident" that we arranged. It's possible Orpheus weren't fooled, that they think the bomb-maker was got at. Beni rose through the ranks of his own organization by stabbing his bosses in the back . . .'

'So Beni had past form, while I'm just a "kid" – which made him the more likely target,' Felix murmured. 'But it could easily have been me they negged instead.'

'Yes,' the Girl agreed. 'Is it possible Orpheus agents witnessed you foiling their car bomb?'

'I don't know. Maybe, I guess.' Felix felt frustration harden into anger. 'What was I supposed to do, leave Coral to die? With all that precious intelligence on Orpheus we're trying to get at?'

'You may have demonstrated a level of training at odds with your cover story.'

He nodded dismally. *To Gregor Manton's girlfriend if no one else.*

The Girl changed the subject. 'What was the merchandise delivered to Orpheus?'

'Chemicals,' Felix told her. 'For weapons, I'm guessing. They could be used to make scores if not hundreds of IEDs.'

'Dirty bombs?'

'Not classic dirty bombs in the radiological sense, but you'd definitely want to wash your hands afterwards, yeah.' He paused while a noisy announcement in Spanish distorted over the speakers. 'There was something else taken, something important that Coral and Deep took for the CAF. Three cardboard boxes – quite bulky but really light. I didn't have the chance to look inside, Chessa and me were taken straight here and dropped.'

'We arranged for someone to keep obs on the apartment,' the Girl revealed. 'Deep and Coral didn't return, and neither did Manton.'

'Right now they're taking the boxes back across the border. Chessa and me are being met at Denver by some other CAF member. I assume we'll be taken to the CAF safe house at Colorado Springs and everyone will meet there.'

'We'll be tracking you,' she reminded him. 'Once your signal stops moving we'll send in other operatives to keep obs.'

'That's comforting,' said Felix. 'So long as they're not spotted and Manton doesn't work out that Beni was nothing and I'm the *real* traitor in the group.'

'You know how well trained they are.'

'I know how easy it is to mess up.'

'For what it's worth,' she said slowly, 'I think you're dealing with this mission incredibly well.'

The words sent his cheeks burning. *I wish we could meet*, he wanted to say. *This thing feels so big now; I'm so far out of my depth . . . I just want to see someone who's a step removed from all this horror, someone who'll say it's OK. Someone I can trust.*

Felix cleared his throat. 'Listen, I know you're only meant to be a resource or whatever, but—'

'Your flight's boarding,' the Girl broke in.

'Wow.' For a moment he was floored. 'Are you hacking into the airport's computer system or something?'

'No, I overheard that airport announcement down the phone.' She paused. 'I wish I was as good as you seem to think I am. Good luck, Felix. Make contact as soon as you learn something.'

'Roger that.' Tiredness seeped back into his bones. 'Felix out.'

Tagging along with Chessa, Felix made it onto the plane without incident – but it was only once they'd taken off that he found he could finally relax a little. He looked down at Mexico City through a scuffed window in the glare of the morning sun. Miles and miles of drab, grey buildings, divided by bulging arterial roads already choked with traffic. Further out, slums sprawling over hills like a blight on the sierra, blending into a thin haze of brown smog. Distance lent the unsightly city an odd serenity.

But the only memories he was taking away were filled with fire and violence.

Chessa shifted in her seat beside him. 'You're quiet.'

'Sorry.' He looked over. Her long red hair lay across her angular face like fine-spun prison bars. 'I thought you were trying to sleep.'

'It's not happening.' She closed her eyes and sighed as if to prove it.

'Stuff on your mind?' *May as well try your luck*. 'You said you wished this whole Deathwing thing wasn't happening . . .'

Chessa shrugged. 'I shouldn't have said anything.'

'I thought I'd passed my tests? Thought I was in?'

'It's just . . . everything's gone so heavy. You saved Coral's life – you two nearly died. Beni *did* die, and took those poor security guards with him . . .'

Felix hesitated. 'One of them was dead already,' he

said gravely. 'Whatever Deep put on those rags, it wasn't chloroform.'

'What?' Chessa looked shaken. 'It . . . it must've been a mistake.'

'Maybe.'

'Deep's changed. Since Coral dumped him . . .'

Felix raised his eyebrows. 'Deep and Coral were an item?'

'A couple of years back. Before she fell for Greg.' She stared into space, her fingers a twisting tangle as she talked. 'Things got pretty messed up for a time. And though Greg and Deep worked stuff out – they had to, the CAF came first – Deep got kind of more extreme after that. More out there. You know?'

Felix nodded. He supposed terrorists got their hearts bruised just like anyone else.

'Felix, I'm scared.' Chessa looked at him, big-eyed. 'I'm just so afraid. Who else is gonna be dead before Deathwing's over? Deep? You? Me?' She shook her head and sighed. 'I never dreamed I would see someone I knew die right in front of my eyes.'

'I thought we'd be saving animals,' Felix chipped in. 'Not killing people.'

'I know. But it's . . . it's just how things have to be.' Chessa rubbed her eyes. 'Peaceful protest gets you nowhere. Manton doesn't want to use violence, but that's what big business is using on animals. Enough is enough.'

There you go, channelling your sister.

Felix nodded fervently, playing along. 'So . . . what

is Deathwing?' he asked casually. 'Coral said it would change the world.'

'Greg will tell you, I guess. When he's ready.'

Felix offered a noisy sigh. 'I don't see what else I can do to convince the CAF I'm onside and up for anything.'

Chessa held his gaze. 'You know, Coral thinks . . .' She shook her head, brushed her hair over her eyes. 'No. It's crazy. Forget it.'

'What?'

'Nothing.'

'Come on, what?'

She sighed again, but a nervous smile was tugging at the corners of her mouth. 'Coral's crazy, is all . . . she had this dumb idea that maybe it's not so much you wanna be with the CAF, but that . . . well . . .'

As she tailed off, Felix swallowed. He sensed where this was going, but played dumb. 'But that what?'

'I . . . I saw how you reacted when you found out I didn't just bump into you at the café,' she went on awkwardly. 'I know you like me, and Coral knows you like me, and . . . Well, I like you too, Felix, OK? You're . . . you're not like a lot of guys I've met. I mean . . .' She reached up and tweaked the air-con nozzle; the cool air blew at her hair. 'Look. There are more Benis than Felixes out there, is what I'm saying, OK? Way more Benis.'

Felix couldn't help himself. 'One less after last night.'

She didn't laugh. 'Look at you. You've been through such a lot . . . but you've come through it.'

'You've been through a lot too.'

'I had Coral watching out for me.'

'And telling you what to do. Like, who to talk to in cafés.'

Chessa shrugged. 'She may tell me what to do. Doesn't mean I always listen.'

'Oh, yeah?'

'Yeah.' She glanced shyly at him. 'Like, she said not to even think about being more than just friends with you.'

'She . . . she did?' Felix hesitated. *Chessa likes you. Use that.* He felt sorry for her, despite her cracked ideals. But he couldn't let that get in the way of the job he was here to do. 'We're not friends,' he said lightly. 'We're just . . . comrades. Brothers in arms.'

'I'm a girl, duh.' Chessa screwed up her nose. 'I can't be your brother.'

'Well, I've met your sister – and trust me, I don't want one of those!'

'Hey!' She slapped his chest reprovingly.

He caught her hand. Held on, just enough for it to signal something – then shammed shyness and pulled away. 'Uh . . . sorry. I didn't mean to . . .'

'. . . let go of my fingers?' Chessa looked him in the eye and put her hand in his again; to his surprise, Felix felt something stir inside. 'You Brits, you're so good at apologizing. I love your accent. You guys have the best accents, you know that?' She bit her lip. 'I . . . I really wish your country wasn't going to get it.'

'Get it?' The words were like a blowtorch to his brain, but Felix tried to keep his composure. 'Chessa, what are you on about?'

'Forget it . . .' She looked down at her lap. 'I shouldn't have said anything.'

'It's no big deal,' Felix insisted. *You've got to act like you're totally on side. You're CAF now.* He lowered his voice and leaned in closer to her ear. 'I left Britain, remember? They'd have put me inside if I'd stayed. If anyone's going to stick it to the Brits, good luck to them.'

Her eyes looked troubled, searching his out. 'Truth is, I don't know exactly what Deathwing is. Not the details. But I caught sight of Greg's notes one time, when he and Coral were going over some plan. And I saw it written down – *Deathwing, GB attack*. GB as in Great Britain . . . right?'

Felix stared at her. 'You're sure?'

'Written there. Black and bold.'

He shrugged and smiled. 'Well, then . . . Good.' Then he turned from her and looked out of the window, hiding his face in case she could read the horror there. The incredible view of Mexico City was long gone; the thick plastic was shaded solid grey-white, featureless in the clouds. Nothing to see. Oblivion.

For Felix, it felt like a glimpse of the future.

Upon touchdown at Denver International, Felix felt the familiar tightening in his guts at the prospect of his cover story facing outside scrutiny. The thought of being plunged back into the dark world of extremists he now inhabited filled him with dread, especially when he needed to talk to Zane about 'Deathwing GB attack' as soon as he could. All the way on the plane he'd been counting off the hours to their destination, planning how he could get word to Minos without Chessa knowing. She liked him, sure, but if he acted suspiciously he was sure Coral would get the truth from her in no time.

They walked through the endless corridors of the terminal. Felix eyed the payphones longingly, still checking all about for security, for any sign the two of them were being watched. If ATLAS agents were here, they might find a way to make contact. If the police were onto them, he would stand no chance.

But no one stood out. Felix and Chessa made their way through customs. They handed over little white forms to a dour-faced official and strolled out through NOTHING TO DECLARE.

If only, thought Felix.

A thin crowd of people was waiting at the arrivals gate. Again, Felix's eyes darted all around for signs of hope or trouble – then settled on the large plasma TV mounted on one of the walls. It showed police cars clustered around an anonymous-looking office block, then a close-up of an ambulance, and a stretcher being loaded on board.

Suddenly Chessa jerked to a stop beside him. There was no sound, of course, but 'Breaking News' scrolled along the bottom of the screen: COSMETICS BOSS TRIPLE ASSASSINATION. CRUSADE FOR ANIMAL FREEDOM CLAIMS RESPONSIBILITY FOR SHOOTINGS IN LONDON, NEW YORK AND MEXICO CITY. ANIMAL MURDERERS WILL IN TURN BE MURDERED.

Felix felt the floor shift beneath him. 'Triple assassination?' As if in answer, the image on the screen cut to another building, ringed with incident tape.

'Manton couldn't come with us,' Chessa said quietly. 'An important meeting, remember?'

Grumpy passengers pushed past them, and Felix steered Chessa onwards. 'Manton couldn't be in three places at once,' he murmured. 'So even if he shot one of them himself—'

'He never uses guns,' said Chessa.

'It's got to be Orpheus,' Felix thought aloud. 'They'd have the resources, and the manpower to arrange synchronized hits. But not the motivation – unless Manton's giving them something big.'

'Deathwing,' they said together.

Felix rubbed the back of his neck. One of the assassinations had taken place in London. Did these murders signal the start of Deathwing? 'You know,' he said, 'I ought to call my uncle, tell him I'm back in town.'

Chessa frowned. 'But I thought you told him you were going camping with friends?'

'I did,' Felix said vaguely. 'But he'll be expecting me to keep in touch. He'll be worried, you know what old people are like.'

She shook her head. 'No I don't. Coral's always looked out for me.'

'Is that what you call it?' Felix couldn't bite his tongue any longer. 'Getting you mixed up with killers?'

'Not killers. Crusaders. Freedom fighters.' She was staring at a woman in tears on the screen. 'People like *her* are the killers – they're responsible for the torture of so many animals. Did she cry over *them*?'

You're trying to sound like Coral, Felix thought sadly. *But I don't think you're like her. Not really.*

'No time to talk to your uncle, anyway. I spy our ride,' Chessa said suddenly. 'It's Kurt.'

Felix looked over. A tall, blond, stocky man in a grubby checked shirt was leaning against a pillar, reading a paper. He looked up and made eye contact with Chessa for a moment, then he glanced at his watch, stretched, turned and walked away.

'Something I said?' Felix joked weakly.

'Coral said we were supposed to follow him out to the multi-storey garage,' Chessa said. 'Once we're in the car, Kurt will fill us in on everything that's been going down.'

They followed the man out onto a crowded forecourt in bright sunlight, then across a road and into the dark shadows of an echoing multi-storey car park. Kurt heaved open an iron door and vanished up a stairwell. Felix felt tremors of wary anticipation as he and Chessa climbed the steps after him.

Chessa quickened her pace to keep up with Kurt, but he had already disappeared through the doorway to the third floor. Felix followed her through – but then a hand slapped down on his shoulder from behind.

Close-quarters combat training and muscle memory kicked in – Felix spun round and hit his attacker in the windpipe with his forearm, slamming him back against the stained concrete wall.

'No, Felix!'

Even before Chessa shouted, Felix realized it was Kurt he had pinned and at his mercy. He relaxed his grip. 'Sorry, man. You shouldn't have come up behind me like that.'

'You're good,' Kurt said. Like Manton, he had a Germanic edge to his hoarse voice. 'I was just going to tell you, you're not travelling with Chessa.'

'That's right,' a voice called over from a battered white pick-up. 'You're coming with me.'

'Manton?' Felix felt a prickle of nerves as he saw the gaunt, speckled face staring out at him through the open window. *He must've put Kurt up to that little surprise, but why? To see how I reacted, to see if it was fluke I handled myself OK with Beni?*

'Felix, Chessa,' said Manton. With a nod of his head he beckoned them over. 'Glad you've made it. Though I see your antisocial tendencies haven't left you yet, Felix.'

'We saw the news,' Chessa began, but Manton's eyes flashed as he shook his head angrily. *A car park's hardly the place to congratulate a guy on his contract killings*, Felix supposed.

'Coral and Deep are on their way as we speak,' Manton said. 'I spoke with them this morning.'

'You heard about what happened to Coral last night?' Chessa looked proudly at Felix. 'He was awesome.'

'Yes, we've talked the matter over. Thank you, Felix.' A grudging smile crept onto his face. 'Now, Chessa – go with Kurt. There have been complications with the New York situation. Luckily nothing major. But Kurt's picked up the final consignment and I must deliver it shortly.' He glanced behind at the back of the pick-up; whatever he was carrying, it was bulky and hidden under tarps. 'We're all meeting at the house – once I've taken Felix on a tour of the works.'

'You're showing him round yourself?' Chessa looked at Felix, impressed. 'Wow. You get the special treatment.'

'He's earned it,' said Manton, his smile growing strained as he glanced about. 'Now, come on. You know my rules – never too many of us in one place. If we're caught . . .'

You will be, thought Felix, cold anger flaring as the news clip of the widowed woman's face replayed in his mind. *Just wait*. He jogged round to the other side of the pick-up and got inside. The car smelled of sweat, and Manton himself looked as though he hadn't slept or showered in days. As the big man reversed smoothly away, Chessa waved, and Kurt gave Felix a long, oddly knowing look.

Then the pick-up was off, down the concrete slopes of the multi-storey car park and out into the harsh daylight.

Felix tried to break the awkward silence. 'I . . . I didn't know what to do when I saw Coral trapped in that four-by-four.'

'It sounds like you knew *exactly* what to do,' Manton returned. 'You wouldn't have risked her life and yours if you hadn't, right?'

'Well, I hoped I—'

'Only Coral is important to me. Very important.'

And he thinks I risked her life. 'If the cause is right,' said Felix, impassioned now, 'I'll do whatever it takes.'

'Meaning you'll take chances. You'll act on your own initiative.'

'Deep tried to contact you but got no answer. We couldn't just leave her there—'

'Coral knows the risks she takes.' Manton looked at him, eyes hard as shrapnel. 'Do you?'

Felix nodded boldly. *Time for a change of subject*. 'You, er . . . you made good time getting across the Mexican border.'

'The border runs almost two thousand miles,' Manton informed him, 'and barely seven hundred miles of it are properly policed. I was flown across in a light aircraft.

Deep is flying Coral over in the same way – straight here.'

'Why couldn't me and Chessa go with them?'

'The same reason I didn't wait till they had joined me so we could all fly together. I never put all my eggs in one basket.'

'Is that why you had three assassinations planned for the same time?' Felix asked quietly. 'In case one or two didn't come off?'

'The New York guy was an added bonus I didn't expect,' Manton said casually. 'Our partners are keen to demonstrate just how they can support us.'

'Orpheus, you mean?' Felix almost flinched as Manton threw him a sharp look, and quickly mumbled: 'Coral mentioned they were working with you . . .'

'I met with their representatives in Mexico to finalize plans and timetables,' Manton said curtly. 'And to ensure they were keeping their side of our bargain.'

Felix shrugged to disguise a shiver. Manton had mentioned *complications with the New York situation* – was that something to do with the Orpheus hitman? 'So, their side of the bargain is bumping off cosmetics bosses?'

'Eliminating certain key targets using skillsets and resources we lack,' Manton said calmly. 'Just as we can supply skills and resources *they* lack. That's why we're working together on Deathwing.'

'Right.' Felix attempted to sound in sympathy. 'Well, everyone's going to be talking about the CAF after those killings. People will see we really mean business.'

'Exactly. And all the planning, all the logistics – and the risks – were undertaken elsewhere.'

'But . . . . what is it that Orpheus doesn't have that they can get from the CAF?'

'Our own expertise can be applied to certain of their . . . issues.' Manton smiled sadly. 'You know, I'm sorry for what will happen. But people must be made to see that cruelty to animals *must* stop. There is no excuse for such prolonged torture and savagery against innocent lives.'

You said it yourself, Felix wanted to yell at him. *Innocent lives*.

But he knew that, to Manton's mind, they weren't. They were meat-eaters, animal-killers who'd forfeited their right to life.

They fell into silence, traffic thinning around them as they reached the city limits and drove on through the rugged western landscape. 'Uncle' Pete's home in Colorado was in a more urban area so Felix had never driven through such wilderness before. The brown plains swept on and on, broken here and there by patches of cactus, coming up short against red, stunted mountains. The wide-open expanse of nature was breathtaking. *All that's missing are cowboys riding the range*, he thought.

'How far away are the CAF's works, then?' Felix wondered.

Manton flashed a tight smile. 'So many questions, Felix.'

'I, uh . . . I just need to use the bathroom.' *That and phone in, tell Zane all I've learned.*

'We'll be there soon,' Manton assured him.

Distance and landscape melted into one. Finally Manton left the highway for a smaller road. There were few other cars in sight as he swung the pick-up onto a dirt track without signalling and accelerated hard away.

The path curved lazily through more wide-open nothingness. They passed a couple of old ranches – dilapidated shacks and outhouses and ancient farm machinery rusting in the shadows of giant cedar trees. Eventually the road petered out completely, surrendering to dusty, scrubby pastureland, but still Manton kept on. The occasional cedar waved wide, bushy arms as if in warning.

A knot pulled tight in Felix's belly. *This is seriously off the beaten track. Is he taking me somewhere to get rid of me?* His instincts were screaming something was wrong. Should he tackle Manton now, try to subdue him, bring him in for questioning? But timetables were being brought forward, and Manton wouldn't talk easily. If he kept quiet for long enough, it might be too late to stop Orpheus anyway; whatever big-time atrocity was in the offing, the CAF was only one part of it . . .

He knew his best chance was to cling to his cover and gain any intelligence he could, trusting that Minos were watching from a distance, tracking him through his pendant.

Finally Manton stopped the pick-up, jerking up on the handbrake in a short, violent snap. 'We're here.'

'We are?' Felix could see nothing but a slope of mottled hillside ahead, rising above the plain with its boulders and thickets of scrub oak.

Manton gestured to the graveyard sprawl of the ghost ranches far behind them. 'In the nineteen-fifties, a group of ranchers gave over some of their land to a guano mining operation. All but forgotten now.'

'Guano?'

'Bird-, bat- or seal-shit, if you prefer. Used mainly as a fertilizer.' Manton threw open the door and unpacked his burly body from the pick-up's cramped confines, stretching in the sun. 'Bats made the guano in this case. Mexican free-tails. There are hundreds of thousands of them in the cave system.' He marched along the track and Felix had to hurry to keep up. 'Apparently the mine never turned much of a profit; ammonia levels were too high in the smaller passages, caused breathing problems, labour disputes . . . It shut down, decades back.'

Felix feigned interest. 'I'm surprised those homes are still standing.'

'The land was bought and earmarked for re-development in the nineties,' Manton continued, 'but the construction company went bust. So the land stays as it was. Good news for the ecosystem. And for us.'

'How'd you hear about it?'

'A friend grew up local. He'd heard stories about the place, you know? I just did some digging round, learned the legal situation.' Manton crouched beside a tangle of barbed wire and wooden planking. 'When we got serious about the CAF, we knew we needed a place we could keep stuff. Stuff that would land our asses straight in jail and be confiscated immediately if the cops caught on to us.'

Nerves washed around Felix's stomach. 'And this is it?'

'A perfect setup.' With a grunt of effort Manton dragged the barrier away from the hole. 'Deserted, abandoned, hard to find – unless you know what you're looking for.' He gestured down to the hole. 'There's a ladder just in there. Go on, lower yourself down.'

Felix peered into the pit of blackness at his feet. 'What's down there?'

'A workshop, used by our previous bomb expert.' Manton smiled, but a second gesture to the hole betrayed impatience. 'Now it's yours. I need you to make something for me.'

Felix didn't move. 'A bomb?'

'Something special.' He pulled a torch from his pocket and shone it into the pit. 'I need it quickly.'

Through the alarms blaring in his head, Felix knew he had to play along – for now. In the torchlight he discerned a glimmer of metal in the blackness: a rung.

With Manton's eyes and the torch trained on his every move, Felix gingerly lowered himself into the pit.

Felix knew he would never forget his nerve-shredding descent into the old mine for as long as he lived. Lost in cold, stinking shadows almost at once. Grasping every rung on the creaking slimy ladder as though it were gold. Feeling the ground beneath his feet squirm as he sank into thick slimy deposits of guano.

Talk about up shit creek. Here I am, down it.

It was a nightmare; hearing the rustling of countless wings and the eerie chitters of bats, invisible in the thick blackness. Itching as the mites that infested the crap on the floor swarmed blindly up his legs, into his clothes. And only the lone beam from Manton's torch to light the way as he was guided roughly through a tangled trail of tunnels and caverns.

How did I ever end up here? Felix bunched his fists, tried to keep calm and take deep breaths – but the air was so rank he almost retched. *I can't handle this.*

I've got to handle this.

A sudden icy flutter cut the air with a thin squeal as something flew overhead. Felix flinched and swore.

'Just bats.' Manton steadied him and steered him onwards.

The nightmare journey continued until they came to a larger cave. The floor was overlaid with wooden planks, and a false ceiling of plastic tarpaulins was stretched taut over scaffolding poles. The torchlight reflected off metal, revealed structures in the dimness. Slowly Felix managed to identify them: a workbench, toolbox, a chair, a bookshelf, a camp bed. Other shapes were less defined. He thought he saw a sleeping bag, a rucksack, bin liners, a large metal case. At his feet were a few snags of detonator cord.

'Of course, saltpetre from guano can be used for making black gunpowder,' Manton said, his voice strangely deadened by the weird acoustics. 'An appropriate place for a bombsmith to work, right? Which is why it still doesn't make sense to me that McGregor – your poor predecessor – blew himself up at his apartment. I mean, I laid on all this for him, instructed him to work here and here alone . . .'

Felix inwardly cursed Zane, who clearly had known nothing of this underground factory. *Sloppy*. No wonder Manton had negged the injured man instead of taking him to hospital; the 'accident' happening at home instead of here must've made Manton still more suspicious. 'It's, er, not the nicest of places to work. Maybe he got claustrophobic?'

'McGregor was a very committed man,' Manton murmured.

'Lucky the accident didn't happen here anyway,' said Felix, trying to keep in character. 'I mean, what about the bats?'

'I would never want to risk their safety needlessly.' Manton played the torch beam on a small metal box on one of the shelves. 'This device generates a high-frequency signal. The bats don't like it. They stay well away; the entire area is clear.'

And I suppose we're far enough from the real world and deep enough underground that an explosion would never be noticed, Felix thought, heavy-hearted.

Manton switched on a large, powerful torch and placed it on its end. It shone up at the plastic ceiling, sending warped shadows in all directions. The speckles on Manton's face seemed to swarm there like tiny flies.

Felix looked away and saw half a dozen small, furry bodies on the table. He shuddered at the thought of how many bats must infest the cave network. 'Those ones can't have heard your signal.'

'They're dead. McGregor must've put them here.' Manton pocketed his torch and then gently, reverently scooped the bodies off the table. 'Hundreds fall from the caverns every day from old age or disease. Invisible as they plunge through the darkness into the filth they've spent their lives creating.' He stroked one of the little corpses. 'In time, their bodies will be buried in the waste of their young, as the cycle starts over. In its own way, it's beautiful, isn't it?'

To a sicko, maybe, thought Felix. 'Did you name Deathwing after them?'

Manton nodded, and placed the bats down in a dark corner. 'It was here the plan was hatched. "Deathwing" sounds a touch melodramatic, I know. But the wings of vengeance *will* be beating . . .' He returned to the shelving and rummaged through a number of bulky black objects before holding one of them up. 'What's this, would you say?'

Felix saw it was an old Soviet assault vest with sticks of C4 explosive stuffed into the ammunition pouches. The design had been modified: lengths of black duct tape blocked the armholes and a larger pouch had been sewn onto the front. 'Some kind of hostage vest,' he said quietly.

'McGregor was working on a microcircuit,' Manton explained. 'One that would operate a release mechanism on a jacket so that its wearer could flee the area before the explosive detonated. I understand Deep talked to you about it.'

'He told me about the vest in theory.'

Manton didn't look pleased. 'Deep forgets himself sometimes. He shouldn't really have told you anything at all.'

'Well, he certainly didn't say anything about a microcircuit.'

'That's because McGregor never completed a working version to fit our needs.' Manton stowed the jacket back on the shelf. 'Reluctantly I've agreed to abandon the microcircuit and pursue a lower-tech version. One that Deep seems to think you can deliver.'

Felix thought back to his conversation in the Passat the night before. It seemed like days ago. 'A pencil detonator to blow the release-catch on the vest so that the whole assembly falls to the ground . . .'

'Igniting a secondary fuse that sets off the main explosive,' Manton agreed. 'Can you can make it work?'

'Yeah, I think so.' Felix nodded to the vest, back on the pile on the bottom shelf. 'Do you want me to adapt that thing?'

Manton shook his head. 'I need you to make me a working version in miniature.'

Felix frowned. 'In miniature?'

'A scaled-down, fully functional prototype,' Manton insisted.

'Um . . . why? Couldn't you just send over the full-sized one to them now?'

'Courier firms scan packages for explosives as a matter of course. You will use the barest minimum, so it will slip past their scanners.' Manton held up what looked to be a small tube of glistening material. 'And you will use this as your "vest".'

Felix studied the curious item. It looked a bit like a miniature wrist support. There were no armholes, just as Deep had specified; it was slit up the front, and hook-and-eye fasteners were attached top and bottom to secure the strip. There was a small pocket, perhaps big enough to hold a data card of the type you got in digital cameras; it looked to be part of the original design rather than added on.

'What is it?' Felix wondered.

Manton looked at him and frowned. 'You don't know?'

'Well . . .' Felix pressed on quickly. 'I mean, the material's very different from the full-sized harness. As scale models go—'

'It'll suffice for my purposes.' Manton's attitude seemed to have grown chillier. He indicated a stone on the desk, one about as big as Felix's fist. 'The vest will fit around this basic mannequin – and must easily detach from it too.'

'Couldn't you just smuggle the full-sized version across the border?' Felix wondered. 'After all, if it's as easy to get across as you—'

'*I say what we do, Felix,*' Manton raged suddenly, his voice rattling off like automatic gunfire. 'You understand?'

A palpable sense of threat hung in the stale, musty air. Felix held very still. 'Yeah,' he muttered. 'I'm sorry. Course.'

'I respect initiative, but obedience and loyalty, whatever the circumstances, are more important.' Manton's towering frame seemed too big for his subterranean bolt-hole as he bore down on Felix. 'Coral said you ignored her direct request to leave her be, and that you convinced Deep to let you try to save her.' He paused. 'She also said you seemed extremely well-trained in bomb disposal.'

Felix bought time to think of his reply with a slow shrug of the shoulders. 'I told you, my dad rammed that stuff down my throat when I was growing up.'

'Ah, yes, your father. Well, now you can prove how well he taught you. You'll find everything you need in here to get on with your work.' Manton selected a handful more of the tubular fabric supports from a box on the shelf and placed them on the desk. 'Here. I don't expect you to get a working model right first time. You can experiment. And later on, I'll be here to assist you.'

Now he stooped to lift a large rusted cylinder from beneath the desk; it was drilled full of holes, like a garden incinerator. 'First, I must take care of another problem that's arisen.'

Felix regarded him. 'Will you be gone long?'

'No.' Manton half smiled. 'I should mention, we have a couple of webcams inside one of those ranches, watching the track and the entrance to the caves. So if anybody comes looking for you, we'll know – and will respond accordingly.'

Felix felt sweat cold and slick on his back. What if Zane *had* sent ATLAS agents after him?

'Nervous, Felix?' Manton enquired.

'No.' Felix shook his head. 'But if I do this, I want to know what I'm doing it for.'

'To belong, Felix. Isn't that what you've wanted so badly all this time?' He shifted his grip on the large metal canister. 'When you've finished the prototype to my satisfaction, I'll take you back to the safe house – and share every detail of Deathwing with you.'

Felix felt a frisson of anticipation. 'I'll get to work,' he said. *But can I make your miniature prototype before the cavalry show up – and get me killed?*

* * *

Ignoring the tickle of bugs exploring his skin, the soreness in his throat from the sharp, acid air, and the ache in his tired, watering eyes, Felix worked as quickly as he could. Down here in this dark, stifling world of rock, wood and plastic sheeting, time had little meaning. But his heart had to be pounding at least four times every second.

He longed to have a good root round, turn the place over. But aside from the risk of disturbing a booby-trap, what if the CAF had rigged hidden cameras in here? He just couldn't take the risk.

Even the most cursory inspection showed the workshop was well stocked. Felix understood now where Deep had got hold of genuine US army kit – there was a stack of it on the shelves, even an amount of counter-IED hardware. He recognized the tools in an instant because he'd been trained to use every one; they'd come straight from a NATO EOD 085 Operator's Toolkit. *To test how easy it is to take their bombs apart*, Felix supposed, *to understand them better.*

It was weird to see high-tech items like a Scanwedge – a portable X-ray scanner – alongside such primitive tech as a stock of pencil-dets. This was newly manufactured kit, though, not ancient army-surplus. *How'd they get hold of this stuff? Samples knocked off from a defence systems specialist?* He realized that the detonators' relatively crude nature could be an asset to the CAF and Orpheus – they would be impossible to detect or jam using electronic counter-measures . . .

Get on with the job, he told himself. *Let's do this.*

Like a surgeon about to perform a major operation, Felix studied the components he'd laid out on the workbench: the miniature vest, the pencil det, the burning fuse and an array of tools. He put on a pair of surgical gloves and began to work, carefully and methodically.

First he took the pencil detonator and clamped it gently into the vice secured on the edge of the workbench – if he crushed its delicate aluminium case, it would probably blow his hand off. Then he took a length of the black burning fuse – closely resembling a piece of washing line – and taped one end of it to the pencil det. Quickly wiping his brow, he lifted from the table a thin foil capsule of lead azide – a highly sensitive primary explosive – and crimped it to the other end of the burning fuse.

The first triggering device was almost complete. All that remained was for him to take a tiny ball of PE4A plastic explosive, and mould it around the capsule. Then he could attach it to the miniature harness.

Felix held one up, and looked at it critically. It was a very crude substitute for a real assault vest – its tubular shape made it look more like a bodystocking. At present, a cold-and-flu remedy capsule was tucked inside its little pocket, representing the payload to be carried.

And I'm supposed to know what this 'vest' really is, thought Felix ruefully. *Though I guess the important thing is to jolt it off this stone mannequin . . .*

Would his improvised solution work?

'Let's find out,' he murmured.

* * *

The cave was soon stinking like bonfire night, as test after test proved unsuccessful. Felix slumped down on a wooden chair. He realized with some surprise that almost four hours had passed.

Suddenly a large shadow loomed over him. Felix jumped.

Manton was back.

'Here.' The big man slapped a bottle of water down on the desk, and a Subway roll that was a couple of days out of date.

'Sort out your business?' Felix asked.

'I've sorted the platforms. We're another step closer.'

Platforms? Felix frowned. *As in, computer operating systems?*

'Now.' Manton sniffed the air like a rangy wolf. 'What progress have *you* made?'

'I've . . . worked out how not to do it.' Felix found it hard not to physically flinch from the displeasure in Manton's eyes. 'I'm not used to dealing with such small amounts of explosive.'

'I need this prototype to work, Felix.' Manton held up the charred remains of one of the miniature test-harnesses with a disapproving look. 'A man called Stevens supplied me with these; he won't be able to do so again. I wasn't expecting you to need to use my entire supply here.'

Felix rubbed his tired eyes. 'The hook and eye fasteners are difficult to dislodge without damaging the whole assembly. I'm aiming for the pencil det to ignite a small percussive charge that will jog the hook from the eye. But I'm telling you, you can't really compare this to the big plastic clasps on the real deal.'

'I've told you it's *this* assembly I must deliver,' Manton said impatiently.

'Wait a minute . . .' Felix nodded slowly. The solution seemed suddenly obvious. 'What if I didn't hook the fasteners directly, but secured them with something like . . . I don't know, fishing wire. Something the charge could sever.'

Manton nodded keenly. 'Or even a length of cotton thread?'

'Depending on how rugged you want the set-up – yeah, that might do the job.' Felix felt wide-awake again. 'The det will light the fuse and burn through the cotton at the same time. Then the hostage vest drops off the victim . . .'

'And the lit fuse ignites the secondary charge, releasing the payload where it's dropped.' Manton smiled, and the torchlight reflected off his horn-rimmed glasses. 'I'm hearing "Eureka", Felix. Are you hearing Eureka?'

But suddenly, all Felix could hear was the screaming victims of some unknown future holocaust. He tried to smile but felt physically sick. Whatever the CAF and Orpheus were planning, he realized he might just have brought them a whole lot closer to achieving it.

. . . 16 . . .

It didn't take too long for Felix to rig another ready-made miniaturized dummy vest with the new improved catch-release mechanism. Manton had disappeared off again; to breathe fresher air, Felix supposed. But at least working unobserved made it easier to concentrate and just get the job done.

After a few failed attempts Felix was able to defeat the cotton catch between the two hooks with just the tiniest fizzle of gunpowder.

Duplicating the charge volume, he fitted another vest onto the blackened test mannequin. The quickest of the pencil dets was five minutes, give or take, so he attached it and waited, ready to give Manton the final demonstration. In case this one failed, he prepared another as a back-up. *You'd better work*, he thought. *I need that intel on Deathwing, almost as much as I need to be let out of this stinking hole and grab some sleep.*

Anxious thoughts flapped in his mind's shadows: *No one's come to find me so far – do they know about the surveillance or have I been abandoned?* He thought of the Girl – *'I wish I was as good as you seem to believe'* – and of Zane giving the order to disable McGregor, not knowing he was under orders to perform explosives work here. He felt more and more vulnerable. *You've made enough mistakes yourself*, he realized. *Learn what you can, get to the CAF safe house, then get the hell out and let Zane take care of everything.*

What would happen to Chessa?

Not your problem. You're kidding yourself if you think you can turn her.

He was shaking his head miserably when the sound of slippery footsteps signalled Manton arriving back at the workshop. Only this time the squelching was louder. With a start, Felix saw Deep was just behind Manton.

'Hey!' Deep said, with a brightness that seemed strained. 'There's the man!'

'You made it back.' Felix forced a big grin. 'How was the flight?'

'I was the pilot, so obviously it was perfect.' That smile that never reached Deep's eyes was back. 'Put us down on private land outside Denver.'

'Is Coral here too?'

'Nah, she got a ride with Kurt back to the safe house while I came on in a copter Orpheus laid on for me.'

'They're getting impatient,' Manton muttered.

Deep shrugged. 'Been rattled, haven't they?'

Felix sensed the undercurrents between the two men,

but couldn't grasp the meaning. *Or am I just starting to imagine things now?*

'Well, anyway,' said Manton. 'I know you went through a lot to steal that equipment. Now here's where you see it dovetail with McGregor's part of the pro- gramme. Although, credit where it's due, Felix has really made it his own.'

'His fuse idea . . . ?'

'Will work, now a little thread's tying everything together.' Manton loomed over Felix, his habitual creepy smile on his face. 'Show us.'

'It's not very spectacular,' said Felix. 'But once I crack the det, in five minutes or so . . .' He pinched the end of the metal pencil with a pair of pliers. 'That reminds me – how were you planning to crimp the pencil end?'

Manton shook his head. 'That can be done manually by whoever's assisting the volunteer.'

I wish I knew just what you had in mind, thought Felix.

The three of them waited in the cold, pungent gloom for the big event. Deep seemed edgy, tapping his foot, his eyes darting between Manton, the vest and Felix. Manton, as ever, stood poised and impassive.

Finally, with the faintest of sparks, the fuse ignited, the cotton thread snapped and the substitute hostage vest fell from the pumice. The fuse in the weird, filmy material burned down into the pocket and ignited the tiny amount of gunpowder in the ampoule, cracking it open.

It was probably the least impressive display of pyrotechnics Felix had ever witnessed. But Manton and

Deep burst into excited raptures of praise and applause. Felix flinched; the noise felt too loud for such an enclosed space.

'The final piece falls into place.' Manton clapped Deep on the back. 'Satisfied, my old friend?'

'Should've been the *first* piece. But that was beautiful.' Deep's relief was marked in every line of his face. 'Have you written out your method, mate?'

Felix patted a piece of paper on the desk. 'It's all there. And I already made a back-up model for you to send off wherever.'

'Then I think we're all done here.' Manton smiled across at Deep, then crossed to Felix and put an arm around his shoulders.

Felix never saw Manton's other hand hurtle towards his jaw, but he felt the strike like a door slammed on his face. Taken completely off-guard, Felix couldn't even roll with the blow – the friendly arm around his shoulders had tightened into a neck-lock. He tasted blood in the back of his constricted throat, felt a thick warm rush of the stuff sticky on his lips and chin. The pressure on his throat increased.

Manton played you, Felix realized. *Promised you intel he would never have shared.*

Muscle-memory kicked in even while his senses reeled; he kicked his heel hard against Manton's shin and then shifted his weight violently, knocking the big man off-balance and breaking his grip.

But Deep was already advancing, a white cloth clutched in one hand. The image of dying guards in the Mexican security hub flashed into Felix's mind.

Don't breathe in, don't breathe in.

But Manton had left him half strangled, and as the sodden rag was pressed against his face he couldn't help but suck in a breath . . .

Just for a moment a sharp, acrid stink forked through his nostrils. He tried to breathe out, spluttering into a hard handful of wet cloth. Felix felt his knees buckle. He shut his eyes and the next thing he knew he was on the ground.

He felt Manton nudge him with the toe of his boot, checking for signs of any struggle left in him. *Fake unconsciousness,* Felix thought. *Maybe if you wait, catch them off guard . . .*

But he didn't have to fake a thing. Wakefulness was already reducing to nightmare flashes. He felt sick, could barely open his eyes. When he did, he found his vision distorted. His senses picked at movement and sound, trying to make sense of them.

Manton's voice: *'The hostage vest . . . always told McGregor we'd need it someday . . . stashed it over there . . .'*

Blackness. Then the caustic rip of Velcro. Loud, like his head coming apart. Hard fabric closing on his chest like the jaws of a mantrap. Two sinister clicks as heavy clasps fastened around his waist. Weirdly detached, he realized:

A suicide bomber's bodywarmer. Old-school.

Deep, hesitant, a way off: *'. . . I'm glad you're doing as Orpheus said you should . . .'*

'I make up my own mind, Deep . . . He didn't even

recognize . . . We're taking no chances . . .' Manton's words wouldn't hold their definition. 'Fetch Stevens . . . we'll take care of them both . . . with the rest of the evidence . . .'

The world went black again. Another voice seeped through the silence, not too far away. He couldn't place it.

'. . . Help me. Please, no. No water . . .'

Deep's voice. 'No cure . . . Kindest to end it . . . Neither of them will know.'

A fourth person was now in the workshop with them. Felix tried to stir. No good. His body – numb.

Absolute darkness consumed him.

It might have been a moment or a year later, but Felix felt sudden sensation prickle through his body, like billions of tiny spiders in his veins.

'Felix. Wake up. Wake the hell up. It is Felix, right? Can't check your chain with this damn rig you're wearing.'

An American voice. Not Zane's. This one was pitched a little higher. It sounded kind of like the dumb bloke off *Friends*. What was that guy's name?

'Joey . . .' Felix croaked.

'I'm not Joey. I'm Brad Rivers. Unless you mean that *you're* Joey? No way. Come on, man, you've got to be Felix. Or you at least have got to know where we can find him 'cos if I try and get this thing off you myself . . .'

Felix's mouth felt dry as a cracker and his head was

pounding, but it was as if he were stretching out of a tunnel, into light again. The sky was grey and fractured with light. He realized he was still in the workshop, the torch was still beaming at the tarpaulin stretched above and he—

He was still locked into a terrorist hostage vest and someone was bent over him. *Brad, he said his name was.* Felix squinted, trying to focus. Brad was a young guy, late teens maybe. He looked to be Chinese with cropped black hair and square-framed glasses.

Felix stared up at him. 'What . . . happened?'

'Don't try to move. You might go bang.' Brad looked grave. 'Your pockets are stuffed full of C4 and we don't know what might set it off, do we?'

'No.' Felix was longing to stretch his limbs as the pins and needles burned through them but held himself still. 'No, we don't.'

'Someone dosed you up with a bad-ass sedative. You had depressed respiration and I thought you were going into cardiac arrest, so I gave you a shot of adrenaline. I brought it along for poor old Doc Stevens over there. But it's too late for him.' Brad frowned, his facial expression ever-changing as he went on gabbling. 'Y'know, it's a pity this damn hostage vest was in the way or I could've given you the shot intracardially – needle in the heart, whack! Right through the chest like they do in that old movie. Only Uma Thurman sits right back up, *you* just lay there and came round slowly 'cos I had to stick the needle in a vein instead—'

'Shut up!' Felix rasped, his voice catching. He glanced

quickly to his side and saw another body lying in a similar vest – Stevens, the man he'd heard being brought here. 'For God's sake get out of here. This whole place could go up any moment.'

'I'd love to, man, but I'm in the Minos Chapter. Split-second Squad, like you. Means I've got to do the right thing right now.' He grinned unexpectedly. 'Sorry – I talk a lot. When I get nervous, I get the verbal craps. Just the way I am.'

Felix stared at Brad groggily. 'So Zane sent the cavalry after all.'

'Only trouble is, my training's more on the "hacktivist" side. Going after future-spook terrorists. High-level espionage. Cool stuff. Not the kind of crap that explodes in your face if you cut the red wire before the blue wire or whatever.'

I don't believe this. Holding very still and starting to sweat now, Felix tried to marshal his thoughts. 'You've had no training in bomb disposal?'

Brad shrugged and smiled. 'A little. But I'm sure you're an excellent teacher. Right?'

Felix wasn't feeling up to superhero-style banter. 'Bring me something to prop up my head,' he said. 'I need to see what's going on in this vest.'

'You'll be seeing what's going on in my bowels,' Brad muttered. 'I'm crapping myself here.'

Me too, Felix thought to himself. 'Listen – I don't know how long I was out. Was there any sign of two guys outside?'

'Didn't see anyone.'

15

The news gave Felix little cheer. 'Manton and Deep could be hiding out there. But how will they know when the bomb's gone off? Anything too big would hurt their precious animals . . .'

'Shock tremors maybe.'

'I guess.' Felix winced as Brad wedged something hard under his neck. 'What's that?'

'Relax. It's a reel of det cord.'

Felix said nothing. He was trying hard not to throw up, even as he assessed the task ahead. The ammunition pouches were super-glued shut, and each was linked to an electronic motion-sensor triggering unit. But for the full lowdown on how the hostage bomb had been rigged he needed more than eyes.

'Fetch me the Scanwedge from the kitbag on the shelf,' he said, licking his dry lips. 'It's an X-ray generator: we can look inside the bomb.'

'Won't that be nice?'

'Just get it.' Felix fought to stay calm. 'There's the generator itself, a flat panel and a—'

'Tablet PC to show the image?' Brad waved the hardware over Felix's head. 'Yeah, I know all that. I told you I had some training. Took tests on this stuff. Nearly passed them, too.'

Felix watched as Brad powered up the tablet. 'You trying to be funny?'

'It takes no effort, I promise. OK, here we go.' Brad tried to slide the flat panel under Felix's back. 'What, you're just gonna lie there? Lazy son of a—'

'Be careful.' Felix held his breath and arched his back

a fraction. 'I may feel like death, but I don't want to go the whole hog.'

'See, now *you're* joking.' Brad smiled tightly. 'Isn't this fun?'

Felix did his best to return the smile. What did they say in training – *Put the victim at ease any way you can, so he's less likely to panic and blow you both to hell*. But it was one thing to do the reassurance stuff when you were the one in control. When you were on the receiving end . . .

'There.' The flat panel, about the size of a tea tray, was square underneath Felix. Now Brad trained the X-ray generator down at him. Felix heard the whir and buzz of the generator firing the pulses of radiation into him. It seemed to take for ever. *I'm a human bomb*. The realization was overwhelming. He felt so rough anyway, a part of him wanted to just shut down completely, to fall apart.

'Aw, man, you never said cheese.' Felix forced himself to focus as Brad turned the tablet round to show him a blurred and grainy image.

'Looks like we've got ten sticks of plastic explosive – about five pounds – and two firing circuits,' Felix muttered. 'The good news is that there's no back-up radio-controlled initiation method. But the triggering device is a mercury tilt switch.'

'That's when if you make a sudden move, a blob of mercury slides down a tube and closes the electrical circuit wired to the bomb, right?' Brad grimaced. 'Good job you didn't have that Uma Thurman moment back there.'

'At least it's nothing too complicated,' Felix muttered.

16

'If Manton was a bomb expert he wouldn't have needed me.'

'But *you* need me. So what do I do with this switch, cut it out of the circuit?'

'Exactly. Scalpel and snips on the workbench.'

'I'm on it.' Brad ran over to the workbench. 'Oh, and just so you know – getting cramp would be a really bad idea right now.'

He returned moments later and began deftly cutting pieces of fabric away from the vest. Holding dead still, almost numb with fear, Felix barely dared to breathe. They both knew there was enough explosive positioned between them to destroy the entire cave, and the slightest movement would cause it to detonate.

Brad took a moment to wipe the sweat out of his eyes, then cracked on, carefully cutting his way through the fabric like a surgeon practising his trade. Centimetre by centimetre he closed on the circuit, getting closer to death with each incision . . .

Finally Brad cut his way through the last piece of fabric and exposed the bird's-nest loop of wires inside the ammo pouch. 'Jeez!' Brad stared at the mess. 'What do I do with this?'

'You've got to trace the wires to the circuit,' Felix told him, 'then hack out the tilt fuse. Come on, you can do this.'

'I guess I'd better, huh?'

Felix watched as Brad traced the wires into the mercury tilt switch and edged his snips forward. If he got the right wire, the tilt fuse would be cut from the circuit. But if he was wrong . . .

Brad hesitated.

Please God don't let him mess this up. Felix had never felt so vulnerable in his life. If his heart drummed any harder it would be enough to tilt the switch. The blood was roaring in his ears. This was about as elemental as it got. Straightforward destiny – live or die.

Brad took a final deep breath and eased the tip of the cutters to the wire.

...15...

Felix held his breath as Brad opened his palm and gently
squeezed the jaws of the snips shut.

Nothing.

The bomb was dead.

It was like a crushing weight had fallen from Felix's
shoulders; relief came with an overpowering rush of
nausea. 'Thanks,' he muttered, breathing deeply to stop
himself puking.

'Don't mention it.' Brad wiped his sweaty brow,
spiking up his hair. 'Actually, *do* mention it. Loudly. To
Zane and the tera-heads and anyone else, let them know
how good I am.'

'OK.' Felix was already undoing the assault vest, free-
ing himself from its confines. 'Should I tell them the part
where you let Manton and Deep eyeball you coming in
here?'

'Why are you so sure they did?'

'Think about it.' Felix carefully put down the explosive vest. 'Why would they leave motion-detectors in this thing when I was as good as dead and not likely to move any time soon?'

Brad winced. 'Because they knew someone was coming who would try and move you?'

'Manton said they had security around here,' said Felix. 'They must've seen you coming up the track and realized you were following me.'

'I wasn't, though.' Brad crossed to the crumpled body in the assault vest over by the workbench. 'I came after Doc Stevens here from New York – as part of my investigation into the Deathwing project.'

'I'm tasked on that too,' Felix told him.

'I know.' Brad smiled wanly. 'Zane said there was someone else working on this thing. But he didn't go into details.'

'Yeah, he only mentioned you to me in passing. The less we know the less we can spill, I guess.' Felix took a swig of warm water from the near-empty bottle on the bench. 'So your Doc Stevens must've been the trouble in New York Manton mentioned . . .'

'The tera-heads were tracking him. Through this.' He reached into the body's jacket pocket and pulled out a gold chain. 'I planted it on Doc Stevens.'

Felix frowned. 'Your Minos pendant? So the tera-heads tracked it and guided you here?'

'S' right. The Girl with the cute Russian accent, d'you know her?'

Felix felt a stupid spark of jealousy. 'I, uh . . . I think

so.'

'She said the signal converged on yours, and that both chains had stopped transmitting.' Brad shrugged. 'It doesn't take a genius to know both chains had to be underground somewhere, where the signal couldn't be picked up.'

'Glad you worked it out.' Felix crouched to study the bomb vest Doc Stevens had been strapped into. 'The mercury tilt switch is way smaller on this one,' he muttered. 'Another miniaturized prototype?'

'I hate to interrupt when you're making theories,' said Brad, 'but Manton must've wanted to destroy all evidence, right? Can't see him pushing off, *assuming* we've all gone up in smoke.'

Felix grimaced. 'He'll want to make damn sure. '

'So, now might be a good time to ask you what you think that PIR sensor in the doorway is for?'

Felix saw with a jolt the small black plastic housing, barely visible at ground level.

'I stepped over it,' Brad assured him. 'It's pretty basic. Don't think I was detected.'

Felix was already on his hands and knees inspecting the PIR sensor with the flashlight, willing his eyes to focus.

'What's that thing attached to?' Brad had lowered his voice to a whisper, as if the PIR could somehow hear him.

'I think,' said Felix slowly, 'it might be a VO trigger linked to a remote-controlled IED here in the workshop.'

'What?'

'First priority would be to destroy all evidence,' Felix

went on. 'But if they can kill someone else they've seen sniffing around at the same time, that's all good. They're not ready to put Deathwing into operation yet.'

'So this PIR must be part of their standard security protocol,' Brad concluded.

'Right.' Felix could see two lots of wires running from the PIR – and realized it was linked to something else pushed into a cavity in the wall just above floor level. 'I think this thing is working just as it would in a home burglar alarm system. They can't use wireless tech 'cos the cave walls would block the signal. So one of these cables must run all the way through those tunnels to an alarm someplace.'

'And when it sounds off, it tells Manton or whoever that someone's inside. What about the second wire?'

'Rapid firing cord.' Felix looked up at Brad. 'There's a command wire IED wedged into the rock.'

Brad closed his eyes. 'Please be kidding me.'

'In most security situations, Manton wouldn't want to blow up his workshop, would he? It's kind of a last resort.' Felix started following the course of the cord, almost invisible as it snaked out of the workshop and along the tunnel at ground level, hugging the cave wall so tightly as to be near-invisible. 'The PIR lets them know when someone's passed through into here, and then they have a choice – come in and catch them or use the command wire and set off the IED.'

'And if Manton *is* waiting out there and hasn't felt the double bang of hostage bombs, he might detonate that thing at any moment.' Brad looked horrified. 'Come on, let's get out of here.'

'But this place is full of forensics, clues to whatever the hell it is they're doing,' Felix argued. 'If we lose all that, everything I've done to get here's been for nothing.'

'It'll be worth *less* than nothing if our asses go up with it too.' Brad grabbed hold of his arm. 'I turn sixteen next month – then I'm out of Minos. Call me sentimental, but I'd like my limbs to leave with me.'

'So go.' Felix shook off his grip. 'There's no point both of us risking it.'

'What is this, my-balls-are-bigger-than-your-balls time? Your CAF friends could get bored and set off that thing off any second. You can't defeat it in time.'

'Probably not,' Felix agreed. 'But I *can* cut the command wire.' Brad instantly offered him the snips but Felix shook his head. 'Not with those. If the cut wires touch it might short-circuit and activate the IED.'

Brad threw down the snips. 'So what will you use?'

Felix was already at the cluttered shelves, sorting through the kit. 'I think I saw . . . yes!' He grabbed a leg pouch and produced a black tubular object like a pocket torch from inside. 'A Korona wire-cutter. Remote-operated ceramic blades slice a fourteen-mil section from the cable—'

'Don't quote the brochure, just do it!'

Felix was sweating like a killer in court as he wound the wire-cutter spring to its maximum and placed it beside the cord. How long did he have? He wiped sweaty hands on his top and used the non-conductive ground anchors to secure it in place, banging it into the hardened guano floor.

'Will you hurry?' Brad hissed at him.

'I'm hurrying.' Felix scissored his teeth through his dry lips, tasted blood. He knew Brad was right. Even now, Manton could be deciding enough was enough – that the unexpected intruder had somehow avoided the PIR or just not located the workshop at all – and was preparing to destroy it himself. The deadly electrical pulse could already be humming down the line, into the circuit, detonating the bomb . . .

Brad's right – work faster, you idiot.

Felix pulled the spool of trigger line from the leg pouch and reeled off several metres. *Manton could be outside right now with his finger on the button.* Then he used the integral snap hook to attach it to the Korona before easing a section of command wire into the tool's cutting slot. Finally he retreated to where Brad was sheltering behind the workbench.

'Here goes nothing,' he murmured.

'Or everything,' Brad shot back.

Saying a silent prayer, Felix yanked hard on the trigger wire. The ceramic blades fired silently.

The silence continued as the det cord lay severed.

Brad released a long, shuddering sigh of relief. 'Nice.'

'We're not safe yet,' Felix warned him. 'I don't know about Manton, but Deep has a gun. They might come looking to check the bomb's gone off. If they find us . . .'

'Well I'm sick of cringing here in this stinking pit,' Brad declared. He pulled a Sig 229 handgun from inside his jacket. 'How about we take the fight to them?'

'You got another of those?'

'I wish. But there's got to be something in this crock of crapola we can use, right?'

Felix pulled out his iPhone. 'I'll take pictures while we look. The analysts might recognize some of this "crapola".'

'You think we're gonna get out. Optimism. I like it.'

Brad and Felix looked around carefully and methodically, wary of activating any traps that may have been left. Felix took his pictures. All the time, he pictured Manton and Deep moving through the caverns like vengeful wraiths, converging on the workshop. The thought was frightening, but Brad was right – with his cover blown and his life damn near taken not once but three times, it was time to fight back.

'This is where we say, "paydirt".' Brad picked out a Glock 179mm from a large pelican case stowed in a dusty corner of the workshop.

Felix took the offered gun grimly and retracted the slide. There was a round in the chamber and twelve more in the magazine – hollow points, for maximum tissue damage. 'Fully loaded,' he murmured.

Brad tutted like a fussing mother. 'And they were going to let this good stuff go up in smoke.'

'Whatever Deathwing is, it's got to be worth a lot of collateral damage.' Felix stowed the phone in his pocket, picked up the torch and crossed to the entrance of the tunnel beyond the workshop. 'Come on.' Gun in hand, he felt the familiar sick thud of his heart as he moved out into the broad blackness of the cave network. The endless rustle and chitter of the bats was a nightmare soundtrack, biting at his nerves. He held the torch to the side of the cave wall, watching for the regular daubings that should guide them back out; but with perfect timing, the thick yellow beam of light was growing weaker. Felix felt the slimy guano suck at his trainers, felt insects exploring his skin again. Close-quarters combat in here would be next to impossible. He spat as something scurried over his lips – then Brad suddenly stopped, gun raised, finger on the trigger. Felix froze too.

'Did you hear that?' Brad murmured.

Felix put out the torch, straining to hear, willing his eyes to adjust in the darkness. There was a point of light ahead in the distance – *how far away?* No, not just one, two – three . . .

Manton's brought back-up.

'Stand still!' Brad bellowed into the darkness. 'We're armed!'

He fired his gun in the air.

Felix flinched; the crack of the shot was deafening in the weird acoustics of the cave. And the echoes bled instantly into a hideous cacophony of screeching and rustling as the bats fled their perches. Suddenly the air around Felix was thick with them. Hundreds, maybe thousands of the creatures – their echolocation senses useless in the living storm – came swooping blindly, colliding, smashing into his body, clawing at his clothes and hair. Felix dropped the gun, flailed wildly, over-balanced and fell.

The back of his head splattered into bat shit.

Felix squirmed, tried to rise, slipped again. The thick muck was in his ears, over his cheeks. Instantly his flesh was crawling with unknown parasites. He kept his mouth tight shut as he struggled to get up. His hand closed on the flashlight, his slimy fingers jerked the switch. He glimpsed the seething mass of the bat swarm, saw Brad on his knees, dragging himself up from the filth – and then a huge, dark figure loomed over him into the failing torchlight. Felix looked up helplessly – *I'm dead, it's game over, it's—*

It was Zane.

'Take it easy, you crazy sons of bitches,' the big man rapped, the scowl on his face deeper than the darkness around them. 'Let off another shot in here and I'll make this rescue party a funeral party. Clear?'

'Crystal, sir,' Felix stammered. He caught Brad's eye and the two of them cracked up into laughter till their sides ached in dizzy, heartfelt relief.

Felix sank into the blisteringly hot soak pool, laid his arms on the marble sides and gazed out over the bushy tree-tops of Central Park and the iconic Manhattan skyline beyond.

What a difference thirty-six hours make, he thought, as his bites and sores stung in the foaming water. Felix closed his eyes and the darkness swept him from the elegance of his hotel suite to those Colorado caves. He remembered being led out by ATLAS troops into the early evening light, revelling in the taste of fresh air, swapping filthy clothes for clean spare uniforms.

Less pleasant were the memories of Zane's gruelling debrief at the Peterson USAF base, a stone's throw from Cheyenne Mountain – and his subsequent defumigation. It seemed there were any number of diseases Felix and Brad could've picked up from the caves, from rabies to histoplasmosis. That had meant an arsenal of shots that would make it hard to sit down for a week.

To add to his discomfort, Felix had been put through a stack of health checks following his exposure to Deep's sedative – a synthetic opioid of some kind. It was too early to tell if there would be lasting long-term effects, but he'd felt OK. Even better once Zane had launched a major security alert initiative in the UK on the strength of Chessa's Deathwing intelligence, and then okayed Felix and Brad to take a break for some R and R.

Cue the private jet to Teterboro airport, just nineteen kilometres outside Manhattan, and a black limo to one of New York's swankiest and most discreet hotels, a graceful arc of dark glass and steel rising high over Columbus Circle. The kingsize bed was buried in soft cushions, the carpet pile was almost as deep as the guano he'd trudged through in the caves. And while there was a huge plasma TV on the wall, so far – except for sleep – Felix's eyes had barely wandered from the gobsmacking view. The attentive staff had asked no questions, treating him like an adult and leaving him to his business. He wondered what cover story the hotel staff had been told; whether they thought he was a prince, or a child star, or . . .

Probably best I don't know. Don't want to louse up another legend.

He opened his eyes again and drank in the wide blue freedom of the September morning sky. *Felix Smith has left the CAF,* he reflected. He looked at the scars on his thigh and hand from past misadventures in the Minos cause. *Back to being plain Felix Smith, elite boy soldier. Expert in bomb disposal. Expendable.*

He thought of Chessa, wondered what she'd been told about his sudden departure. If she knew about his lies now, and if so, how she was feeling. Zane had tried to trace her through her phone, but it had gone dead. No great surprise there. She'd have dumped it long ago.

More importantly, what was the CAF planning next? Zane had reported that Manton and Deep escaped by helicopter as the ATLAS Humvee tore up the track, converging on the twin signals from Felix and Brad's chains. The copter – the same one Orpheus had supplied to Deep, Felix supposed – was soon traced, of course – abandoned in scrubland in Peyton, close to US Highway 24. The fugitives could've escaped anywhere.

Felix kept staring out over the wide-open city. He sometimes wished he could escape too.

Around noon, after a five-mile run through Central Park to clear some of the cobwebs, Felix made his way downstairs to the hotel bar, a cavernous collision of oak and brushed steel with brown and orange accents. Brad waved to him as he came in, suited and seated on a squishy leather sofa with a pitcher of some cocktail or other.

'Glad you could make it,' Brad said, pouring him a glass and passing it over.

'Alcoholic?' Felix wondered.

'How dare you! I've kept off it since midday.' He honked with laughter at his own joke. 'Anyway, it's just juices and ice.'

Felix sipped. 'Like to stay in control, huh?'

'No,' Brad shot back. 'I just don't like the taste of alcohol. Cheers.'

'Cheers.' Felix sank into an armchair opposite. 'Got rid of those lice yet?'

'All except the pubic ones.'

'Gross!' Felix grinned. 'Too much information!'

'It was kind of horrible in there, though, wasn't it?' Brad shook his head. 'I'm telling you, that's the last time I come round saving your ass, man.'

'I owe you one, mate.'

'Best you pay me back quickly. One more month and I'm sweet sixteen—'

'And out of here. Yeah, you said.' Felix looked at him. 'What d'you think you'll do then?'

'Take my pension and walk,' Brad declared. 'I've lived through enough crap.'

'And *waded* through enough of it after Colorado.'

'Exactly.' Brad put down his glass, his mood suddenly sombre. 'It's all made me realize life's too short. I mean, I'm always going to be proud of what I've done in Minos, but I'm moving on. I want to work in video games. Architect. Twist that code around my fingers and play.'

'Good for you,' said Felix.

'You don't mean that.' Brad sized him up. 'How long you been with Minos?'

'Three months, give or take.'

'Makes you quite the veteran in the Split-seconders,' Brad noted. 'Me being ancient and all. So . . . what do you think you'll do when your year in Minos is up?'

'I dunno. I'd quite like to join the Technical Gaming Team at JIEDDO . . .'

'The where-do?'

'Joint Improvised Explosive Device Defeat Organization, over in Maryland,' Felix clarified. 'The technical gamers there kind of imagine the IEDs of the future, and work out how best to stop them.'

Brad grinned. 'I knew when you said "gaming" it was too good to be true. Wouldn't you miss London?'

'Nah. There's nothing there for me any more.'

'And with Minos, the world is your oyster, right?'

'Right – slimy, overpriced and it stinks . . .'

The two of them sat bantering together for a good hour. Felix felt a rare sense of contentment as he looked around his opulent surroundings, sipped his drink from heavy cut-crystal glasses and eyed the businessmen seated with papers and laptops. *Did they appreciate moments like this?* Felix wondered. He doubted it. This was their world. They took it, and the luxury, for granted.

I'll never be like you, thought Felix. *I'm going to savour every minute of the life I have.*

Almost guiltily, he found himself switching the conversation back to the CAF task. 'So, how'd a hacktivist like you get involved with that guy Stevens – he was, what, a biologist?'

'A mammalogist,' Brad corrected him. 'He was attached to one of the big applied science labs out in Westchester. He did a lot of animal testing.'

'So how come the CAF got together with him instead of taking him out?'

'They used him.' Brad paused while a smart waiter came over to check they didn't need anything; when he spoke again he lowered his voice. 'Your friend Coral knows Sammy, one of the code-junkies I've been hanging with. A few months back Coral paid Sammy to hack into Stevens's PC and dig up some dirt. And she found plenty to use against him.'

Felix nodded. 'Blackmail?'

'Black male, white male – judging by the photos on his hard drive and the emails from a gay dating site, Stevens didn't care,' Brad quipped. 'Only his wife and kids didn't know a thing, see, and he wanted to keep it that way.'

'I guess underground workshops don't come cheap.'

'It wasn't a workshop that the CAF wanted funding.' Brad leaned forward. 'They were making him do experiments for them.'

'Huh?' Felix frowned. 'The CAF performed its own animal experiments?'

'They got after-hours use of this lab in Westchester and a fully trained scientist doing stuff for them. Just what kind of stuff, we don't know.'

Felix felt a familiar sense of unease growing. 'But those guys would never harm animals . . .'

'You'd think so, right?' Brad brooded over his juice. 'I was tasked to find out what the hell he was doing.'

'What was your cover story?'

'Not a hundred miles from the sweet and simple truth. I told them I hung with the girl who'd got inside his computer and that I'd heard about what was going down

– and that, for a fee, I could erase all malicious code, restore his PC privacy, and get back everything the CAF took, so he didn't have to take their crap any more.'

Felix nodded. 'Smart. Did he take you up on it?'

'Man, the poor bastard almost bit my fingers off.'

'He was into that too, was he?'

The two of them laughed. Then Felix pictured the man's corpse in the workshop and the simple tragedy of Stevens's life and death struck him, straightened his face.

Brad went on breezily: 'Of course, I couldn't really get back what he'd lost – by this time, months after taking it, the CAF most likely had backed it up all over. But Stevens didn't know that. He was ready to clutch at any straws.' He shrugged. 'What I did do was install my own spyware so I could check out his emails and see what was going down. But the juicy stuff must've been taken care of already. It was all "these specimens are suitable" and stuff.'

'Suitable for what?'

'I'm not sure. He used the word hibernation a lot. It might have been a code for something. Whatever the specimens were, there were a hell of a lot of them, anyway. Hundreds.'

Felix sipped his drink thoughtfully. 'How'd you plant your chain on the guy?'

'Me and him met up a few times. I installed privacy software on his PC and showed him how to use it. And each time the CAF made demands, he called me to come round and check they hadn't done anything. But towards the end . . .'

'What?'

'He got kind of weird. Like he was taking something, you know? The last time I met with him, he was holed up in some cheap hotel in Brooklyn. Said he'd left home, that the CAF was after him 'cos he knew too much. He didn't want them to find him.' Brad shook his head. 'Well, if he did know anything, he didn't spill his guts to me. He was burning up, talking crazy. Said something about a Project X.'

'Project X? Sounds straight out of a crummy sci-fi movie.'

Brad shrugged. 'It was just fluke I was there when this guy Kurt came for him. Stevens saw him pull up outside through the window and flipped out. He . . . he made me hide in the cupboard. In case they saw me and blackmailed him about being with a kid . . .'

'Brad Rivers, international operative, hides in cupboard,' said Felix. 'Once he's sneaked his special-agent transmitter in the crazy man's pocket.'

'I guess I could've tried slugging Kurt and taken him in for questioning, but I figured if the guy could lead me to the CAF's HQ . . .' He swigged the last of his cocktail. 'Course, if I'd known he was only going to lead me to you, I wouldn't have bothered.'

'Yeah, course,' Felix agreed with a smile.

'Still, it's no joke, is it?' Brad put down his glass. 'The whole of the UK's on full terrorist alert, and after these assassinations all cosmetics and pharmaceutical companies are being protected – but what do we really have to go on?'

'Zane's got a whole stack of leads,' said Felix. 'If ATLAS can figure out what was stolen from that lab outside Mexico City, if they can pick up some intel from that workshop or even pull up Manton or Deep, or Coral—'

'Or this Chessa chick,' Brad put in.

'Or Kurt,' Felix shot back. 'I mean, God, can't the tera-heads trace anybody?' Even as he spoke, his mobile buzzed. He didn't recognize the number, but picked up. 'Hello?'

'It's me.'

Felix sat up straight at the sound of the Girl's voice. 'Uh . . . Hey.'

'I'm downstairs in the reception of your hotel,' she said briskly. 'Don't tell Brad it's me. Can I see you?'

'I, er . . .' He frowned. 'Well, yeah, of course. What's happening?'

A pause. 'Oh . . . I just want to talk. Can we meet in your room? That's 3830, yes?'

'Um, yeah. Give me five?'

'I'll see you there.'

The phone blinked back to the home screen. Felix was left fizzing with sudden nerves and excitement. He barely knew the Girl, but that one and only time they'd met he'd felt something. Some kind of connection.

'Who was that?'

'Just a friend of mine.'

'Blonde, brunette or redhead?' Brad grinned. 'You've flushed scarlet, man. Very uncool.'

Felix laughed awkwardly. 'Just someone I met on my first night in Minos.'

'A night to remember, huh? Either way, you want to keep her waiting. Have another drink.'

'Best not.' Felix got up and offered a sweaty palm to shake. 'Catch you later.'

Brad took the hand, but his smile lacked its usual warmth. 'Happy making out. Enjoy.'

'You know our motto.' Felix turned to go. 'Live each day like it's your last . . .'

Brad nodded. ''Cos soon enough you'll be right.'

Felix threw open the door to his suite and ran to the bedroom. He barely had a chance to hide yesterday's socks and boxers under the pillow before there was a knock at the door.

He wondered if he'd remembered to put on any deodorant this morning as he rushed to the door and opened it.

There she was. The Girl. Her eyes were deep and brown as he remembered, her black hair swept back from her high forehead. Her fine arched eyebrows echoed the shape of her high cheekbones. She was dressed simply in black trousers and a grey blouse, and with a pinch of disappointment he saw she carried a document wallet. *It's business, then.*

She smiled briefly, flashing straight white teeth. 'Good afternoon, Felix.' The eastern European edge to her English seemed a little less pronounced in person. 'It's been a while.'

'Hasn't it just,' Felix agreed. 'What brings you here – come to see how the other half lives?'

She pushed past him. 'I'm not supposed to come to operatives in person.' She sat on the edge of the sofa, her eyes wide and nervous. 'But I asked to . . . I was scared for you.'

'You were?' Felix felt flattered, half smiled. 'I thought you were just a resource, something we could use. You're not meant to have feelings, are you?'

'This work does things to people, Felix.'

'Too right it does. It damn nearly gets them killed, for one thing.'

'You're always joking around, Felix.' The Girl didn't look amused herself. 'Zane will be coming here soon. New information has come to light. He'll want to speak to you, and to Brad.'

Felix regarded her more cautiously now. 'So why are you here?'

'Chessa and her sister have been seen in New York.' She opened her case and pulled out a grainy photograph, clearly blown up from a long-distance lens shot.

Felix sank into the leather chair opposite and took it from her. He felt a pang somewhere inside at the sight of Chessa, looking downcast as she trailed along in the wake of her sister. Coral was holding a large box wrapped in a bin liner. Her face was stony, impassive.

'Now I know why I was sent to rest up in New York,' Felix realized.

The Girl nodded. 'No one knows those two like you do.'

'Why would they be in New York if Britain is the target?' Felix muttered.

'We no longer believe that it is.'

'But Chessa had been told Deathwing was going to take place in Britain—'

'Not really. You told me she saw *Great Britain attack* written down in Manton's office. It's likely what she saw meant something else.' The Girl looked troubled. 'We finally got a report in on what was stolen from that lab you blew up. Several chemicals were removed in bulk — sodium fluoride, dimethyl methylphosphonate, phosphorus trichloride . . .'

Felix shrugged. 'I don't think I passed a single chemistry test.'

'These chemicals can be combined with ethanol to create sarin.'

Felix froze. 'Sarin?'

'It's a Schedule One nerve agent, production of which was outlawed by the Chemical Weapons Convention of—'

'I know what it is,' Felix interrupted. 'Just breathing in a tiny amount of that stuff . . .'

'Can be fatal, yes,' she agreed. 'In the 1990s Japanese terrorists released a tiny amount of only thirty per cent pure sarin on the Tokyo subway system and the resultant casualties—'

'Wait a second.' He remembered the dry facts and figures he'd absorbed back in training, when studying the use of biological warfare agents. 'Sarin was one of the G-agents, right? G for Germans, ''cos they discovered that series of nerve agents – the first ones ever synthesized.'

She nodded. 'Taban was the first, discovered in 1936 and code-named GA. Soman followed in the 1940s, designated GD. And when Sarin was first created—'

'It was code-named GB?' Felix felt cold to his core. 'I guess you're right, then. That's what Chessa saw – GB. And she *thought* it meant Great Britain.' He slammed his hands to his temples. 'I should've known . . .'

'You didn't. You were tired, over-stressed.'

'And so I sent ATLAS on a wild-goose chase to the UK.' He felt gutted. Absolutely gutted. 'We don't know where their target is at all.'

'If Chessa and Coral are here in New York City, if the CAF were using a New York mammalogist as part of Deathwing, then it's possible somewhere around here is their target. On the other hand, we haven't been able to trace Manton, Deep and Kurt. It's feasible they sent Coral and Chessa here to keep them safely out of the way while they commit a terrorist act closer to home in Colorado . . . or anywhere else. We just don't know.'

Felix nodded, a queasy feeling in his gut. 'So what do you want me to do?'

'You know Chessa and Coral,' the Girl pointed out. 'You've spent a lot of time with them. Did either of them ever mention New York; friends they had here, or recon missions, or likely targets . . . ?'

'Brad's in with the female hacktivist who helped the CAF blackmail Doctor Stevens,' Felix mused. 'She might be helping Coral and Chessa now.'

'We've already sent an agent to Samantha Tilson's rented apartment in Queens. She's cleared out her stuff. No forwarding address.' The Girl's voice betrayed her impatience. 'And a thorough search of Doctor Stevens's home and files has also proved fruitless. Please, Felix. Go over every conversation with them you can remember. There might be something.'

'If my memory was as good as yours, there wouldn't be a problem.' Felix paused. 'I don't get it though. You could've told me all this over the phone. Why *did* you come in person?'

The Girl rose and took a tentative step towards him. Felix felt a twinge of nerves as she approached. She fixed him with her eyes. She looked hot. He realized he was holding his breath. What was she . . . surely she couldn't be . . . ?

'If you had to eliminate Chessa to prevent an act of terror, could you do it?'

Whatever spell Felix felt was forming suddenly shattered. He blinked. 'Huh?'

'You've spent a lot of time getting close to the CAF's inner circle,' the Girl said calmly. 'Possibly too close. You've formed a bond with Chessa and—'

'And now I'm a liability, is that it?' Felix stared at her. 'I will always do my duty. You know that. You know I've already done stuff I never wanted to.'

'And that sort of necessity has been known to create resentments against your controlling organization.' She was still so bloody calm. 'No one is expecting you to be Superman, Felix. We just need to know how you're doing. Your first time in deep cover ended badly and that's bound to have affected you—'

'So this is why you're really here,' Felix realized. 'To watch my reactions, see if I'm lying?' He mimicked her: '*Oh, I don't normally visit operatives in person.*'

'As it happens, I don't. But I do need your answers.' The Girl looked away. 'This is big, Felix, bigger than your hurt feelings. And mine.' She looked back at him. 'You know the Minos Chapter has enemies in high places. You know how a lot of GI5 runners regard using minors to perform key functions in global anti-espionage as a big mistake, a disaster waiting to happen. Your failure to secure full intelligence on the CAF–Orpheus connection is being blamed on your inexperience.'

Felix felt every muscle tense. '*What?*'

'Your failure to convince Manton of your status as an activist . . . your giving the CAF the specialist explosives knowledge they required to aid them in their joint venture with Orpheu—'

'Oh, come on! What else was I meant to do?'

'It's being claimed that the ATLAS agent posing as your uncle in your legend is now at risk of discovery himself.'

'Pete?' Felix felt a sense of creeping dread. 'He's in danger because of me?'

The Girl shook her head. 'I've assessed the situation personally and I believe his cover is still intact—'

'I don't believe all this!' Felix could feel long-repressed anger surging up inside. 'What about the forensics in the cave I saved from being blown to bits? I've been through hell for Minos these last weeks. I almost died!'

The Girl looked genuinely downcast. 'I know. And your life was only saved when Brad reached you – and then again when Zane's recovery team scared Manton and Deep away. That's what the critics of Minos are saying. They don't want to see the bright side of this. Because you made it out alive, some of the head-sheds seem keen to make you a scapegoat – to hold you to account, to damage Minos's credibility.'

Felix wanted to spit. 'A couple of months ago I saved the whole of west London from going up in flames. And this is how I'm thanked . . . ?' But even as he spoke he knew he was acting exactly as those nameless spooks longed to paint him – a whining kid. Not a professional agent. He took a long, shuddering breath and whispered: 'This isn't fair.'

The Girl's expression had softened. 'That's why I came here myself. So I can give Zane and his superiors my own sworn testimony that you are fit for duty and can continue in active service.'

Felix slumped down in a chair. 'It's as serious as that? I've really got an axe over my head?'

Her silence was an eloquent answer.

'Well, then. To answer your original question . . .' Felix swallowed hard. 'If there was no other way, then yes. I'd "eliminate" Chessa. I'd have to. But I don't believe she would let herself be directly responsible for killing others. She was so upset by the security guards being killed, and by Beni. He'd been such a pig to her, but she was shaking so badly I had to hold her . . .' He looked up at the Girl. 'She's the weak link in the CAF chain. Zane always thought so, I know – that's why he assigned me to the task. To get through to her.' The Girl was looking down at the ground; he took it as an indication of hopelessness.

'Look, if we could find her, and I could talk to her, make her see what her sister's been blinding her to for so long—'

'Did anything happen between you and Chessa?' she asked quietly.

That was a change of tack. 'No,' he told her.

'But she is fond of you, isn't she?'

'Well . . . I guess she used to be. She was my way in. I played her, as ordered.'

The Girl nodded a fraction. 'Do you think she would respond to you in an interrogation?'

'She most likely hates my guts now for feeding her such a pile of crap.'

'Do you really know any particular weak points we could exploit to gain intelligence?'

'Uh . . . yeah, I'm sure. I know her.' Felix felt he was talking for his life. 'She's got a conscience; I can get through to her.'

The Girl looked awkward. 'Felix . . .'

'We need to find her and Coral. Do something practical—'

'Felix, if you say you can do this, and you can't . . .'

'Then, fine.' Felix jumped up again. 'I'm finished. You're finished. Minos is finished. Just 'cos a bunch of asshole spooks want an excuse to shut us all down . . .'

Suddenly the suite door shook with a barrage of rapid knocks.

Felix frowned, instantly alert. He gestured to the Girl to back away, and approached the slab of oak stealthily, muscles tensed as he reached for the handle and suddenly yanked the door open.

There was Zane, bearing down on him, framed in the doorway. His face was grave. Felix glanced at the Girl, suspecting some new game developing. But if it was, she looked as surprised about it as he did.

Zane pushed inside. Brad followed him, head down, his customary good humour gone.

I'm through, thought Felix. *It's all over*.

'First of all' – Zane turned to the Girl – 'd'you talk to our boy here? Happy to give your testimony?'

The Girl hesitated, and Felix held his breath again. But then she nodded stiffly. 'It's my professional opinion that Felix Smith's emotional connection with Chessa Lopez will not compromise his continued active service on this task.'

'Hallelujah,' said Zane wryly, with a brief smile that Felix hoped was bordering on the kindly.

'Never in doubt,' said Brad quietly, 'was it?'

Felix shook his head, felt his cheeks burn, relief and resentment tangling up inside. 'No way,' he murmured.

'Then we can cut the crap and go forward.' Zane parked himself in the leather armchair. 'Gents, this is a private summit, a pooling of intel and opinion.' The Girl made to leave but he held up a hand. 'No, no, you can sit in. Minos needs all the opinion it can get.' He pushed out a long breath. 'We have found not a damn trace of Manton and his merry men besides their safe house – or what was left of it – burned to the ground. Arson. They torched their tracks, like pirates scuttling their own ship.'

'Any forensics?' asked the Girl.

'Nothing we can use. But further intelligence *has* come out of that lab works you roasted back in Mexico.'

'So I didn't entirely screw up,' Felix muttered.

'It's a point back to us, and we could sure use it right now,' Zane growled. 'The dumbass police investigators there could've told us sooner, but they didn't figure it was important.' He levelled a stare at Felix. 'It's my belief they were wrong. It's my belief that the United States is facing an actual terrorist threat involving CBRNE material.'

Felix knew the initials well enough, but as always felt a frisson of fear as his mind translated automatically – *Chemical, Biological, Radiological, Nuclear or High-energetic Explosives.* 'Orpheus and the CAF are all set to pull off a miniature apocalypse?'

'That's the score, Felix.' Zane heaved a weary sigh. 'And forgive me if I crap myself on your luxury furniture, but I think I know how they're gonna do it.'

... 13 ...

Felix sat down heavily on the minimalist arm of the hotel room's elegant sofa. The look on Zane's face was one that demanded total attention, and more than a little raw fear. Brad moved a big fruit bowl and sat on the coffee table while the Girl hovered near the door. It wasn't exactly the typical location for a briefing, but then he supposed that Minos was hardly a typical military operation.

Felix struggled to push aside his tangled thoughts on the Girl and all she'd said to him. At least he'd salvaged something from the situation and she and Zane were backing him. He wasn't finished yet. As an active operative he still had the chance to take down Orpheus and the CAF's joint venture . . .

But he found himself taking something else first, as Zane reached into his jacket and pulled out a slight and flimsy object. 'Recognize this?'

Brad opened his mouth to speak but Felix jumped in

first. 'Looks like one of the miniature harnesses I had to rig to blow apart on a timed fuse.'

'Actually, it's a testing suit for a rodent,' Brad drawled. Felix was about to round on him for joking out of turn, but then Coral's words the night of the car bomb rang in the depths of his memory – when he'd asked her what was in the boxes that barely weighed a thing . . . *'Little jackets for mice,'* she'd quipped.

The boxes Coral and Chessa took that hardly weighed a thing . . . That's what we were stealing?

'You're dead right, Brad.' Zane took back the tube of fabric and then tossed it onto the glass coffee table. 'Hundreds of lucky rats get to wear these things with all kinds of potential health risks tucked inside – like microwave transmitters from cell phones and stuff.'

Felix felt a guilty prickle of envy. 'How'd you know?'

Brad picked up the testing suit. 'Doc Stevens used them a lot in his research. I saw photos when I was raiding his laptop.'

'Manton must've got that lot from the lab where Stevens worked.' Felix shook his head. 'And I didn't recognize them. Maybe that's why Manton tumbled me in the end. Some hardcore animal activist I'd make.'

'Or maybe he was always gonna kill you when you'd done your bit.' Zane helped himself to an apple from the big fruit bowl. 'As you pointed out in debrief, we negged Manton's last expert in suspicious circumstances. It was always a risk that your coming along would seem a little too timely.'

Felix felt a pang of relief that Zane didn't blame him

completely. 'But Manton was just using that thing as a scaled-down version of a full-size assault vest. Pretty poor match, I know, but he insisted.'

Zane looked at him. 'A poor match like thinking GB for Great Britain and not sarin, right?' He took a crunchy bite out of the apple. 'And like thinking Project X instead of Project X-*ray*.'

'X-ray?' Felix looked at Brad, but he seemed just as baffled.

'Back in the 1940s, X-ray was the codename for a whack-job plan to win World War Two in the Pacific. Even President Roosevelt got behind it for a time. Attach small incendiary devices to millions of bats – Mexican free-tails, just like the ones we met in that damn cave – and release them over Japan's major cities.' He took another crisp bite. 'The bats go to roost – then they go boom.'

'A lot of Japanese buildings were made of wood and paper back then,' the Girl realized. 'If millions of fires broke out . . .'

'You'd be left with cities of ash,' Zane agreed.

'Yeah, but it's a crazy idea,' said Brad.

'You think?' Zane's teeth crunched noisily on the core of his apple. 'On their first airborne test, the bat bombers burned a brand-new military airfield to the ground. You can't predict exactly where the fires will start – which makes it tough to guard against.'

'But the CAF would never harm animals, would they?' the Girl pointed out.

'Oh, God,' said Felix as an especially nasty penny dropped. 'The quick-release harness was never meant as a scaled-down version of an assault vest like Manton said. It was always going to be the end-product.' He put his head in his hands. 'If that harness was on a bat it would fall off when the fuse burned through the catch-threads, but before it triggered the secondary device.'

'But buildings aren't made of wood and paper now,' said Brad. 'A bomb that size couldn't do much damage, could it?'

'A dirty bomb could,' said Zane. 'And the CAF supplied Orpheus with enough precursor chemicals to make a vat of sarin. A dose of fifty milligrams by inhaling or one hundred through the skin is fatal in fifty per cent of cases.'

'How much sarin could one bat carry?' asked Felix. 'How many people could they hurt?'

'Project X-ray showed that a healthy Mexican free-tail could carry a payload of between fifteen and eighteen grams,' said Zane grimly. 'There's a thousand milligrams in a gram. You do the math.'

Felix swore under his breath. 'So if just one of the bat bombs goes off in a populated area . . .'

'And it's impossible to predict where each bat will go.' The Girl sounded as calm as ever, but was hugging herself as if for comfort. 'I suppose you don't need a target if all you want to do is spread terror.'

'But Brad was right,' said Felix. 'The CAF still wouldn't risk harming living animals. What about putting the bats into those harnesses? If that isn't cruel, then—'

'Bats can be made to hibernate,' Zane informed

him. 'Lower their body temperature, they go sleepy-byes, easy to handle. Warm 'em up, they wake again.'

'Stevens kept talking about specimens and hibernation!' Brad banged his fist against the table. 'There's me thinking it was code for something else.'

'And let me tell you, the CAF were real choosy about their bomb squad.' Zane stared at Felix. 'Remember there were dead bats in the CAF underground workshop? Well, they died of rabies. And if Doctor Stevens hadn't been killed by Deep's knockout juice, he'd have died of rabies too.'

Brad sat up straighter. 'Stevens had rabies? That's why he was sick?'

'The same strain of bat rabies as we found in those caves.'

'Once symptoms appear, I think rabies is fatal,' the Girl put in. 'I suppose the CAF could better justify Deathwing if the bats they were using were already infected and going to die in pain.'

'And from the Orpheus viewpoint, the damn things are set free to spread a deadly contagion,' Zane muttered. 'Two bites at the same sick cherry. Someone finds one lying sick, picks it up . . .'

'Like Stevens. He must've got bitten or something when he was handling them,' said Brad. 'Those emails I saw – "These specimens are suitable . . ." Jeez, the CAF must've got him identifying the rabid bats they could use.'

'And then put them into hibernation till they're ready – and so the CAF can dress 'em up in their bomb vests without a hitch.' Zane looked at Felix. 'As if it wasn't bad enough the CAF got away with high-grade precursor chemicals . . .'

'How many of those harnesses did they bag?'

'Over a thousand.'

Felix felt sick. 'A thousand?'

Zane nodded. 'If we only knew for sure Orpheus's exact target area, or how they plan on deploying the damn things . . . Project X-ray planned to drop millions from bomber planes in special containers.'

'I can't see terrorists getting away with pulling a stunt like that in American airspace,' said Brad.

'And I can't get how animal rights activists as hardcore as the CAF can use any animals in that way,' said Felix. 'Even dying ones.'

'Maybe they've trained the bats to volunteer?' Brad joked feebly.

'And what about all the animals that could be harmed by the sarin?' Felix argued. 'Pets, wild animals . . . . There are bound to be animal casualties. I just can't believe Chessa in particular would be a party to that.'

'She's completely in thrall to her sister,' the Girl said coldly. 'You've admitted as much.'

'But even Coral, she'd never . . .' Felix saw Zane looking at him. 'Look, I'm not kidding myself or sticking up for them. I just can't believe they would do something to hurt animals.'

'Maybe their target's industrial,' Brad suggested. 'No animals on site.'

'That's possible,' Zane agreed. 'But until we know for

sure we're just pissing in the wind.' He straightened. 'Our first priority has to be to locate any CAF personnel.'

Felix chewed his lip. 'The All-Points Bulletin should get a result, shouldn't it?'

'In a city of more than eight million?' Zane shook his head. 'Maybe. But will it be in time?' He got up, plucked another apple from the bowl and looked at the Girl. 'Time we were headed back to the ops room. You got a lot of CCTV footage to go through. I want it scoured for any trace of Coral and Chessa. And Brad, set up a meeting with your hacktivist friends – take Felix and pump anyone you can get hold of for anything they know about the CAF plan. Me, I got a meeting with ATLAS top brass, an FBI Special Agent in Charge, and a big bunch of head-sheds from the DHS Homeland Security Operations Center and the National Counterterrorism Center. They're going to decide if the threat posed by Deathwing is credible.' He shook his head. '*In*credible, maybe. Whatever, they're gonna be real stoked when I turn up with the good news: Technical Feasibility of the project? Check. Operational Practicability? Check. Behavioural Resolve of the terror groups concerned? Check.' He shoved the apple in his pocket. 'Should impact nicely on the level of the Federal response we get. We're gonna have to tell the good people of America to get packing and know where they're headed in case of emergency.'

Brad nodded. ''Cos until we know where this thing is gonna go off and what scale we're talking about . . .'

'We're just shooting in the dark,' Felix agreed gloomily.

'Then let's get shining the light. Starting with a defence of our boy wonders here to keep them on the case.' Zane nodded his head to the Girl, who walked quickly to the door and opened it for him. Once Zane had stalked away, she followed him out without a backward glance.

'I think our vacation just ended,' said Brad gloomily.

'Today, the vacation,' Felix murmured. 'Tomorrow, the world.'

. . . 12 . . .

Felix barely noticed the doorman wishing him and Brad a
good day, or the September sunshine on his skin as he
stepped out onto the wide white pavement and turned
right onto Eighth Avenue. The sheer size, scale and
spectacle of the city impacted on his mind only vaguely;
all he could think about was his precarious position, the
mistakes he had made, and what terror might come
down if the good guys couldn't win through in time.

A terror he'd had a good hand in helping to create.

I had to do it, he told himself. But a louder voice,
mocking and sneering, was drowning him out. *You're a
failure, Smith. Everyone knows it. And when people start
dying . . .*

Brad hailed them a yellow cab nosing out from West
58th Street and asked for an address in Blissville, Queens.
The cabbie grunted and his car jerked away, hacking
into the thick traffic choking the asphalt.

'There's a few places on 35th Street where some of Sammy's gang hang,' Brad explained. 'Good a place to start as any. Though if my cover's been blown by Manton seeing me go into his cave . . .'

'You think that could be why "Sammy" cleared her apartment?'

Brad shrugged. 'Speaking of apartments . . . sorry to interrupt you and the babe, man.' He smiled knowingly. 'She's a tera-head, right?'

Felix nodded.

'You been dipping your pen in company ink, huh? Dangerous game. Even if she does have a great ass.'

'It's not like that,' Felix assured him. 'And it's my ass I'm more worried about right now. It's on the line.'

'Yeah, I picked up on some of that. What the hell . . . ?'

'I messed up big-time and now the head-sheds at the top of GI5 want to bury me and Minos too.'

'Before I retire next month on full pay? No way!' Brad put a hand on Felix's shoulder. 'We can turn this round. I mean . . . we've got to. Right?'

Felix nodded sullenly. 'Right.'

The cab took them onto the gigantic sweep of the Queensborough Bridge. The rows of distant skyscrapers filled Felix's vision, dominating the skyline like some vast glass-and-concrete curtain. Criss-crossed beige girders complicated the view above and either side and caused the sunlight to flicker distractingly in Felix's eyes. The Hudson River was calm and still, a vast stretch of turquoise interrupted by the thin, tree-mobbed splinter of Roosevelt Island. Soon they were entering a low-rise landscape, boxier, drabber. Felix was reminded of the Mexico City streets he'd raced through, in the wake of the lab explosion in Azcapotzalco. It felt like half a lifetime ago.

And it seemed to be almost as long again to reach Blissville through the afternoon traffic – and it wasn't really worth the wait. Whoever named it had to have been a great joker. The numbered streets weren't prefaced with compass directions here as they were in Midtown – perhaps because wherever you were, you felt lost. Derelict blocks were caked in graffiti. Shut-down strip clubs and delis displayed flyposted boards and metal shutters in place of windows. A hotchpotch of garages and storage spaces crowded the dowdy streets.

Brad motioned the driver to pull over and pressed a twenty dollar bill into the gnarled hand that flew up the moment the car stopped. Felix stepped out onto the sidewalk and Brad joined him. 'Café on 34th Street's where we're headed,' he said. 'But not cool for the cover to jump out of a cab.'

Brad led Felix through the seedy neighbourhood. Felix waited outside the small café while Brad quizzed any 'buddies' who might be hanging out inside.

'Rufus ain't seen her all day,' Brad reported when he re-emerged. 'Said she was staying with friends and expecting visitors yesterday. He doesn't know who.'

'Hmm. I think we can hazard a guess.' Felix looked all round, wishing he could somehow will Chessa and Coral to appear from behind a parked car or slung-out trash-bag. 'So now where?'

'Sammy used to hang with some dudes in Dutch Kills. We'll go check them out.'

'In where?'

'Another top neighbourhood, north of Queens Plaza. Trust me – you'll hate it.'

And so the afternoon wore on – trailing after Brad and his latest lead. Felix walked lonely stretches past dilapidated blocks and sprawling construction sites, crumbling brownstones and cheap chain hotels, feeling more helpless and discouraged with every passing hour. Dutch Kills proved a dead end in just about every way, so they hunted out a girl Brad used to hang with in case she had any clues to offer. Brad managed to charm out of her the names of a couple of Asian guys Sammy knew over in Jackson Heights on 74th Street. One was out, the other hadn't seen her – but he knew the address of her ex-boyfriend in Brooklyn . . .

Night was drifting in as Felix and Brad jumped and slumped on a bus to the Red Hook Houses, a massive sprawl of red-brick buildings just south of the Gowanus Expressway, reeking of menace and decay. Wispy trees swayed behind high chainlink fences. A distant gunshot rang out, and Felix noticed that the kids in a nearby play-ground didn't even look up.

'Nice neighbourhood,' he murmured.

'Uh-huh.' Brad slouched towards the main door of one of the blocks. 'Used to be known as the crack capital of America. Things are actually improving.

These days the muggers smile before they stab you.'

'You ever think about becoming a tour guide?'

'Mmm . . . better prepare ourselves for trouble.'

As they approached, Felix could see that the heavy lock had been prised out of the door. The communal hallway stank of sick. Felix followed Brad up a flight of grimy concrete steps to the sixth floor, past a couple of young teens slumped silently on the stairs. Broken glass and syringes were strewn everywhere. A young man lay face down in the corridor, vomit on his clothes, not moving. Felix thought of the sweet sterile safety of his hotel suite with a guilty longing.

Brad came to a halt and knocked on a battered door. His only reply was a steady drone of noise from inside; the TV or a radio, Felix supposed. 'Hello?' Brad called. 'I'm a friend of Sammy's.'

No one came to the door. Music thumped and thudded. 'Someone's obviously in there,' Felix muttered. 'And we don't have time to dick around.'

Channelling his frustration, he raised his leg and kicked hard just below the lock. The door jumped in its frame and started to splinter as the bolts were jarred loose. Brad then took over, shoulder-charging the slab of plywood, which crashed suddenly open, allowing Felix to steal sharply inside. Senses alert and wired for action, he kicked open another door to his left – a man's bedroom, a mess but empty. At the same time, Brad moved further along the corridor and burst his way into a grungy bathroom. He glanced back at Felix and shook his head – the room was empty. Felix edged past him towards the

remaining closed door and the source of the blaring
music. Heart pounding and muscles tensed, he readied
himself to confront whoever was inside and smashed his
way in . . .

Then he saw her. The girl in black lying twisted on the
carpet, her long blonde hair in greasy streaks across her
face. Her eyes were pale blue and staring; she was
obviously dead. Thick sticky drool from her nose and
mouth glistened on her face. The room stank of urine.
Sarin attacks the muscles, Felix remembered, *removes all
control. Your body goes into spasm. You can't breathe.
Snot and saliva run like a tap. You lose control of your
bladder and bowels . . .*

'Sammy,' Brad whispered.

He started towards her, but Felix grabbed hold of his
arm. 'Are you crazy? She's dead and it looks like sarin
poisoning.' He backed away, dragging Brad with him. 'If
it is—'

'We could be breathing it in right now,' Brad realized.

Terrified, Felix turned and ran outside the apartment.
Brad tried to close the broken door shut behind them –
but Felix was looking at the man lying face down in the
corridor in a new light. Maybe the poor bastard wasn't
some drunk or junkie – maybe he was another victim. The
guy who owned the apartment even, trying to get clear.
And those kids on the stairs . . .

Oh, God, everyone in this block could be affected.

From the look on Brad's face he'd had the same
thought. The two of them turned and ran, panic-stricken
for the staircase. Sarin didn't smell; it didn't taste of

anything. You couldn't see its vapour. It just killed. It had no other point or purpose. It could linger in the clothes of a victim for thirty minutes after release. *I could already be dying*, thought Felix. *Any second now my eyes could start burning, my body start to convulse . . .*

He and Brad came hurtling through the outer door of the block, panting for breath. Felix was already pulling his Minos sat-phone from his pocket. 'We've got to call in and get this place cordoned off. We need a hazard team in there to get forensics, maybe then we'll—' The shrill ring of his phone interrupted. 'Good timing, saves me calling in.' He hit answer. 'Felix Smith, passcode one-one-seven-nine. We've found Samantha Tilson and at least one other dead—'

'There have been sightings flooding in. The bats.' The Girl's voice was low and urgent. 'Hordes of bats, swooping in from the river over the Lower East Side and Chinatown, Dyker Heights, Glendale, Long Island, City . . .'

Felix opened his mouth to speak but no words came. *Oh my God*, he thought uselessly. *Oh my God, oh my God.*

'News just broke,' the Girl went on haltingly. 'Hundreds dead underground at the World Trade Center Transportation Hub. They just went down, falling like flies . . .'

'Wait.' Brad shook Felix's shoulder, pointing at the sky. 'Man, will you look at that . . .'

Felix lowered the phone numbly. An unearthly rustling noise was building out of nowhere, triggering some primal, instinctive fear. A sudden swelling of shadow robbed the fading light from the sky.

A seething column of bats came swarming overhead. It was as though a billion dollars in black bank notes had come billowing across the horizon, tumbling, fluttering, borne on the shockwaves of some silent explosion. Felix pictured the tiny harnesses wrapped around each body to the design he'd helped provide, a deadness building in his chest.

Then Brad was grabbing at his sleeve, hauling him away towards the block that neighboured Sammy's. 'Inside! C'mon, move!'

The spell was broken; Felix scrambled away with Brad into the communal hall. Unlike Sammy's, this one was not deserted. One of the apartment doors was open, and people of all ages were crammed inside – old women, young dudes, children, gathered around a huge plasma-screen TV too large for its cramped surroundings. CNN was showing rolling news, the anchorman's tones vibrating from the set.

'*Absolute panic on the streets of Manhattan . . . The police are already overwhelmed. Major situations in Times Square and Broadway – people literally dropping dead where they stand . . . hundreds of them . . .*' The slick delivery halted, the voice cracked. '*Police officials are warning all New Yorkers to stay in their homes and await further instructions . . .*'

Felix realized he was still clutching his phone, still connected to the Girl. *Why has the CAF done this? Why?* He crossed back to the block entrance; the bats had passed, but their shadow seemed to linger. He pressed the phone again to his ear, though he could barely speak, his mind reeling at the sudden scale of the horror breaking around them. 'Deathwing,' he said hoarsely. 'It's underway.'

'Yes.' The Girl's voice faltered, as though she were struggling to hold back tears. 'And this is just the beginning.'

EVACUATE NEW YORK CITY.

Four words, thought Felix. *A single command. But the repercussions, even forty-eight hours later . . .*

Wearing his full-length chemical protective undersuit, he sat slumped in a swivel chair in the middle of a makeshift field operations command centre, in a commandeered school. The first priority of the National Response Plan – the law enforcement and investigative response to terrorist incidents – was to preserve life and minimize risks to health. Given the scale of the threat in this instance, full evacuation was the only way to meet that priority.

Great theory. Felix rubbed his gritty eyes. *But in the real world . . .*

He was sitting in a classroom. It was hot and sunny outside, but the windows were shrouded in canvas taped to the walls. A fan whirred, pushing muggy air between the two-dozen desks – each one buried beneath laptops, printouts, plastic cups. Some soldiers slept where they sat, others sat typing at a furious pace. Felix was on a break, but he was too dog-tired to do anything but stare into space. He'd spent a couple of ten-hour shifts helping to harry the disbelieving population out of the city. He'd seen so many ugly, painful scenes . . . Streets full of corpses. Hospital halls choked with shrieking casualties. Police officers in tears, unable to count the dead fast enough to give realistic reports of fatalities . . .

And to add the final insult, at the end of it all he was forced to come here – back to school. The group of buildings had been constructed in the 1970s for a student body of 3,500, but ordinarily over 5,000 pupils attended. Its size and facilities – and its strategic location on the borders of Manhattan and the Bronx – had seen it commandeered as a forward base for the counter-terrorism agencies.

From here Federal forces could co-ordinate the mass exodus from Manhattan Island via two secured routes, over the Broadway Bridge and the Henry Hudson Parkway. With the Trans-Hudson subway and transit lines down to the south, most evacuation routes led north towards Westchester, or out west into Nassau and Suffolk, or into New Jersey from Staten Island. That was the idea anyway.

As far as Felix could see, the reality was a confused hell. The media wasn't helping any. Since no one had claimed responsibility so far, the press was trying to blame everyone from the Taliban to the US military or the entire government, whipping up public hysteria further. Mobile phone networks, overloaded with panic calls, went down – leaving New York's terrified, bewildered residents more isolated still. With buses crammed past safety limits, people crushed into trucks or pleaded for lifts or used force to take others' transport.

No one knew why New York had been singled out for this. No one knew when invisible death might strike again. They only knew they had to find a way out, at any price.

The US had its contingencies in place for meeting an emergency like this, of course; and as the significance of the incident had escalated, so had the response. Ordinarily, the FBI would convene a Joint Operations Center – an inter-agency command and control hub – tasked with responding to the terrorist threat. But since Deathwing was an 'Incident of National Significance', the JOC had swiftly expanded, drawing on assistance from regional and national assets to support the huge range of ESFs – Emergency Support Functions, spanning everything from transportation and communication to mass care and long-term community recovery.

But how can New York ever recover from something like this? Felix wondered gloomily. *How can the world?*

Nowhere will ever feel safe again.

A myriad of different policy, planning and response units had come together in an attempt to manage the incident, a bewildering collective of authorities masked by mind-melting acronyms – the Command Group of the JOC – itself a section of the JFO (Joint Field Office) – took advice and expertise from the JIC Team (Joint Information Center, managing media and information release to the public), the SLT (Strategic Legal Team, giving legal advice on crisis resolution strategies) and the DEST, the Domestic Emergency Support Team . . . The baffling list of faceless, formless entities went on.

Throw enough bureaucracy at a problem and you'll bury it, thought Felix cynically. *That's what the head-sheds must've thought.*

But we're the ones getting buried.

Felix wondered how the Girl was coping. Many of the tera-heads worked in intelligence; analysing any and all relevant information and disseminating it to all JOC units, FBI Headquarters Strategic Information and Operations Center and the JFO Co-ordination Group, while keeping head-sheds from ATLAS, the DHS Homeland Security Operations Center and the National Counter-Terrorism Center informed. He'd last seen the Girl ten hours ago, looking drawn and haunted.

Having a photographic memory and total recall was great most of the time, Felix supposed. But there were some things you couldn't wait to forget.

While the military and civil cope-and-counter divisions came together like a Federal colossus, the police force, armed troops and law-enforcers from all over the world worked to clear the most densely populated major city in the United States of its eight million inhabitants – an operation unprecedented in size, scope and challenge. Under plans for coping with a terrorist attack, the city had been pre-divided into 151 sectors based on terrain, location and population, ready to be moved out by train, boat and city buses along preset routes. But the problem with a biological attack like Deathwing was that the threat was dispersed over time and distance, with no real 'incident site' – instead there were hundreds of incidents scattered all across the boroughs.

Central Park and countless smaller green spaces around the island had swiftly become death-zones, as the bats made for the shelter of trees as well as the high-rise overhangs and crevices in the boundless skyscrapers. As the free-tails' harnesses burned free, most times they plummeted to the ground, spilling the deadly ampoules of liquid with no need for the secondary cap to detonate. And the hideous death toll at the World Trade Center Transportation Hub had demonstrated graphically that if even a small amount of sarin penetrated the area, the fans that ventilated the tunnels would circulate deadly vapour through the crowded platforms.

As a result, the evacuation had been severely compromised, with all underground transit routes shut down. But subsequent events had proved the precaution a wise one, as phials of sarin had been found inside several major stations – along with several bat carcasses. Either the creatures had gained entry through one of the many blast shafts integrated with the ventilation systems, or else they had been dead already and simply dropped there.

Either way, thought Felix, *it demonstrates there's no hiding place from Deathwing*.

And there was no escaping the painful truth that the

Federal response teams had been entirely overwhelmed trying to clear out so many people. As if he hadn't seen enough harrowing snatches of the exodus, the TV reports kept running fresh ones. Fights breaking out at closed petrol stations; the injured and infirm, abandoned in hospital corridors by terrified staff, waiting for help; hysterical crowds leaving their cars, trampling each other in their desperation to escape; devastated families, searching for lost children and pets, being hauled off the streets and bundled into troop trucks; old people's homes, mental hospitals, special needs centres – their un-comprehending charges being bundled into buses and ambulances to join the backed-up traffic. The city was choked with every kind of vehicle, the highways grid-locked and seething with fumes.

And always, in every view of the stricken city, there were soldiers and police officers and exhausted volunteers struggling to manage the overcrowded rest centres and refugee stations. Day and night the dispossessed arrived by the truckload – rich and poor side by side, fighting to be seen, to be heard, jockeying for preferential treatment. Felix had heard them begging officials to bend the no pets rules, or pleading for help to find loved ones, demanding that the President step in to do something, *anything* to end this madness ... And as facilities broke down under sheer weight of numbers and conditions grew steadily worse, it wouldn't be long before law and order did too. Pretty soon, the peace-keeping forces would have full-scale riots on their hands.

Felix ran his hands through his sweat-stiffened hair as if he could rake his head free of the memories. For the thousandth time he felt a rush of red-hot anger at the CAF, at Orpheus, at the bastards who'd brought about this terror . . .

And at himself, for failing to stop them.

'Get over yourself,' he muttered. 'This isn't a movie. How could anyone, however old or however good, stop an operation like Deathwing?'

River police CCTV had shown a storm of bats being released from a motor yacht in Wallabout Bay that first night. Several perforated metal canisters like the one Manton had taken from the cave had been found on board – filled with drop-down cardboard compartments for storing scores of bats, a direct copy of the original Project X-ray designs. A couple from Westchester who owned the yacht had been found shot dead; the double homicide had occurred just hours before the first casualties were recorded. Wallabout Bay sat between Brooklyn and Manhattan, and the incidents of sarin deaths had all taken place within a six-mile radius of that point.

Only the beginning, Felix brooded.

Several free-tails had been captured, and further bat corpses recovered from buildings or parkland. Pencil dets with timers ranging from fifteen minutes to forty-eight hours had been identified. And it seemed some were carrying not sarin but improvised explosive devices made from nitrate fertilizers. Chillingly, one had even been found to contain a payload of anthrax spores.

Mix-and-match biological warfare, designed to stretch the resources of the victim state to breaking point.

As the first day of emergency had drawn to a close, CCTV cameras showed more bats in flight over the terrified city – a second wave that seemed to have originated not from the water, but from within the confines of the city itself.

And what if there was a third wave, or a fourth, waiting to be released at any time?

There's got to be something we can do to stop it, thought Felix hopelessly. *With all the people we've got looking for Manton and his gang . . .*

He closed his eyes. How many times had his thoughts chased their tails down that particular route? *Save your strength*, he told himself. He swigged cold coffee from a plastic cup, grimaced, and got to his feet. *I'll go outside. Not exactly fresh air, but it's no good sitting here moping.* Like everyone else remaining in the city, he'd had his low-level PON-1 pre-treatment shot to ward off the onset of sarin intoxication, and carried his syringes of atropine and oxomine for use at the first sign of symptoms.

Couldn't make me feel much worse, Felix thought sullenly.

Until he was rostered for patrol he wasn't supposed to leave the designated base. That just left the playground for breaks and exercise. Protective CBRN bio-suits – shielding the wearer from Chemical, Biological, Radiological and Nuclear material – hung surreally from pegs in the kids' cloakrooms. You were supposed to kit-up before leaving shelter in case of attack, but after hours spent sweating into them on patrol, many chose to take their chances without.

A large part of the playground had been designated a smoking area, and a crowd of soldiers, police and admin staff stood about in a fug of their own smoke. *Should've brought my gas mask after all.* Felix held his breath and walked until the air was less stale. A few men and women were playing soccer, a bizarre sight in their olive-green hazard gear. Beyond the school gates, the world was eerily quiet and still. No traffic, no people.

It was the same all over New York City.

'Hey, *boet*!'

Felix started at the familiar South-African accent, and turned to find a handsome, stocky girl his own age striding towards him in a navy-blue bio-suit, her grin nearly as big as the bags under her eyes. 'Hannah!' he said incredulously, a smile tugging at his lips for the first time in days. He'd been tasked with her on his very first assignment; and they'd wound up in hospital together. 'Where'd you spring from?'

'I'm Minos too, aren't I?' She grabbed him in a tight hug. 'I've been pulled off surveillance ops in Warsaw. Literally about to plant a listening device on some scumball, when I'm diverted, dragged onto a plane and sent here. Not even time to change. I've been wearing the same underwear for two days.'

'Are you coming on to me?' Felix deadpanned.

'You wish. Seriously though – this is a real shitstorm, huh?'

Felix nodded. 'Zane's desperate for the Chapter to

be seen to be going all out to tackle this situation. The situation that I messed up.'

Hannah snorted. 'Thought you were golden boy?'

'Not any more.'

'What's the matter – forgotten how to save the world single-handed?' She whopped him on the arm. 'We both know that crap happens. I got shot, remember? That was my fault – if I'd only been faster than that murdering . . .' She trailed off, and suddenly smiled again. 'See what I did there? I let it go. If you can't win 'em all, at least you can play nice.' She leaned in and kissed him hard on the lips. 'There. Did that make things better?'

Felix smiled despite himself. 'Thanks. What have you been doing?'

'Using my big mouth.' Hannah grimaced. 'You know what a melting pot this city is. Something like eight hundred different languages are spoken – there's still people who don't understand the evacuation, who're separated from their folks and scared to death. So multi-linguists like me have to talk to them. Tell them everything's OK. And try to mean it.' She sighed, pulled out a chocolate bar and bit off a big chunk. 'It's like working in the call centre from hell.'

'But it helps people,' said Felix.

'*Ja*, I'm a regular girl scout,' she agreed, chewing sullenly. 'I just wish I could see some action.'

'Greetings, amigos.' Brad breezed up to them in an olive-green bio-suit, looking chipper and alert.

Felix smiled. 'Hey, Brad.' He was about to introduce Hannah when his attention fixed on a sheet of laminated paper in his friend's hand; one stamped with the five-spiked star of the ATLAS logo. 'What've you got?'

'Something to make us feel useful, at last,' Brad said. 'The tera-heads have tracked down Coral and Chessa.'

Felix jumped as though a hundred thousand volts had just slammed through him. 'They have?'

Hannah grabbed Brad's hand in a firm shake. 'Howzit, Brad? I'm Hannah. You're cute.'

'Which translates as, "You have a pulse,"' Felix told him. 'Now, come on, where are Chessa and Coral?'

'In a secured hospital down on 1st Avenue,' Brad said. 'Turns out Coral's real sick. One of the first admitted with signs of sarin poisoning. She and her sister checked in with false ID. But the military took mug-shots of every patient to circulate around the rescue centres for friends and family, and—'

'Is Chessa all right?' Felix demanded.

'Who are these girls?' asked Hannah, baffled. 'What's going on?'

Felix ignored her, grabbing Brad by the shoulders. 'Well?'

'Whoa, man, I don't know. But they've been down there since the start of all this, and if they're still breathing now, that says something, right?'

'We've got to get over there,' said Felix.

'That's what this letter of authorization says.' Brad showed him the paper. 'Zane's giving you first crack at interrogating Chessa. You know her best, he thinks she might open up to you or something.'

'He wants Minos to get a result out of this,' Felix muttered. 'And God knows, so do I.'

'I thought Manhattan hospitals would be among the first to be evacuated?' said Hannah.

'Most were.' Brad shrugged. 'A handful have been commandeered by Health and Human Services as emergency medical centres for the worst hit casualties, first responders, search and rescue teams . . . They've been turned into miniature garrisons.'

'Has Zane laid on transport for us?' asked Felix, nerves sticking needles into his guts.

'Yeah, there's a Humvee outside.' Brad mimed pulling on a gas mask. 'Get the rest of your MOPP together and we're good to go.'

Felix sighed as he followed Brad back inside the main building to the well-stocked cloakroom. MOPP stood for Mission Oriented Protective Posture – the military term for all protective gear in a toxic environment – and since the threat of biological exposure could come literally out of the blue, the highest level of protection was necessary when going out on task. Mask, gloves, overgarments and rubber overboots had to be worn at all times. Felix struggled into his drab green jacket with little enthusiasm; the MOPP was designed to be as lightweight as possible to extend operational endurance, but it was still a pain in the ass to wear.

Hannah followed Felix and Brad inside. 'So who are these girls you're chasing?'

'Animal rights activists who helped make Deathwing happen.' Felix explained the basics of his mission while he secured his Powered Air-Purifying Respirator system to his back with the belt harness and connected the air-tube to his full-facemask. Because he wore glasses, Brad couldn't wear the close-fitting mask and had to opt for a more cumbersome rubbery hood/tunic combo with an integrated breathing hose. He looked like a reject monster from *Doctor Who*.

Hannah pulled a PAPR system from one of many boxes on the floor. 'I wanna come too,' she said. 'I'm on break, and I bet I can help around the hospital if they've got patients with no English.'

'Yeah, right,' said Felix, affixing a strip of M9 protection tape to his jacket; in the presence of chemical warfare agents it would change colour. 'You just want to be in on the action.'

'*Ja*,' Hannah agreed. 'Who wouldn't after eight hours stuck on the phone? You can brief me on the way.'

Brad looked disapproving. 'You're only allowed out if you're on the roster.'

'We're Minos Chapter: officially we're not even meant to exist. I am so sick of pig-ignorant guys asking me if I've lost my parents and am I OK?' She spat on the floor. 'Besides, I bet your tasking letter doesn't say I *can't* come, huh? Who's going to notice one more soldier out and about in all this mess?'

Brad opened his mouth to reply but Felix covered it with a gloved hand. 'Save your breath, mate, trust me. Let's just shift.'

... **10** ...

In under two minutes, Felix was sat in the back of the covered transport, breathing through his respirator. His breaths sounded over-loud in his ears, but there was something comforting about that. The PAPR filtration system delivered a constant purified airflow into his face-mask, and its batteries were good for up to eight hours. There was even an audible alarm that told you when power was running low. Mind you, eight solid hours on-task would be pushing it – while the carbon fibres of his bio-suit were constructed to be air-permeable to reduce heat stress, they didn't come with a built-in toilet. And stripping out of the thing was a nightmare.

Hannah and Brad sat opposite him in the truck. Their suits and masks, like his, left no human features visible. They rumbled across a bridge and into the eerie emptiness of Manhattan. It felt to Felix like he was touring some movie set, that the huge stretches of glass and stone looming so high either side of him were nothing more than plywood facades.

Empty of crowds and traffic, the streets looked wider and longer than ever. There were clues left behind to mark the calamity – hazard-marker triangles and bright striped tape marked out incidents. Scribbles on the sidewalks and outlines in the roads denoted where bodies had fallen. Then there were the signs of panic and looting – overturned trash cans, abandoned cars with their doors gaping wide, the occasional broken store window . . .

An air of funereal peace had settled over New York City. It felt so totally wrong and unnatural, it chilled Felix to the core. *No, they're not film-set facades*, Felix decided, eyeing the unbroken run of skyscrapers. *They're more like tombstones*.

They continued motoring south, along First Avenue. From the way the traffic lights were ranged away from them, Felix realized they were going the wrong way down the one-way thoroughfare. It didn't matter. There was no other traffic and no one to book them. The sky-climbing tower blocks thinned out as shorter red-brick buildings and brownstones took precedence. *Come on*, thought Felix, tapping his heel against the metal floor, barely feeling it through his protective boots. *Chessa'd better still be there. She'd better be alive*.

He wasn't sure if he'd hug her, or scream in her face.

Finally the truck braked abruptly, swerving onto the sidewalk at the corner of First Avenue and 16th Street. Felix jumped out and surveyed the medical centre. It was maybe ten storeys high, its windows shrouded in huge blue swathes of tarpaulin. Armed troops in full hazard gear stood on the roof and outside the large glass frontage, armed with flame-throwers. Felix saw that all the trees on East 16th Street had been reduced to charred stumps, and a small park at the end of the block was now a square of bulldozed ash.

'They're trying to make the place bat-proof,' Brad remarked, the words coming crisply through the voice-mitter in his mask.

Hannah nodded. 'If those things are still getting into the city, can you blame them?'

Felix raised a hand to thank the driver, who was under orders to wait with the truck and take instructions from his passengers. He didn't know they were fifteen-year-olds with no official military rank, and neither did the guards on the door. Brad showed his statement of authorization to the men, and one of them stepped aside and hit a door control in the wall. The glass doors slid open and Felix was first inside.

Almost immediately, a balding doctor in scrubs and a surgical mask ran up to them. 'Do you know when evacuation will be completed?' he began. 'My staff are severely overworked and over-stressed, our mortuary is overflowing with corpses and supplies of key drugs are dangerously low. If you need a field hospital then you must take over with your own people, you . . .'

He trailed off as Felix removed his gas mask and Brad did likewise. 'You're just kids.' His face crumpled. 'Things really must be desperate if they're drafting in boy soldiers.'

Hannah pulled off her own gas mask. 'And girls,' she said pointedly, running a hand through her cropped blonde hair – although in fairness she could easily pass for eighteen. 'Look, we appreciate what an amazing job you're doing in near-impossible conditions. We don't want to give you extra hassle—'

'But we need to see two of your patients,' said Felix, cutting to the chase.

'You'll have to speak to Admissions. I've got fresh victims coming in – a couple of looters in the Bowery. It sounds as though another wave of bats has been released.' The doctor turned abruptly and walked away, shaking his head. 'We go on trying . . .'

Brad watched the doctor go. 'Guys like him are the real heroes in all this.'

'Can you believe still *more* bats?' Hannah stuck out her tongue. 'Some *skelm* in the city's got to be releasing them from someplace.'

'Start praying Chessa and Coral can tell us who and where.' Felix walked to the deserted Admissions desk and rang the buzzer. The smell of disinfectant was overpowering, but it couldn't mask fear's stink lingering in the white-tiled corridors – a deeper odour.

A harried young nurse, who looked like he hadn't slept in days, hurried up to the desk. 'What is it?' he said.

Brad gave him the aliases used by Coral and Chessa, told to him by the Girl. The nurse checked and, sure enough, their photos came up on a computer screen. Felix's heart pumped.

'They're on the fourth floor,' said the nurse. 'Elevator's that way. Turn left and out into Parson's Ward. The house RN's on duty, she'll take you to them.'

Felix looked blank. 'RN?'

'Registered Nurse,' Hannah told him. 'She manages the regular nurses.'

'Right now she can barely manage a damn thing,' the nurse muttered.

'Thanks for your help,' said Felix, already crossing to the bleach-stinking lift, Brad and Hannah just behind him. 'OK, guys. You two talk with Coral. I'll handle Chessa.'

'Sure that's wise, man?' said Brad. 'You'll be, like, her worst enemy now.'

'Maybe so. But she's squeamish – not like her sister. She didn't like it when the security guards died in Mexico, or when those cosmetics bosses were taken out by Orpheus hitmen.' Felix shook his head. 'So with all the deaths that have happened since then, she'll be feeling . . . well.'

'Like the rest of us,' Hannah suggested quietly. 'And her own sister almost bought it, from the sound of things. You may be right, *boet*. Any familiar face might see her break down a little.'

'Let's go in wearing headgear,' said Brad. 'More intimidating. We want Coral to take us seriously.'

'And I don't want her seeing me at all,' said Felix. 'Not yet, anyway.'

They donned their masks and pressed onwards. Much of the hospital stood dark and empty. Felix supposed that those patients with relatives in the out-of-city shelters, or who could reach family further afield, had been discharged once they were well enough, and evacuated to the safe zone by the military. But there were plenty more with nowhere to go – or who were in no condition to be moved.

As Felix peered into a private room just off the ward, it seemed Chessa would be classed as the former – and Coral very much the latter.

There you are. Felix felt his heart thump. He hadn't seen Chessa in days, since they'd parted in different cars at the airport. She sat in a white dressing gown, curled up asleep in a stiff-backed chair with one hand resting on her sister's. Coral was lying motionless in the bed, her face part-obscured by tubes between nose and mouth, an IV line in her arm drip-feeding a colourless liquid into her veins.

'Can I help you?' Felix turned to find an attractive dark-skinned woman with long straightened hair had come up behind him.

'If you're the house RN, you can,' said Brad, passing her the letter of authorization. 'We're here to speak to these patients.'

'Who must now be considered prisoners of the Anti-Terrorist Logistic Assessment Service,' Hannah added, deepening her voice to sound older than she was.

'What happened to them?' Felix asked.

The RN shrugged. 'Sarin happened. This one had

it bad.' She gestured to Coral. 'Problems with respiration, convulsions, visual darkness, vomiting . . . Fell into a coma for a while. Almost left it too late to get treatment. Her sister brought her in – and got sick from the contact. We pumped her full of pralidoxime iodide till her symptoms subsided.' The RN said the words as though she'd learned them by rote; Felix imagined she'd had to take on a doctor's role as well as her own these last two days. 'They both responded well to the drugs.'

Coral's eyes flicked lazily open. 'Drugs you tested on animals?'

The sister sighed wearily. 'Reckon so, honey.'

'I don't deserve to live if any beast died for me.'

Brad toughened his voice. 'There's plenty who'd agree with the first part of that sentence, at least.'

'Who's that?' Coral held herself rigid. 'I . . . I can't see . . .'

'We're with ATLAS,' said Hannah.

Chessa jerked awake – eyes red and swollen from tears or treatment – and recoiled from the sight of her intimidating visitors. 'ATLAS?' she breathed. 'What do you want?'

'We know you're both members of the CAF,' said Brad. 'We know you're responsible for Deathwing.'

'It wasn't us!' Chessa protested, her voice shrill. 'We didn't want any of this to happen—'

'Shut up,' snapped Coral. 'Say nothing.'

'Where's Manton?' Brad demanded.

Chessa looked down at her lap. 'I wish I knew.'

'Shut up, I said.' Coral grabbed blindly for Chessa's hand.

'No.' Hannah stabbed a finger at Chessa. 'Get her out of here.'

Felix stepped forward and took hold of Chessa's arm. 'No, please,' she began.

'You can't hurt us,' Coral said hoarsely. 'We're sick. We're patients here.'

'She's right,' said the RN, a spark of defiance in those weary eyes. 'We have a duty of care. Whatever she did—'

'No one has to get over-excited,' Hannah said. 'We just want to talk. Alone, please.'

The nurse looked set to object. Then she nodded. 'I'm going off-shift now.' She left the room. 'If you need me, I'll be crashed out in my office.'

'Don't leave us with them. Don't let them take me away.' Chessa struggled in Felix's grip. 'Please. Coral's all I've got.'

'And now we've got you both,' said Brad, moving into Chessa's chair. 'And you're going to spill your guts.'

'I want a lawyer,' Coral snapped.

'*We* want a deal,' said Brad.

'Don't say anything to them, Chess. Chess?' Coral wasn't even sure if her sister was still in the room. Felix felt an unexpected flicker of pity.

'I won't talk, Coral. I love you.' Chessa's face was twisted with trying to hold back tears. 'It's OK. It's OK.'

Felix dragged her through the door and down the corridor, past the disapproving nurse and out of earshot.

'Please,' Chessa said, pulling free of his grip. 'Coral's right. We want to see a lawyer.'

Felix pulled off his gas mask. 'How about a ghost?'

... 9 ...

'Felix?' Chessa breathed his name, her red eyes wide with disbelief. 'Oh my God . . .'

'I've been so worried about you,' Felix admitted. 'I thought you might be dead, or —'

She made to hit him round the face. He blocked the blow. She tried again with the other hand, but he gripped her wrist and propelled her into another ward close by, dark and airless with the tarps over the window. She struggled against him, twisting and writhing.

'All right, whatever,' Felix hissed. 'You want to hit me, go ahead.'

She did, too. A real knock to his cheek that jerked his head to one side. She stood staring at him, breathing hard, her whole body trembling, eyes wide and afraid.

'I . . . I'm sorry.' Felix held out his hands, palms up. 'I don't know what Manton has told you about me, but . . .'

She sat heavily in one of the visitor chairs beside an empty bed, and looked away. 'Deep told Coral you'd sold us out. Done a deal with the FBI or someone.'

Logical assumption, thought Felix. *And something I can work with.* 'It was ATLAS. But I only *said* I'd give them info. I wasn't really going to . . .' He put on his most sorrowful face, which under the circumstances wasn't so hard. 'They told me if I didn't do as they said, they'd deport me back to Britain. That I'd do time there.'

'What are you doing *here*?' she muttered. 'Dressed like one of them?'

'After what the CAF's brought down on New York City, I *am* one of them,' Felix told her. 'I never dreamed you'd all go to these kinds of lengths.'

'I didn't either.' Chessa was hugging herself, still looking out at the dark sprawl of the tarps outside the window, flapping like wings as the wind took them. 'I didn't think Deathwing meant all this. Even Coral had no idea . . .' She looked up at him. 'I knew we'd be found out. We're in, like, the deepest shit ever, aren't we?'

'I can't think of any deeper.' Felix sat on the bed beside her. 'You have to help ATLAS.'

'Like you've helped them?'

Felix licked his dry lips. 'They've cut me a deal. They can make one with you too.'

'And Coral.'

'Sure. It's Manton they really want.'

'I don't know where he is. Coral doesn't either.'

'He's walked out on you. Left you to take the rap while he goes off—'

'No! He wouldn't leave Coral. He . . .' Chessa began to sob. 'Oh God, Felix, this is such a mess.'

'But ATLAS can dig you out of it,' Felix promised. 'You and me, we're small fry in all this. But if you can get more information out of Coral . . .'

'I'm not selling her.'

'No. You'd be saving her skin – and yours.'

Chessa glared at him. 'Why should I trust a thing you say? You acted like everything was fine . . . pretended you liked me . . . but all the time . . .'

'Not all the time,' he said vehemently. 'After I blew up the lab and Manton said I could join you – that was when this ATLAS handler approached me. I'd been tailed.'

'And ever since then you've been tricking us?' She wiped her nose on the sleeve of her gown. 'Beni was right not to trust you.'

'I told you, I was never planning to go along with them. I saved Coral's life in that car bomb, didn't I? I didn't have to. I did it 'cos I care, Chessa. You have to believe that. And I've been scared, just like you. So scared.' He allowed a little self-righteous anger to surface. 'Manton and Deep tried to kill me in their secret caves, did they tell you that? They left me for dead. And now they've killed thousands of people here.'

Chessa sank her head into her hands. 'It's horrible. All of it.'

'Yes.' He put a hand on her shoulder; she looked at him, and he kept the eye contact. 'And if you don't come through for ATLAS with the information they need, it's going to be more horrible than anything you can ever imagine.'

'I really don't know where Manton and Deep are. Nor does Coral, I'm sure of it.' Chessa wiped tears from her cheek. 'The last contact either of us had was when he texted through instructions to her phone.'

'What instructions?'

'Told us to collect these rucksacks from a storage place on the Lower East Side.' She shuddered. 'There were respirators inside and . . . bottles.'

'Bottles of what? Sarin?'

'It looked just like water . . .' Chessa swallowed hard. 'We were told to unscrew the caps and leave the bottles in places all over the city – in the subways, Penn Station, Grand Central Station . . .'

'The subway massacres . . .' Felix looked at her, appalled. 'Down to you?'

'Coral said it would make people sick, that's all.' Chessa was close to tears again. 'But we were staying with this girl, a friend of Coral's who's good with computers, Samantha. And Coral must've told her too much 'cos Samantha kind of got cold feet, got mad at Coral. She busted in on us when we were checking how many bottles we had left, saying all kinds of stuff about telling the cops. She grabbed one of the bottles off Coral, and Coral tried to get it back, and then . . .'

Felix shuddered as the memory of the blonde woman lying dead on the floor of her apartment flashed into his mind. 'The bottle broke?'

'We were wearing the respirators, but . . .' Chessa

shook her head miserably. 'We ran like hell. But the respirators weren't good enough, I guess. We still got sick.' She looked at him. 'I know, we deserve jail for this. We deserve to rot in a cell for ever.'

'You deserve a second chance,' Felix told her, without much conviction. 'But you've got to earn it.'

'By ratting on Coral?'

'On Manton,' he corrected.

'Manton? But Coral—'

'She can't still care about him after all this?' Felix was incredulous. 'You know how many animals have been poisoned? How many more will slowly starve in abandoned homes?'

'Don't. Please . . .' She looked down at the floor.

Yeah, thought Felix. *You know.*

'All right,' Chessa whispered at last. There was anger in her eyes as she looked back up at him. 'I'll sell him down the river, just like he's sold us.'

Felix nodded. 'You must find out everything you can from Coral about other contacts in NYC, where Manton might be staying, anyone he met with, anything like that.'

Chessa scowled. 'She'll never tell me. She doesn't trust her stupid kid sister enough.'

'You're her eyes now, she's going to have to trust you a whole lot more.' Felix gave her a hopeful smile. 'Please – don't tell her we've talked. Don't tell her I'm here.'

'And you'll honestly help us? You'll speak up for us?'

Felix nodded. He could tell she longed to believe him. He only wished he was really empowered to deliver on his promises. After all she'd been a party to, chances were

Chessa's head would roll no matter what efforts she made to atone. But that was tomorrow's problem. First he had to tackle the present.

'I promise,' he said, 'you'll be all right.'

The lie was warm and well told.

Slowly Chessa pushed out a long, shuddery breath. 'How will I get you the info?'

'I'll talk to you again,' Felix assured her. 'Don't worry, I'm going to be sticking like superglue.'

Suddenly the door opened behind him. Chessa froze and Felix quickly pulled the gas mask back over his face as Brad and Hannah pushed inside the room.

'Hey,' said Brad. 'I think you should put her back, now.'

Felix saw Hannah nod slowly. They were up to something. 'OK,' he said. Chessa looked beyond tears now, completely beaten.

'You'd better move.' He pushed her gently along the corridor. 'And I mean it, don't tell Coral about this. However tempting it might be. If you do, and she clams up . . .'

Chessa nodded weary understanding. Felix opened the door for her. Coral was still lying on the bed, apparently unmoved by Brad and Hannah's visit. Chessa took her hand. 'It's just me.' She looked over at Felix, her expression unreadable. 'Just you and me . . .'

Felix turned and left the room, conflicted after his weird reunion. He marched straight up to Brad and Hannah, still waiting in the abandoned ward.

'Why'd you burst in like that?' he demanded.

'Shh.' Hannah cupped her hand to her ear.

Brad looked at Felix. 'Get anything out of her, man?'

Felix briefly explained all he'd learned.

'Never were such devoted sisters, were there?' Brad muttered. 'Spreading poison around half the city, giving Deathwing a helping hand. Didn't you say the CAF would never want to hurt animals?'

Felix shrugged. 'I guess Coral thought she was targeting places that were animal-free – stations, subways . . .'

'Coral and *Chessa*,' Hannah said heavily, her hand still pressed to her ear. 'Just 'cos you like her, *boet*, that doesn't mean she's not in this up to those big, puppy-dog eyes of hers.'

'It's Coral who's pushed her into all this,' Felix shot back. 'What did you get out of her? Anything?'

'Not much – not yet. Now, I told you, *shh*.'

'What's up with your ear?'

'Remember I told you I'd come straight from surveillance in Warsaw?' She pulled her hand away to reveal a sleek black earpiece. 'I brought the wire with me. Seemed a shame to waste it. I know a hospital's the last place you want to find a *bug*, but . . .'

The penny dropped in Felix's mind. 'You put a listening device on Coral?'

'It's in a square of sticking plaster, stuck to the lining of her gown,' said Hannah.

'The bitch is blind, she didn't guess a thing,' said Brad, smiling. 'That's why we barged in on your little reunion –

now we've stirred them both up, they'll go talk to one another.'

'Sharing their secrets like good sisters should,' Hannah agreed, 'while we listen in. We can hear for ourselves if Chessa's gonna play ball.' Felix opened his mouth to congratulate her but she waved a hand. 'It's OK, I know I'm brilliant . . .'

But even as she spoke, a chime from the lifts signalled new arrivals to their floor. Felix watched through the thin strip of safety glass set into the door as four soldiers filed past; their hazmat suits were blue and their gas masks came with binocular lenses. Each figure sported a black and gold patch on his chest depicting a spearhead – the emblem of the United States Special Operations Command.

'What are they doing here?' Felix muttered.

'The Girl only told Zane, and he was keeping things under wraps till we had our talk with the girls.' Brad was frowning. 'So how the hell did USSOCOM get on this?'

Hannah swore and banged her fist against the door-frame. 'We can't lose those two to Special Ops before we've even begun.'

Felix opened the door. 'Let's challenge them . . .'

'Challenge them to what?' said Brad. 'A quick game of Total Warfare? We can't go in there and say—'

'That they're Minos prisoners? Of course we can! We've both been on deep cover—'

'USSOCOM won't know Minos from Jack, numbnuts.'

'Shut up, both of you,' Hannah hissed, one hand to her earpiece. 'They're not Special Ops . . . They're bogus.

Coral and Chessa just got way excited. One of them's called Kurt . . .'

'Give me that.' Felix ripped the black receiver out of Hannah's ear and pressed it to his own, shushing her fiercely as she protested. 'That voice . . . Got to be the same Kurt I met. The CAF guy.' The rush of blood through his temples almost drowned out the babble of hushed voices. 'I don't know who his friends are but they're here to spring Coral and Chessa.'

'And take them where?' Brad hissed.

'Shhh.' Felix was straining to listen. 'If Chessa tells them I'm here, they might decide to find and neg us first.'

'*When you didn't make the rendezvous for pick-up,*' Kurt was saying, '*we thought the worst.*'

'We're alive.' Coral's voice, low, angry. '*I'm just blind.*'

'*I had to bring her here,*' said Chessa. '*She nearly died. I got sick too. I gave false names for us, but I thought we'd be caught for sure, and then . . .*'

Felix held his breath.

A heavy male voice he didn't recognize filled the silence. '*Lucky for you, you have a powerful friend, yes?*' The words were spoken with a trace of a Russian accent. '*A friend watching out for you.*'

'*Is Greg here?*' Coral said quickly.

The Russian sounded almost amused. '*I'm not talking about Manton.*'

'*Manton was hurt in the escape from those ATLAS bastards,*' Kurt said quickly. '*Took a shot to the arm. He'll be OK, but . . .*'

'*He didn't say anything about that,*' Coral whispered.

'*He couldn't. You don't know what's been going down,*' said Kurt. '*We'll explain back at Helios.*'

'*Where?*' Chessa's voice sounded faint and fragile.

'*Orpheus place,*' Kurt explained. '*We stayed there during the evacuation.*'

'*Has its own panic room,*' said the Russian. '*Completely secure.*'

'Helios?' Felix muttered. He saw Brad and Hannah looking blank. 'One of them said it has its own panic room, it's where they hid out during the evacuation. They must be based there. What the hell is Helios?'

'Look it up,' Hannah said quickly. 'The computer at Admissions must have net access.'

'Shh,' Felix hissed, straining to catch Chessa's voice.

'*I don't think we should go,*' she was saying.

'*Staying here is suicide,*' the Russian said.

'*Getting in here is one thing,*' Coral said quietly. '*But can you get us out?*'

'*If you do as we have planned, all will be well,*' the Russian voice assured her. '*We have a requisition order for your transfer to another medical garrison. And I do not think the nurses will fight to keep you, hmm . . . ?*'

Felix crossed to the door and checked the corridor was clear. 'You're right, Hannah – we should get down to Admissions.' He tapped the receiver. 'What's the range on this thing?'

'About four hundred metres,' said Hannah. 'But the signal's not going to carry through six storeys. We won't be able to listen in.'

'I'll go,' Brad offered. 'You stay here.'

'See if they've got transport out front,' Hannah added. Brad nodded and left quickly, taking the stairs this time.

Felix heard Kurt's voice asking for a stretcher on a trolley. The voice of a male nurse answered wearily in the positive; the RN must still be crashed out in her office.

While Kurt started telling the nurse about his requisition order, Hannah looked at Felix. 'How did they get hold of USSOCOM gear, and a letter that would fool the hospital guards?'

'How did the CAF have so much NATO kit back at their stores?' said Felix. 'How did they know Coral and Chessa were here? One of those "Special Ops" guys said Coral and Chess had a powerful friend . . .'

Hannah stared. 'A double agent in the military? Inside ATLAS?'

'Makes sense, doesn't it?' Felix peered out to see a bio-suited figure pushing a stretcher into Coral's ward. 'The leak could even be in Minos for all we know.'

'Brad brought you the news,' said Hannah. 'Who'd he hear it from?'

'Zane, I guess, but . . .' He frowned. 'You're not saying Brad could be playing us?' Hannah was about to respond when Felix heard a low hubbub in his ear again. 'They're getting ready to move out.'

'What do we do?' Hannah asked.

'Get outside ahead of them.' Felix flitted across the corridor to the stairwell door. 'If we can follow them, find Manton and Deep and whoever's been helping them . . .'

'There's no traffic in the whole city,' Hannah hissed,

joining him on the Dettol-stinking staircase. 'I think they might just notice a tail, don't you?'

'Maybe Brad's found out something on this Helios place.' Felix started running down the stairs three at a time, Hannah right beside him. They burst out onto the ground floor together, and Felix slapped his hand on the lift button. 'When they call the lift back up, we'll know they're coming.'

Hannah nodded and ran on to where Brad stood behind the Admissions desk. 'Anything?'

'Helios,' he read aloud. 'It's an investment bank with two premises in Wall Street.'

'Two on the same street?' asked Hannah.

'Wall Street's what we call that whole financial district,' Brad told her, drumming his fingers nervously on the desk. 'One of those addresses is probably the main business and the other one—'

'Whatever.' Felix jumped as the lift doors opened. His stress levels were maxing out. 'Which one are they going back to?'

'Who knows?' Hannah muttered something nasty-sounding in Afrikaans. 'Brad, did you check their transport?'

'Armoured ambulance. Four-litter. A stack of uniforms in the back. Driver waiting in the cab.'

The lift doors closed again, and the upward arrow above the doors illuminated – the elevator was being summoned, no doubt to the sixth floor. 'Kurt and his friends will be on their way down with Coral and Chessa any minute.'

Brad thought aloud. 'Can we stow away in the back of the ambulance?'

'A four-litter ambulance?' Hannah snorted. 'You're talking room for maybe nine or ten people, how do you suggest the three of us hide in—'

'Not three of us,' said Felix. 'One of us.'

Hannah raised her eyebrows. 'You, I suppose?'

'I've got the most to make up for.' Felix eyed the up arrow as it suddenly extinguished. 'You two tell Zane what's happening in person – we can't risk telling him over the radio in case Kurt's driver out there – or anyone else – is listening in. By the time you reach him, I should've arrived where the action is. The tera-heads can track me by my chain.'

'Or track your dead body, anyway,' Hannah retorted. 'What if it's a tera-head who leaked Coral and Chessa's location? Or what if Zane's the traitor?'

'What the hell?' Brad looked shaken. 'Leaks, traitors . . . ?'

'Those *skelms* upstairs got their intel, kit and requisition orders off somebody in the know.' Hannah folded her arms. 'Didn't they?'

'Are you making out that "somebody" is me?' Brad shook his head. 'You're lucky I'm too busy crapping myself right now to take offence.'

'Brad's legit,' Felix insisted. 'Or if he isn't, he's bloody stupid bringing me back to life in that cave when he could've let me die.'

'Though actually, I have been kicking myself ever since,' Brad added.

Felix felt his heart skitter as the elevator's down arrow snapped on. 'Enough of this.' He pulled his mask and hood down over his head. 'I'm going to need something to distract the driver of that ambulance while I get in the back.'

'Covered.' Hannah jogged out through the sliding doors, past the guards with their flame-throwers and made a show of peering about. Then she walked up to the ambulance driver, whose features were obscured by his gas mask. 'Got a light?' she asked. 'And if you do, d'you have a smoke to go with it?'

Felix was glad the steering wheel was on the left on American cars – it meant the driver had to look away from the hospital entrance to address Hannah at his side window. Felix jogged over to the back of the ambulance. The doors had been left open by Kurt and his buddies; clearly they were up for a quick getaway. And there were the suits and uniforms all piled up in the back like a military dressing-up box – camouflage gear, combat dress and army blues.

Felix climbed on board stealthily, not wanting to rock the vehicle, and started to bury himself beneath the uniforms, praying that his own bio-suit would not stick out. He heard Hannah thanking the driver for nothing, followed by her rapidly retreating footsteps. Then, through the earpiece, he heard the swish of the automatic doors, and a noisy rattling as Kurt and friends wheeled out the stretcher, the harsh noise biting into his ear.

Felix held dead still, hardly daring to breathe, as Kurt

and one of the others loaded Coral and her IV drip on board the ambulance and the others climbed in behind her, sitting on the flip-down seats ranged right and left. The toe of someone's boot came to rest centimetres from Felix's face; he felt horribly conspicuous. Any second now they would spot him, grab hold of him, and . . .

Kill him.

The engine growled into life and two metallic bangs on the side of the vehicle told the driver to pull away. As he did so, and the vehicle turned the corner, Kurt let out a whoop of relief, which Felix got in stereo.

'Thank God,' Chessa muttered. 'Thank God, thank God.'

'Thank you, Kurt,' said Coral quietly, without much conviction. 'And the rest of you. I can't believe Orpheus would let you risk your lives just to get us out.'

'Told you,' came the Russian's low voice. 'Powerful friend.'

'Deep squared it with him,' Kurt confided.

'Deep?' Chessa sounded puzzled. 'Not Manton?'

'You . . . don't know what's been going down.'

'So tell us!' Coral must've grabbed blindly for Kurt; the listening device under the plaster rasped as something rubbed against it. 'Well, Kurt?'

'Manton . . . disagreed with Orpheus about the use of Deathwing.'

'Disagreed? But he told us where to leave the sarin,' Chessa protested.

'No. Deep did – from Manton's phone.'

A long pause followed, before Coral spoke again: 'Deep's gone with Orpheus over Greg?'

'The big man wants to see us,' said Kurt. 'All of us.'

Felix lay beneath his flimsy cover, each nerve wire-sharp as the atmosphere thickened and his suit filled with sweat. He wondered if lab animals felt this way, trapped and terrified in their cages, free will and freedom things of the past, their life and future in the balance . . .

Felix tightened his fists. *Well, this animal's ready to test himself all the way.*

Justice for the beast.

Felix wasn't sure how long the journey from First and 16th to Wall Street took. It probably wasn't long at all; the driver seemed happy to take full advantage of the zero traffic, flinging the ambulance round every corner. Felix grabbed hold of the coveralls around him, afraid they'd fall loose and leave him exposed. He couldn't see a thing, his limbs were cramping, and his chest ached from so many shallow breaths. *What if I sneeze? What if I cough?*

Finally the ambulance slowed. Felix heard a heavy grinding noise, like a gate opening or a shutter rising. Then the vehicle dipped, accelerating down a slope. *Into a private garage*, he supposed. His heart started jumping so hard he was certain someone would see it shaking the whole pile of clothing on top of him.

Chessa didn't give you away, he told himself for comfort. Surely if she'd said anything in the hospital they'd have talked about it on the journey. But she had stayed silent the whole way here. *Stuff on her mind.*

And a whole lot of blood on her hands.

Felix tensed as the ambulance stopped. He heard the rear doors clunk and squeal as they were thrown open – the echoes carried, sharp through his earpiece; he wished he'd had the chance to take it out. The vehicle rocked as the big driver got out and came round the back.

'Are we going to this panic room you mentioned?' Coral said.

'Deep wants everyone together in the board room,' said Kurt. 'Better view than down in the basement, I guess.'

'I wouldn't know,' said Coral icily.

Just so long as you stay ignorant of what's stuck to your robe and don't change out of it anytime soon, thought Felix. As Kurt, Chessa and the others wheeled her away, the dizzying stereo effect of their movements dwindled until the only sounds he could hear were those seeping from the earpiece.

'Where are they going?' he heard Chessa ask softly.

Who's they? wondered Felix. *Their escorts?*

'Places to go, I guess,' Kurt sighed. 'Good riddance. They've been giving me the creeps.'

So the CAF's been left to it, noted Felix. He heard the click of a button, a hum. An elevator, maybe?

Cautiously, when he was certain no one had stayed behind, Felix peered out from the pile of uniforms and packaging.

All clear.

Soundlessly, he got to his feet and rifled through the clothes for anything he could use as a weapon – but the knock-off kit didn't extend to guns, it seemed. The best he could find was a field-surgeon's kit with a couple of scalpels. *Better than nothing*, he decided. *Just*.

The earpiece had gone dead. Coral must be out of range. The boardroom was most likely a long way up if it had a good view.

Stepping down from the ambulance, Felix found himself in a strip lit concrete garage, white and bright, familiar from any number of US movies and crime shows. Bad stuff always happened in garages like this. He peered around from behind the ambulance, checking the place out. But it seemed empty.

How long till Brad and Hannah get here with backup?

Felix checked the exits. Steel-mesh shutters were barring all movement in and out; and the manual override required a key code. CCTV cameras were pointing down at the general area. *Stay back. There could be someone watching.*

If the Orpheus escorts had pushed off somewhere, there must be a more obvious way out. Through the main reception, most likely. He crossed to a fire door and edged it open. No alarms. He could recce the area, try to get out, advise and direct the ATLAS troops when they arrived. Leave everything to them – armed, suited, booted, they'd get the job done. Maybe Felix would win back some brownie points for his derring-do in smuggling himself here.

Just to go straight back out again?

'Screw that,' he muttered, and started scaling the stone steps of the stairwell. He moved quickly, dry-mouthed and still sweating. He pulled off his gas mask with one hand, the two scalpels still clutched in the other. He waited tensely for the signal to steal back into his ear. The lift ought to give a clue as to where Chessa, Kurt and Coral had gone – no one else would be calling it away, so he'd know what level they were on at least.

He'd trudged up to the twenty-ninth floor, and his stress levels had risen way higher, when another voice burst from his high-tech receiver. An angry voice. Manton's.

'. . . you came to me, remember? Deathwing was *my* project before you bought your way into it. I was the one who got the dirt on Stevens, I was the one who made him vet the bats and keep them in hibernation till they were ready to use.'

'And I was the only one who could make sarin so pure so cheaply.' Felix recognized Deep's rough accent. 'The CAF is more than just you, Greg.'

'We could've brought in our own experts,' said an American voice, broad and imperious. 'We could've taken our own animals. But duplicating the work of others is a waste of time. And as I recall, Manton, you were happy enough to accept our assistance in removing certain targets.'

Finally, thought Felix, his pulse quickening. *This guy's got to be a big link in the Orpheus chain of command.* He continued stealthily up the steps, hanging on every word.

'Legitimate targets, yes, and set by me.' Manton's fury had not abated. 'You took out men who'd sanctioned the torture and murder of thousands of animals. But I made it clear to you that Deathwing was to be employed in small, selective strikes against business parks, oil refineries, fast-food HQs . . .'

'Come on, mate, you've got to see the bigger picture,' Deep broke in. 'Something on this scale makes the CAF real players.'

'Players?' Coral broke in with something close to a roar. 'You've made animal killers of all of us! We were set to be taken seriously, a radical group with a clear agenda and the capability to strike—'

'Listen to yourselves.' The American again, haughty, aloof. 'You sound like whining children not allowed their own way.'

'Whining?' Manton railed. 'Coral's blind! She and Chessa could've been killed dispersing the sarin by hand!'

The scoosh of an inhaler. 'I didn't know that would happen,' Deep said quietly.

'Finally got your payback for me dumping you,' Coral sneered. 'Is that it, Deep?'

'Oh, get over yourself, love!'

'It's you who needs to do that!' Manton's German accent was becoming more pronounced in his anger. 'You take it upon yourself to treat my wound with "pain relief" that knocks me out for twenty-four hours, then send Coral a text so she thinks *I'm* telling her what to do!'

'We should never have switched from incendiaries to that stuff,' Coral murmured.

'No. You shouldn't have.' Chessa's words were closest in Felix's ear. *She must be right on top of her sister.* 'What it does . . . It's evil.'

'It's a tool,' said the American impatiently.

'And Manton agreed the switch,' Deep added.

'What's the big deal here?' The American voice again. Already Felix had learned to loathe it. 'The CAF has demonstrated many times that it will kill for its cause.'

'We didn't know what this stuff could do!' Chessa argued. 'The scale of it.'

'I did,' said Coral. 'But I thought, if Greg really wanted it . . .' Her voice cracked. 'I thought, there are no animals allowed in these places, it . . . it made a kind of sense . . .'

'Oh, Coral,' Manton groaned, 'I would never have asked you to risk—'

'Why didn't you tell me Orpheus was pushing you into doing all this?' Coral shouted. 'I might not have believed that text came from you. I wouldn't be like this now!'

Spellbound by the drama unfolding, Felix nudged open the door to the thirtieth floor. The lift hadn't stopped here. He returned to the stairwell.

'I hear what you're saying,' Deep said; and for a paranoid second, Felix thought he'd been rumbled. 'And Coral, love, you've got to see it's 'cos me and the Chief want everything out in the open now that we're here.'

'You and the Chief here, yes,' growled Manton. 'Very cosy. You were less open with me about Orpheus making private overtures towards you. You, the big man at last. Is that it?'

Another puff from the inhaler. 'I keep telling you, Orpheus can help us do so much more,' said Deep. 'What's happened here in Manhattan is just a means to . . .'

He trailed off. *Go on*, Felix willed him, climbing higher, higher. *Don't mind me.*

'It's all right, Deep,' the American said calmly. 'Tell them.'

'Shouldn't we wait for Kurt to get back?'

Kurt's not in there with them? Felix felt a shiver rocket through him. *Which means he's roaming the building.*

'The cradle's in place now,' said the American. 'Kurt will be here soon enough.'

'Cradle?' Coral echoed.

'What are you talking about?' Manton demanded.

Glad it's not just me who's lost. Felix kept going up – until suddenly he found he'd run out of steps. The last flight led up to a fire door that gave onto the roof.

And the next moment, someone kicked it open.

The glare of bright blue sky blinded Felix for a moment, until a burly silhouette stole his focus.

Looks like you just found Kurt.

Shock and then anger twisted the teutonic features as Kurt yanked off his mask. 'You . . .'

At the same time, Felix heard the boardroom discussion spark through his earpiece, the plot unfolding as though he'd tuned into some radio drama. 'The bats haven't been released *just* to kill random targets,' said Orpheus Man. 'We needed the city empty for a good reason . . .'

Kurt hurled himself down the steps. Felix turned and started to run . . .

MANTON: *Hundreds, maybe thousands of animals will have died.*

ORPHEUS MAN: *Their sacrifice will be worth it.*

Timing his attack for the moment he sensed Kurt was about to grab him, Felix swivelled round and punched the man hard in the neck. Kurt gave a strangled shout as he was knocked back into the wall.

DEEP: *With Manhattan evacuated, Orpheus agents posing as US troops have gained unhindered access to strategic positions around the city . . .*

Kurt pulled a flick-knife from his belt. He slashed at Felix's face. Felix ducked and retaliated with his fistful of scalpels. *Have to end this fast. If he raises the alarm . . .* The two thin blades sliced through Kurt's gloved knuckles – he yowled with pain and the big knife fell from bloodied fingers.

DEEP: *They're building thermobaric bombs in key locations . . .*

Felix froze for a second as the words sank in, his mind dizzying with thoughts of the consequences – all the time Kurt needed. He kicked Felix in the groin, making him double over. But Felix gritted his teeth and charged forward, headbutting Kurt in the stomach, knocking him back against the wall.

CORAL: *Thermobaric? What's thermobaric?*

Kurt punched Felix's ear, knocked loose the receiver. But Felix already knew the answer to Coral's question; now he had to focus fully on ending Kurt's threat.

He dodged another blow and landed one to Kurt's jaw. *Thermobaric bombs comprise a stack of fuel and two explosive charges. The first detonates and disperses the fuel into a billowing cloud – which in turn is detonated by the second charge.* He landed another blow to Kurt's face. And another . . .

The destructive blast travels at more than two miles a second. Kurt spat out teeth in a crimson rush and collapsed, unconscious. Felix stared at his beaten enemy, trying to calm his breathing, to slow the blood-drum in his temples. His knuckles throbbed, his left ear felt red hot – he pressed the receiver into his right and listened for any sign that the sounds of his struggle had been overheard.

'. . . far more damage than could be caused by conventional high explosive.' Orpheus Man was concluding his explanation – no alarm bells. 'The devastation to New York will be truly epic in its scope. And if still the rulers of America don't capitulate, we will poison the reservoirs with gallons of sarin that will kill millions more in the wider Tri-State area . . .'

Felix tried not to shake as he started stripping off his protective bio-suit.

Deep put in: 'It's all right, we won't really have to detonate. Don't you see? With just the threat of that under our control, we'll be able to ask for anything we want.'

'An end to animal testing?' breathed Chessa.

'Damn right,' said Deep. 'That's true justice for the beast.'

'What about justice for the ones *your* poison has killed?' Manton's hold on his temper sounded to be slipping. 'Their blood's on your hands.'

'If their deaths help guarantee the well-being of millions more animals, then the end justifies the means.'

'That's what the Nazis said,' muttered Coral.

'We'll be making other demands of the United States government, naturally,' said the Orpheus man. 'The return of scores of terrorists currently in detention, a ransom running to several billion dollars, access to new experimental weapon technology in development.'

'It's some scam, huh?' Deep said smugly.

And speaking of scams . . . Felix started to wrestle Kurt's bloodstained hazmat suit from his body and checked the PAPR-system was still operational. *If it's Kurt you're expecting, you'd better get him.*

'Your demands will never be met,' sneered Manton.

'You think not?' Orpheus Man sounded almost amused. 'The evacuation was a slow and clumsy nightmare. Once the bat threat has been neutralized and New Yorkers return, we'll have demonstrated – graphically – the shortcomings in their systems. Unless our demands are met within six hours, the city will be levelled.'

As Felix heaved the breathing apparatus from Kurt's hazmat suit onto his back, his hot sweat turned to chills.

'They'll never believe you,' said Coral.

'I imagine not,' said Orpheus Man. 'Not until we

obliterate Wall Street, anyway. Detonating the thermobaric device placed in the subway vent close to the Stock
Exchange should serve as a small demonstration of our
power . . . wouldn't you say?'

Power that I helped to give you, Felix realized. *Power
to commit the biggest act of blackmail in history.*

...7...

'See?' Deep's rough accent though the earpiece jolted
Felix from his grim reverie. 'With that one act, we achieve
what no one else could – a permanent end to animal
testing.'

'Get a grip, Deep,' Manton snapped. 'You really think
Orpheus will put animal rights on their agenda? I agreed
the Deathwing deal as a one-off for mutual benefit – but
you can't expect an ongoing commitment.'

'Yeah, here we go,' sneered Deep. 'What's really
bugging you – the fact that I made this happen when you
couldn't?'

'You think *you* made this happen?'

'On the back of my contribution, I've been offered
a place in the Orpheus hierarchy. I've got skills, mate –
practical skills that you don't.'

'Gassing and poisoning people?'

'Tools to make governments listen!'

That's it, guys, keep yourselves distracted. Felix tucked Kurt's flick-knife into his belt along with the two scalpels, and then, heart pounding, fixed the man's gas mask in place. *'Kurt' is coming to get you, and he'll need all the distraction he can get.* He went down another flight of stairs and through the door to the lift area. A sign beside the steel doors promised an EXECUTIVE BOARDROOM on this level. 'Finally,' Felix muttered, pressing the lift call button. The doors opened instantly.

Getting closer. He followed the arrow, through a door onto a carpeted corridor. Opulent offices in oak and steel flanked one side of the passage, boasting the prestige of their fat-cat owners, while on the other stood neat little workstations where personal assistants sat at their desks and took calls for their bosses. Was this whole company a front for terrorist activity, or had it been secretly infiltrated by Orpheus? Felix didn't know, didn't care. All he could picture were these fine offices crashing down to earth in a conflagration that would rage for miles around . . . the deaths, the panic, the numbing fear . . . Like 9/11 and Day Zero all over again, only God knew how many times worse.

It can't happen. Mustn't happen. He felt weirdly calm as he pressed on along the corridor. Was he in the zone or in denial? *Come on! All it takes is a single fifteen-year-old kid with surprise and a flick-knife to stop the whole sickening thing in its tracks. Easy. Right?*

He almost imagined he could hear hollow laughter. Then he realized it was real voices carrying – in sympathy with the tinny scratches in his ear. He was close. Right outside.

He reached under the mask and took out the redundant earpiece, placed it on one of the PAs' desks. Then he hesitated, a few metres from the boardroom door. How was he meant to play this situation? Brad and Hannah must surely have reached Zane . . . in which case crack troops could be showing any moment to take care of the situation.

But when? They're not here yet, are they? The voice of doom whispered in his ear, as though through a new receiver. *When they do arrive it could be too late.*

He closed his eyes. He should call in what he'd found out. Except if there *was* a traitor in ATLAS and they got wind of all he knew—

'Kurt?' Deep's voice rang out through the door; he must've glimpsed movement through the glass of the door. 'That you?'

No getting out of it now.

Felix tried to think how Kurt had moved. He barely knew the guy and he was a half-head shorter. 'A half-head's all you'll have left by the time this is over,' he breathed, and pushed open the door.

'About time,' said Deep.

The lion's den. Through his mask, Felix took in the scene and its surroundings in a series of brisk appraisals. The room was large and airy, with a huge dark slab of mahogany dominating the space. The wall opposite was glass from floor to ceiling, offering an incredible view over the southern tip of Manhattan and the waters beyond.

To his left stood Manton, looking tired and angry in equal measure, wearing the same jeans and checked shirt he'd worn the last time Felix had seen him. Coral was propped awkwardly in a high-backed chair beside Chessa, who looked simply terrified. On the other side of the table stood Deep, dressed in a hazmat suit. An older man was seated beside him, greying, dignified, nondescript, his stolen stripes and star declaring him a chief master sergeant in the US Air Force.

He really is the Chief. A large black holdall sat on the table in front of him. *Not military issue*, Felix noted.

Deep motioned that 'Kurt' should join him on his side of the room. Felix walked warily round the boardroom table. Manton barely acknowledged him.

'So what's this really about, Deep?' Manton demanded. 'You arranged for Coral and Chessa to be rescued just to show me how much clout you have, is that it?'

Deep shook his head angrily. 'You have to decide, all of you,' he said. 'Whether to join Orpheus, like me, or . . .'

'Or what?' sneered Manton. 'I've only ever worked for justice for the beast. Now you want me licking *your* boots in return for being a part of the corporate terrorists who've hijacked my Deathwing and wrecked it—'

The Orpheus man broke in. 'I think you mean, who've implemented it flawlessly and enhanced its effectiveness a hundredfold?'

Felix looked around discreetly, trying to formulate a plan of action. If he could somehow incapacitate Orpheus

Man and lock the others inside until back-up came . . . It wasn't as though the CAF could escape through the window . . .

Then, as Felix glanced out, his heart thumped to see a large window-cleaner's platform, suspended by taut wires.

'The cradle's in place,' Orpheus Man had said. *And that thing's the cradle. That's what Kurt was doing up on the roof – positioning it outside. Why?*

Orpheus Man looked up at Deep. 'Well, I think Mr Manton's made his position quite clear. And these charming ladies . . .'

'Don't,' hissed Chessa. 'Just don't.'

'We're with Greg,' Coral said. 'I hate you, Deep. Hate you.'

'Well, there we are, then.' Orpheus Man got up and slid open the thick, soundproofed window. No noise but the wind's faint whistle gusted in from the deserted city, and he took a deep, satisfied breath. 'I suggest we conclude this charade.'

'I agree,' said Manton. Felix watched the Orpheus Man size up the distance down to the cradle – a few metres only. *He's bailing out. What is this?* 'Kurt, what about you? Surely you can't seriously be siding with Deep over . . .' He tailed off, looking at Felix.

He knows, thought Felix, freezing.

But it was Deep who spoke first. '"Over" is right, Greg.' He stooped and pulled a carrier bag from behind a laptop case at his feet. 'I really wanted this to work out for all of us. New start, you know? I'm sorry . . .'

Felix saw Deep reach for what was inside the bag – two gas masks and a small grey canister. *Oh, here we go . . .*

'No!' Felix lunged forward to grab the bag first.

Deep started in surprise, swung round – and recognized the face behind the visor. *'You?'*

Further accusations were cut short as Felix's fist landed in Deep's face. As Deep fell sideways into a chair, Chessa screamed and Coral shouted, 'What's happening?'

And at the same time, Manton took his chance and jumped up onto the table, fury twisting his features as he made for the American—

There was the cold thud of a silenced pistol firing. Manton's shoulder jerked and he cried out, falling backwards. Chessa shrieked again. At the same time, Felix rounded on Orpheus Man, and found the pistol aimed at his chest. He slapped the man's wrist away; a wild shot tore splinters from the thick mahogany.

'Down, Chessa!' Felix yelled, propelling himself into an awkward backward roll over the table, clumsy in his hazmat suit, dropping out of sight as another bullet fired. Felix bellowed with pain – *Let him think he hit you, play possum, then—*

But the next thing he heard was a metallic rattle – and a hissing like a dozen cobras. *Deep's canister.*

A thick, white cloud was billowing up from the floor where it had landed, beside Manton's bloody body.

'I've set it, come on!' Orpheus Man's voice was muffled by the gas mask he'd grabbed from Deep's bag. Snatching up the laptop case, he swung himself out through the open window and Deep, also masked now, jumped after him.

Felix hesitated. *Follow – or help Chessa and Coral?* The pall of white fog had almost engulfed the whole room, but Coral couldn't see it and Chessa seemed in shock.

'Out!' Felix scrambled up, threw open the door. Chessa was already starting to cough as he grabbed her arm and shoved her out through the door. 'Run to the end of the corridor.'

'But Coral—'

'I'll get her out. Go!'

Coral had fallen from her chair to the carpet, retching, reaching out blindly. 'Greg? Chess!'

'No,' Felix muttered, 'just me.' Stepping over Manton's body, he grabbed her under the armpits and hauled her out of the boardroom, her drip dragging along beside her. The toxic cloud mushroomed through the door as if in pursuit.

'Coral!' shouted Chessa, running towards them from the other end of the corridor. 'I'm coming!'

'No, stay back!' Felix ordered. 'I'll bring her to you.'

'Greg!' Coral screamed, eyes streaming tears, coughing and shaking. 'Where is he? What's happening?'

'I'm going back for him,' Felix yelled, pushing the drip bag into her hands. 'Now, this corridor's straight.' He managed to get her onto her feet. 'Chessa's standing at the end. Run to her. Or you're dead.'

As Coral stumbled away, Felix turned back and braved the smoke. *Thank God Kurt's respirator's still giving pure air.* He almost fell over Manton. He gave him a cursory check – the big man had stopped breathing. Looking up, he saw that both Deep and Orpheus Man had gone. The whine of a powerful motor described the descent of the window-cleaner's cradle.

Anyone who said no to Deep and his new boss was always going to end up dead, Felix realized. *That's why Coral and Chessa were sprung – join up or die. No loose ends left untied*. He skirted the table, running to the window. The two men were already far below. He threw both of his scalpels down at the cradle, more in frustration than in the hope of really stopping them. The window beside him shattered as another bullet narrowly missed his head. He reeled back and fell onto the table just beside the holdall that had been left there. It hadn't been zipped up all the way, and inside it he could just about make out a transparent box of flimsy plastic.

'*I've set it,*' Orpheus Man had said: '*Come on.*'

'Oh God,' Felix murmured, staring at the black leather bag. 'You're a bomb.'

He realized he was looking at the edge of the bomb's Timing and Power Unit, with switches, LEDs and a digital timer inside.

His laboured breathing was causing the lenses in his mask to steam up, he had no tools; not exactly ideal conditions for going to work on a ticking bomb. And while he wasn't short on self-belief, imagining he could tackle this device and win was taking optimism to a whole new level.

I could run, take a chance that I can get Chessa and

Coral out of the building before the bomb detonates.

The gas was clearing a little and Felix looked once more inside the partially unzipped holdall. His stomach lurched as he registered the countdown.

Two minutes and nine seconds to detonation.

...6...

No time to get out. A wave of panic surged over Felix and he fought to ignore the nausea welling up inside.

Get a grip . . . Focus. You have to do this!

He peered deeper inside the bag, but there was no sign of the detonators, battery pack or explosives. He would have to cut his way into the power unit. *Idiot – why'd you throw away both scalpels?* That left him with Kurt's flick-knife. But once he'd hacked his way inside, what then?

You need tools. Now.

Felix skirted the table, jumped over Manton's body and ran outside, his vision restricted by the mask as he searched frantically around the PA's cubicles, yanking open drawers and filing cabinets, looking for something, anything that he could use to work on the bomb. Soon he'd assembled an array of improvised tools – paper clips, eyebrow tweezers, nail-clippers, a make-up mirror. *Not much, but it'll have to do.*

He raced back to the bag, barely able to bring himself to look at the display.

One minute, twenty-three seconds.

Not enough time. Beads of sweat had formed on Felix's forehead and were now trickling down into his eyes, making them sting, but in the stifling confines of the suit, he couldn't even wipe them dry. *Just keep going. You've got to stay focused!*

Felix could hear the familiar voice of his instructor in his mind. *The Timing and Power Unit is the brain of the bomb, but the power source is its heart. It's your job to rip it out.* He had to go for the battery pack . . . but first he took the mirror and lowered it through the gap in the bag; he needed to make sure there were no nasties inside – no booby traps or trip switches that would blow him to bits the moment he unzipped the holdall . . .

There were none. He supposed Orpheus and Deep had expected to be setting this off in a room full of gas and corpses. But then, why set the bomb off at all? To destroy the bodies, thwart any further investigation?

Or maybe the explosion here's meant to draw military attention, making it easier for Deep and his new boss to go to ground . . .

One minute and eight seconds on the timer.

Felix gritted his teeth. 'I'm going to stop you.' Fighting to keep his hand steady, he unzipped the bag further and noticed a microswitch underneath the lid of the TPU. The microswitch was a classic anti-handling trigger and it had been built into the bomb so that if he removed the lid he'd be blown to pieces.

With a shaky breath, he took the flick-knife and forced the blade through the flimsy plastic shell of the TPU. With what felt like agonizing slowness he managed to hack out a square incision in the box, about the size of a pack of cards. His eyes flicked back to the countdown.

Thirty-nine seconds.

This is insane. He felt sick enough as it was just being inside the suit; but the feeling of claustrophobia, mixed with the heady rush of adrenaline made it ten times worse. As he worked, he fought against an overwhelming primal instinct to turn and run, get as far away from here as he could.

If you die now – and if Chess and Coral are killed too – there'll be no one to warn Zane what Orpheus is planning. Terrifying images flashed through his mind in an unending blur – screaming faces, twisted bodies piled up in the streets, buildings ripped apart by tumultuous explosions; a nightmare vision of a city consumed by fire . . .

He forced himself to blank the hellish images from his mind. Sweating profusely now, he lowered his head right down into the bag – until he had his eye right up against the opening – and, holding his breath, identified the first pair of wires leading from the digital timer to the TPU.

Behind them, a further pair of wires led from the six-volt battery to the TPU.

. . . the power source is its heart.

He glanced across to the digital timer. *Only twenty-four seconds.* Another surge of panic, a voice screaming in his head. *No way! You've failed!*

But he could only carry on.

Cut corners and you cut your own throat. The timer could have a hidden collapsing circuit inside and the first he'd know about it would be when he'd painted the room a new shade of crimson. But the colour scheme wouldn't stand for long.

He was going to have to go for the battery – there was no other way now.

He pulled out the tweezers, and gingerly slid them through the opening. Then, moving the first pair of wires aside, he carefully reached behind them and gripped the second set of wires – leading from the battery to the TPU.

He took another breath, then cautiously pulled them back towards the opening.

Eleven seconds. Ten . . . nine . . . eight . . .

Still holding the wires firmly in the grip of the tweezers, Felix reached up onto the desk with his other hand and fumbled around for the nail-clippers, cursing the thick gloves he was wearing.

. . . seven . . . six . . .

Finding them at last, he opened them with one hand and edged them towards the bomb.

. . . five . . . four . . .

He placed their jaws either side of the battery's two connecting wires.

. . . three . . .

He felt a clunk as he worked them hard against the thick-wound strands of wire.

He was still there.

Just two seconds left and he'd done it.

Felix closed his eyes, allowing himself to bask for a moment in the heady euphoria that had engulfed him. He could scarcely believe he was still alive – and by rights he shouldn't be. At least the gas had cleared now, with the windows wide open or shot to smithereens. But he didn't dare remove the mask. Instead he turned from the holdall, avoided looking at Manton's grisly corpse and walked back outside into the corridor. By rights he should've been exhausted but instead he was buzzing.

No time to rest in any case.

He picked up the in-ear receiver he'd left on the PA's desk, and jogged back along the carpeted corridor to the lift area. Kurt lay sprawled in a small puddle of blood. He was still breathing. *Hopefully that means we're gas-free out here.* Cautiously Felix removed the mask and put the earpiece to his still-painful left ear. He could hear tinny squawks, filtering out of range.

A man's voice. '. . . *come on, this way.*'

'*Get off me!*' Coral muttered between coughs. '*I can manage.*'

'*You and your sister are going back into hospital for treatment.*'

'*What about Felix?*' That was Chessa's voice. '*He's still up there!*'

As if in response, the lift chimed and its doors opened to reveal three figures in bio-suits. Felix tensed himself instinctively for another fight . . . .

'Hey!' Zane's voice was instantly recognizable, even muffled by his visor. 'Cavalry's here. Again.'

Felix slumped back against the wall. 'You're meant to arrive in the nick of time – not five minutes after it's too late.'

'So sue us, *boet*.' Hannah pulled off her gas mask. 'You all right? Chessa said something about a gas grenade . . .'

'And it looks like you've taken some knocks,' Brad added, taking off his own mask.

Now Zane did the same, his dark skin beaded with sweat. 'When these two told me what you were doing, I thought you were on some kinda "death before dishonour" kick.'

'Manton got there first,' Felix said breathlessly. 'Shot and gassed. Deep's defected to Orpheus.'

Brad frowned. 'He's what?'

'It's all gone crazy. Orpheus killed Manton when he wouldn't come over, and nearly killed Chessa and—'

'The girls already told us that much,' Hannah assured him.

Felix looked at Zane. 'Do we have back-up?'

'Five good men. Minos agents only.' Zane looked pained. 'Couldn't take a chance on involving ATLAS troops in case this traitor crap you're spouting turns out to hold water.'

Hannah shot him a look. 'And one of those "good

men" is taking Chessa and Coral back to that medical centre. Leaving us with four.'

'We've got to get after Deep and this man from Orpheus,' said Felix. Zane, Brad and Hannah all opened their mouths to speak but he waved a hand for silence. 'He's some kind of senior figure. He said Orpheus are priming thermobaric weapons all over Manhattan, ready to detonate once everyone's moved back in—'

'Jesus, Felix,' Zane exclaimed. 'Slow down a minute.'

'I can't! The Orpheus guy and Deep got away, they'll go to ground, we'll never find them.'

'Wait.' Brad pointed to the bloodied body in the hazard-gear undergarments on the floor. 'Is that Kurt from the CAF? The one who kidnapped Doc Stevens?'

Felix nodded briefly. 'Ran into him once he'd set up the getaway for the others in a window-cleaner's cradle, taking them to ground level, away from the gas and the bomb they tried to detonate.'

'Bomb?' Zane interrupted. 'One of these thermobaric—'

'No – way smaller: I defused it. But there's a thermobaric placed in a sewer tunnel near the Stock Exchange. We need the mother of all ECM jammers down here, blocking remote detonation.'

Zane swore and pulled out his radio, barking off a series of instructions to have that area searched.

'Wait . . .' A thought bolted through Felix's brain. 'Kurt was good to go with Deep and Orpheus Man – he might know where they're headed.'

'And that unconscious act is a sham.' Hannah nudged him in the ribs with the toe of her boot. 'Wakey-wakey.'

'Go to hell,' Kurt said, his words slurring through his blood-crusted lips. 'I'm not telling you a thing.'

'Yes, you are.' Zane pocketed the radio, pushed Felix and Brad aside and marched over. 'Right now, your clothes are telling me a lot. That hazmat suit is military issue. Makes you a soldier.'

Kurt snorted a thick clot of blood from his broken nose. 'I'm no soldier.'

'Funny. I mistook you for one.' Zane pulled out a Sig 229 from his holster. 'And you know what else? I could've sworn you were armed.' He pointed the gun at Kurt. 'Which means, when I shoot you, it'll be one soldier killing another in self-defence.'

'You can't!' Kurt glared up at him. 'You wouldn't dare.'

'I got three witnesses gonna back me up,' Zane said quietly. 'Who've you got?'

'Go to hell.'

Zane just smiled, shifted his aim a fraction and fired his handgun. The bang battered at Felix's ears, the marble floor spat dust and shrapnel over Kurt's leg.

'No!' Fear gripped Kurt's bruised features as he stared up at Zane. 'You're crazy!'

'Uh-uh. I'm impatient. And I want answers.' Zane smiled again. 'Where's Deep headed with this Orpheus man? What's his name?'

'We call him the Chief. I don't know where they're headed.'

Zane tightened his grip on the gun and aimed at Kurt's leg. 'I think you do. I think you're playing for time.'

Felix swapped an uneasy look with Brad. Hannah stood quiet and impassive.

'You can't do this,' Kurt moaned. 'There are rules . . . I've got rights!'

'Thought it was only *animal* rights you cared about. Justice for the beast and all that.' Zane smiled coldly. 'Well, there used to be a rulebook, my friend. But most of it burned on Day Zero and the rest got ground into the dirt when New York's millions walked out of here. So, tell me where your friends are headed, or so help me, I'll *show* you justice.'

Kurt shook his head. Zane squeezed the trigger of the Sig. Felix flinched from the loudness of the retort – and Kurt's scream. Stomach churning, he saw blood pooling from a hole in the CAF man's boot.

I thought Zane was bluffing.

'Tell me, Kurt,' Zane repeated calmly. 'Or the next bullet goes in your kneecap.'

'The heliport,' Kurt hissed, eyes wide with terror. 'Downtown Manhattan heliport.'

Zane straightened. 'Pier Six, on the East River?'

'The holdall bomb going off up here . . . was supposed to bring . . . the soldiers running.' Kurt was clutching at his foot, his face deathly pale behind his bruises. 'Leave the heliport less secure . . . for our getaway.'

'Then what are we waiting for?' said Brad grimly.

Zane turned and called the lift.

'Kurt, do you know the location of the thermobaric bombs?' Felix asked quickly. 'Or the sarin you were going to use to poison the drinking water?'

'Only . . .' Kurt hissed, close to tears now. 'Only the Chief knows.'

'I don't believe him,' said Hannah.

'Stay here and question him some more,' Zane told her.

'Lekker,' Hannah breathed slowly in approval.

'I need a hospital,' Kurt called hoarsely.

'Hannah's trained in field medicine,' Zane told him as the lift doors opened and Felix and Brad piled inside. He handed her his Sig. 'And all kinds of other things.'

'I'm a regular Florence Nightingale,' Hannah agreed, aiming the gun with practised ease. 'For good boys, at any rate . . .'

The doors slid shut, blocking out the scene. Felix felt sick. It must've shown on his face.

'This is how it has to be, Mr Smith,' Zane said quietly, as the elevator began its downward plunge. 'Big boys' rules. You should know that by now.'

'So this Chief character's heading for the heliport with Deep,' said Brad. 'It's, like, one of the few gateways to New York left, and his bomb's not gone off. So it'll be heavily guarded, right? They'll never get through.'

'Kurt and those other Orpheus people got into the hospital without a hitch,' muttered Felix. 'They've got real ID and pukka uniforms. And if there is someone helping them—'

'They could have a flight out of here already chartered,' Zane agreed. 'I got tera-heads checking all orders relating to passage in and out of Manhattan. If anything dodgy shows up, Minos will find it – and those head-shed sons of bitches trying to close us down can eat our dust.' He looked at Brad and Felix, eyes dark as the proverbial coals. 'I have faith in you. But, by God, if you don't make me proud out there . . .'

The lift slowed to a stop, and the doors duly opened. Without another word, Felix and Brad ran out into a huge, well-appointed reception and through revolving doors onto the street outside. A Jeep was waiting, its open boot loaded with firepower and ammunition. As Zane, Brad and Felix approached, its driver gunned the engine. They'd barely clambered inside before Zane signalled the driver and they went roaring away towards the river, through the boxy manmade mountains of the financial district, heading for the heliport.

Brad took two M4s with telescoping stocks and close combat optical sights, loaded a fresh magazine into each and passed one to Felix, who took it without thanks or comment. Looking up at the sheer sides of the sky-scrapers around him, he felt like a lab-rat trapped in some colossal maze. Some half-remembered poem from his schooldays came back sharply to him.

> *Theirs not to make reply,*
> *Theirs not to reason why,*
> *Theirs but to do and die . . .*
> *Into the jaws of Death,*
> *Into the mouth of Hell*
> *Rode the six hundred.*

'Or the four of us at least,' Felix muttered, as the driver stepped on the accelerator, as they rushed at suicidal speed towards the heliport – and a final reckoning.

... **5** ...

The Jeep screeched in a hard right turn onto a wide-open road fringing the East River. Suddenly Felix heard the relentless sputter of machine-gun fire in the distance, somewhere further along the shore.

Brad had heard it too. 'What the hell . . . ?'

The rattling grew louder as they neared the grey-and-yellow striped tarmac of Downtown Manhattan Heliport, jutting out straight and sharp as a draughtsman's T-square into the cobalt river. Six or seven helicopters sat parked on their pads – and with a chill, Felix saw dozens of soldiers scurrying around in apparent confusion, using them as cover.

'Pull up,' Zane bellowed, and the driver stamped on the brakes. As the engine cut out, the air thickened with the terrifying sounds and screams of bullets and battle.

'With me!' Zane ordered, leading the way as Felix,

Brad and the driver abandoned their wheels, clutched hold of their weapons and sprinted down the deserted freeway towards the heliport. Sweating in his cumbersome suit and with no body armour, Felix felt horribly exposed.

As they drew nearer, he tried to make sense of the scene out on the takeoff/landing area. It seemed that the helicopters were being defended by a troop contingent, exchanging fire with their own side. It wasn't hard to guess that the men pressing forward towards the copters were Orpheus Man, Deep and their cronies, intent on securing an escape route from the city. Something must've gone wrong; their ID had failed scrutiny, or a lack of military etiquette had given them away . . .

And now hell was throwing a wild party here on earth.

'All right . . .' Pausing on the asphalt approach to Pier Six, Zane turned to Brad and Felix. 'We're going to secure the entrance building. You know the drill – anticipate attack and return fire. The hostiles are wearing our uniforms – that means every combatant in that heliport must be considered a threat. You will shoot to wound, or to kill if you have no alternative. Felix, we have a visual on Deep, but only you can ID the Orpheus man. Anyone else is expendable, but I want him alive.' He faced the small heliport reception that obscured their view of the carnage. 'Let's go.'

Heart like a brick trying to bounce up his throat, Felix followed Zane and the driver, Brad at his side. Zane opened fire with his M4, and the glass doors blew to pieces. At once, returned fire tore up the tarmac ahead of them. Felix dived for the cover of a car parked outside the building, tucked in his head, struck the ground in a shoulder-roll and jumped back to his feet. Aiming his gun across the bonnet of the vehicle, he let off a round of covering fire as Zane and the driver pelted inside. More shots fired, cracks echoing across the asphalt. Brad ran into the reception after Zane; seconds later the hulking form of a soldier came flying out through the shattered windows, landing in a twitching heap.

Breathing hard, trying to stay in control, Felix raced from behind the car and flattened his back against the brickwork beside the doorway. The suddenness of the violence was almost overwhelming. Real fighting had none of the polish or choreography he'd seen on films or TV. It was ragged, brutal, desperate. He heard shouts in a foreign language, the deadened slap of fists on flesh. Inside, Zane was fending off a burly attacker while the driver struggled with another man, writhing in a bloodied carpet of broken glass.

Felix felt a rush of anger, fear and outrage boil through him. *It's them or us, kill or be killed – and deal with the fallout later.*

Steeling himself, he started forward to help Zane – then heard the creak of a door opening behind him. Whirling round, Felix brought up his gun – to find Brad coming out of the staff room.

'Friendly!' Brad shouted. 'This room's been cleared.' Then a bullet hole split the wood of the door centimetres from his head. Brad threw himself backwards and Felix spun through 180 degrees to spy a man in hazmat gear outside the building, crouched behind a concrete bollard. He returned fire, striking shrapnel from the base of the squat stone post – then ducked down beside the reception desk as Brad took up the firefight, shooting back at the man who'd almost killed him.

Felix tried to keep calm; he'd been involved in fire-fights before, but never right in the thick of it like this. He focused on his surroundings, trying to take stock of his position. To his right was the first of two sets of double doors leading straight out onto the helipad. Looking left, he could see the approach to the heliport, the way they'd just come.

He saw five more uniformed men racing towards the little building, and swore under his breath. Were they ATLAS reinforcements or more Orpheus infiltrators? If he shot them down and they were friendly . . .

'Troops incoming,' he shouted desperately.

Brad fired off another round. 'Kind of got my hands full,' he shouted.

Felix jumped as Zane, still struggling with his assailant, rolled into sight behind the desk. Felix crawled over and jammed the business end of his rifle against the hostile's head. The hostile froze – and Zane put him to sleep with a meaty punch to the temple. 'Sir,' Felix said breathlessly, 'we have more combatants approaching.'

'Sir, I'm pinned down here!' Brad shouted. The driver couldn't help, crouched behind a shot-up chair, blood staining the left side of his uniform, his M4 clutched uselessly in a ruined hand. Zane rose up, fired his own weapon at the man behind the bollard and then bounded across the reception so as not to obscure Brad's own line of fire. Bracing himself against the shattered doorway he fired off a round of warning shots at the approaching soldiers. 'Identify yourselves and your unit . . .'

'Get going, Felix,' Brad urged him between bursts of fire: 'Deep and the Chief are gonna get away!'

Felix nodded, pushed through the first of the two sets of double doors, and with a jolt sighted his targets. They'd taken cover behind a burning copter parked across the concourse. The Chief was clutching his case tightly under his arm, staring keenly at the chaotic battle raging across the pier, while Deep held his pistol cocked and ready. From what Felix could tell, the other Orpheus men were trying to clear a path to one particular helicopter; looked like a Little Bird, a two-man light-attack craft designed to support special operations. *And Deep can fly a copter, we know that* . . .

Presumably the Chief and his new recruit were Orpheus priorities to escape, with their mercenaries and followers left to secure their own way out – or die in the attempt.

And now it's my turn . . . Felix gripped his gun, psyching himself up to break cover. His legs felt frozen. If Felix didn't hit Deep or the Chief first time, he'd surely be shot dead, like so many other good men out there on the pier, cut down – their flesh and organs torn apart by the gunfire . . .

But before he could move, Deep and the Chief

suddenly sprinted across the tarmac to the Little Bird. Deep fired wildly as he ran.

Felix bolted through the double doors after them, out onto the forecourt. The sound of gunfire was deafening. Panting, heart racing, sweat pouring off him inside his suit, he saw a soldier to his right aim his rifle, ready to shoot him down. *My side or theirs?* 'Friendly!' he screamed . . .

And was knocked off his feet as a copter exploded behind the soldier. The man was engulfed in a raging fireball, his burning body hurled into the ranks of the enemy. Felix was blown over, landing painfully on one side. His ears were ringing, senses stunned. He saw combatants on both sides floored by the blast before thick black smoke billowed over the scene.

Choking, Felix got back to his feet, clutching his gun, hoping he wouldn't have to use it. He heard the whine of an engine starting up nearby, and then the thick, roiling air seemed suddenly torn apart by noise. Felix was nearly knocked off his feet again by the gale of the rotors beating down on him, and by the sheer deafening din, but he struggled onwards through the churning grey soup of smoke and air. The Little Bird was operational, Deep at the controls, the Chief clutching his case beside him.

Felix swung up the assault rifle and fired at the cockpit. The recoil made his whole body judder as the rounds spat from the slim black muzzle. The glass cracked – but then the copter began to rise upwards, arcing slowly to one side. Felix switched targets, aiming first at the rotor joints then at the engine's air intake, battering the metal beast till his ammo was spent. But the copter was still rising.

No, thought Felix, *you're not stopping me this time*. He took a determined leap forward and grabbed hold of the copter's landing skids. The vibration through his gloved hands was savage as he dangled there, the rush of smoke and air in his face disorienting as the copter rose higher. Hauling himself up like some insane stuntman, he grasped hold of the strut connecting the left-hand skid to the base of the Bird . . .

But the Chief had seen him. He swung open the cabin door, his features set in a twisted snarl, aiming a gun straight at Felix's head.

Felix felt as if his heart had stopped. Time slowed around him. *Drop*, he thought. *No, too high*. He closed his eyes tight, ears filled with the din of the copter's engines and the rattle of gunfire below, waiting for the Chief to pull the trigger.

Then, suddenly, the helicopter banked sharply to one side, almost causing Felix to lose his grip on the strut. He opened his eyes – the Chief had gone, the door left flapping like a broken wing. Felix glanced down at the helipad, now some forty metres below, and with a dizzying rush saw Zane pointing his assault rifle up at the Little Bird.

Felix swung both legs up onto the skid, clinging on grimly as the helicopter spun round in a tight circle. Either Deep had lost control of the copter or . . .

A figure in a hazmat suit plummeted from the other

side of the copter, trailing blood from its head in a deadweight dive till it vanished into the dull blue expanse of the East River.

Deep, Felix realized numbly. Had he been shot dead or—?

The questions fled his head, pushed out by panic as the helicopter lurched and swooped once more, like a crazed untamed horse determined to shed its rider. The Chief must've disappeared inside to try and bring the heli under control himself – and was doing a lousy job. It was like being trapped on a rollercoaster without the safety bar.

Felix edged along the slippery landing skid, praying he wouldn't lose his grip – or the contents of his stomach. The helicopter dipped sharply sideways and he grabbed hold of the flapping door with one arm to steady himself. Now he could see the Chief grappling with the controls, wide-eyed with fear, the walls of the cockpit behind him splashed red with Deep's blood. As Felix pushed himself inside, the Chief looked up, saw him and reached with one hand for the gun beside his case on the passenger seat. For a second Felix thought he would fall straight out again, but just managed to brace his feet either side of the doorway.

The Chief brought up the gun, but Felix lurched forward and grabbed his wrist, twisting hard. As the man cried out, his grip on the cyclic shifted and the helicopter pitched violently to the right. Felix tumbled on top of the Chief, head-butting him sharply on his jaw. The man cried out and lost his tentative grip on the gun, which clattered to the floor. The engine screamed even louder as the helicopter rolled the other way, losing altitude. Felix was thrown backwards, almost tumbling out of the open door. The Chief turned back to the controls, his mouth a gory mess, desperately trying to bring the copter back under control.

But Felix guessed it was already too late. He caught a pitching view of the yellow-striped helipad through the thick smoke still belching from the chopper wreck, snatched hold of the Chief's case and threw it outside. The Chief snarled in anger, swiped at Felix's face with the side of his hand, knocking him backwards and almost out of the passenger door. But there was no follow-through. The Chief had a sat-phone in his hand – he jabbed a button.

Who's he calling at a time like this – God?

Then, with a grinding, wrenching noise, a huge broken sheath of metal hurtled past the windscreen. *Rotor blade*, Felix realized in wonder. *I must've hit one of the struts before, weakened it . . .*

The heli began to drop like a stone, spinning round and round. Smoke was everywhere. The Chief was yelling into his phone over the screeching engines – hard, guttural words in a language Felix couldn't place. Was there sea or concrete below? Felix could see nothing through the dizzying spin of the copter's death throes; then he felt his grip on the doorway slip—

Suddenly he was shaken free into the maelstrom of noise, heat and smog like a leaf in a hurricane, tumbling over and over through the air. He thought his fall would never stop. He opened his mouth to scream.

Then his body struck blackness and all his senses slammed into shutdown.

... 4 ...

The heavy smell of burned diesel filled Felix's nostrils and made him choke. A sharp ache defined every muscle as he tried to sit up and open his eyes. Something cold and wet rubbed against his cheek. A sodden blanket. He realized he was soaked through and shivering.

He opened his eyes and found himself still at the heliport. The gunfire had stopped, and an uneasy calm hung over the battle-ravaged pier like the last, lingering trails of smoke. Since none of his bones seemed broken he supposed he'd splashed down in the East River; barely less toxic than a dose of sarin, he imagined, but since he was still here, he guessed . . .

I did it, thought Felix, strength and elation rising in his worn-out body. *I actually came through in one piece.*

'Howzit, *boet*?' Hannah loomed over him, reaching out a hand. 'You damn nearly got your head sliced off by a couple of rotor blades, and then you nearly drowned. What's it take to get rid of you?'

'I guess I'm just lucky.'

'Charmed, for sure.'

Felix took her hand and let her haul him to his feet. He coughed again, chest tight with pain. 'What happened to the Chief?'

'Negged. Brains all over the windscreen when the copter hit the water.'

Should I feel glad? Felix could only feel dissatisfaction they'd got no intel out of him. 'How long have I been out?'

'Of the water? Or out cold?' She smiled. 'You've been sleeping an hour or so. Wimp. You're as much of a pussy as that *skollie* Kurt.'

Felix frowned. 'What'd you do to him?'

'Got him to talk. And then got him a doctor. He's being held along with Chessa and Coral.' She snorted. 'The only three people alive who'll be sad Deep and Manton karked it.'

'Deathwing lived up to its name even for them,' Felix murmured, wondering how Coral must be feeling right now. 'What did Kurt talk about?'

'Oh, real fun stuff. He said these thermobaric bombs have been sited strategically to cause maximum damage. Duh, big surprise. He doesn't know the specific locations. And we haven't found the one in Wall Street yet. Zane's ordered in special gear that can scan underground . . .'

Felix started taking a keener interest in his

surroundings as the awful flashes of memory began to settle into sense. 'Where's Zane now?'

'In meetings. He'll be back here soon to see what Brad's come up with.'

'And where's Brad?'

Hannah pointed to the wrecked terminal building. 'Using the heliport's wi-fi to hack into the Chief's laptop you saved for us. If it had gone in the drink like you, him and the whirly-bird, it'd be useless. As it is . . .'

Felix rubbed the back of his aching neck. 'It's still working?'

'So Brad says. Guess he's not our traitor after all.'

'Have you said sorry?'

'Like hell.' She grinned cheerily. 'There'd better be some good intel on there. Those *breekers* playing soldiers for Orpheus down here didn't know a thing. Mercenaries, most of them . . .'

'Fighting for money, not dying for the cause. I guess the Chief wouldn't trust them with the thermobarics' locations, or where Deep's left his stockpile of sarin.' Felix shuddered. 'But if Orpheus agents are waiting to tip that stuff into some reservoir somewhere . . .'

'Zane's talking to any head-shed he can get hold of, from regular army and ATLAS through to GI5 spook-handlers, pulling search and destroy teams together from different units. If Brad comes through with locations, Zane will lead the operation himself.' She smiled. 'No one can deny that Minos has made the breakthrough where the traditional units failed. The Chapter's back on track.'

Felix nodded a little hesitantly. 'Zane shot an unarmed prisoner to help get it there.'

'Oh, boo-hoo,' said Hannah. 'How can you be so soft? When it comes to balls, you've got the biggest I've seen.'

He smiled grudgingly. 'Did you peek while I was asleep?'

'Couldn't. Sore hands.' Hannah held up skinned knuckles. 'Kurt still needed a bit of persuading to open up.'

Sickened by the violence he'd lived through today, Felix couldn't muster a convincing smile back. 'I don't suppose Kurt took a call on his mobile during your Q and A sesh, did he? Only the Chief made a call when he knew he was on his way out. And I don't think he was calling home to tell wifey he loved her.'

'Neg on Kurt. But we don't know how many other agents Orpheus have in NYC.' Hannah looked troubled. 'They could still be placing those bombs, right now.'

'Nice thought. Guess we need to let Zane know.' Felix turned and limped unsteadily over to the burned-out reception. Hannah walked with him, supporting him with a hand under his elbow, as he stepped through the smashed glass double doors.

'Hey!' Brad straightened from hunching over a titanium laptop on the trashed desk inside the terminal and held out a hand. 'Here's our have-a-go hero!'

'Pretty cool, wasn't I? Or do I mean freezing.' Felix shook hands, glad to find Brad alive. 'Any luck hacking your way into Orpheus's files?'

'We're looking at full-system drive encryption with a

256-bit key,' Brad said. 'It would take a supercomputer a week to crack this – or me an hour or so.'

Felix tutted good-humouredly. 'Mate, if you're trying to trump my helicopter action with a bit of geekery . . .'

'Backdoor cracking,' Brad explained. 'See, it's easier to decrypt the code *behind* the encryption software and replace it with an override code so it translates into cleartext . . .'

Hannah gave a pantomime yawn. 'You ever think about getting a girlfriend, Brad?'

Brad grinned. 'Thanks for the offer, sweets . . . but I got standards.'

'OK,' said Felix, 'so what have you found out?'

Brad opened his mouth to reply when light, crunching footsteps on glass announced a new arrival. It was the Girl. She looked tired as hell, but animated with a nervous energy. 'Is Zane here?'

'Not yet.' Felix crossed to her. 'Are you OK?'

'Are you?' She placed a hand against his arm, just for a moment, then stepped back self-consciously. 'I'm fine. Just kind of dizzy, right now. Helping co-ordinate the evacuation, I've had to absorb petabytes of data . . . my head's so full of family names and statistics I feel like I'm drowning in them.'

Felix smiled weakly. 'Drowning's not good. Just tried drowning.'

'And then one statistic in particular stood out . . .' She hesitated, uncertain. 'It's Zane I should speak to.'

'I can't trump Felix's action-hero bit, but I bet I can

trump you,' said Brad suddenly. 'I know the whereabouts of the bombs. All twenty-eight of them.'

Felix, Hannah and the Girl all stared at him.

'Twenty-eight?' Felix whispered.

'Uh-huh. And placed at key points, just as we knew. There's one positioned under Penn Station, one under Central Park, the Plaza District . . .'

'So we can get them all now . . .' Hannah whooped. 'Job done!'

'And we need to do it fast,' Brad went on. ''Cos one of these thermobaric devices is bigger than all the others – and for a not good reason. In the Deathwing sales pitch our man from Orpheus says that if the scheme should be compromised, triggering this big mama will start a chain reaction that will initiate most of the others. We're looking at around thirteen square kilometres of the most expensive real estate in the world being levelled.'

'The whole of Midtown,' the Girl murmured.

'Well, which is the big bomb?' Hannah demanded.

'Give me time.' Brad was back tapping at the keyboard. 'I'll find it.'

'I think . . .' The Girl swallowed, her sharp features haunted. 'I think it's somewhere below ground in the World Trade Center Transportation Hub.'

'Ja, well, I think it's under Frankie's Meatball Shack on Bleecker Street,' Hannah retorted. 'Anyone else got any wild guesses?'

'It's more than a guess,' the Girl said. 'That statistic I mentioned. We've been monitoring all cellular and satellite phone signals in the run-up to jamming all frequencies. The Orpheus agent Felix brought down made a call . . .'

'I saw him make it, right at the end,' said Felix. 'In some foreign language.'

'With local telecommunications close to zero it was easy to get a fix,' the Girl continued. 'Whoever took that call was in the vicinity of the Transportation Hub – one of the first places to be hit by the sarin.' She looked at Felix. 'Now, Chessa is co-operating with our interrogation experts in the hospital. She claims Coral was given instructions that the Hub was their priority target.'

'Well, it connects all over – to New Jersey, thirteen subway lines, to JFK airport . . .' Brad noted.

'And it's on the site of the Twin Towers,' said Felix. 'It's meant to be part of that whole rebirth thing after nine-eleven. Maybe that's why New York was chosen as a target – to make a point that terror won't go away.'

'But this is just guesswork,' Hannah argued. 'Brad, you've got to find more than that—'

'I checked the bat sightings,' the Girl interrupted, 'looking for patterns. Each time a new wave has been spotted since the original mass release, it's been in that area. There are plenty of pipe subways and vents running close to the surface . . . I think Orpheus agents have been down there all along, reviving Deathwing bats from hibernation and setting them loose at intervals—'

'Keeping the city empty till they finish assembling their bombs.' Felix felt the hairs prickling on the back of his neck. 'That phone call the Chief made . . . he could've been ordering a suicide strike.'

'He knew he'd blown it,' Brad agreed. 'He can't hold the city and its people to ransom – but he can still destroy New York.'

'And if the big bomb's finished . . .' Felix stared around at his friends. 'It could detonate at any bloody moment!'

. . . 3 . . .

Within a half-hour, Felix stood in a thirty-strong throng of
hazmat-suited soldiers outside the entrance to the World
Trade Center Transportation Hub.

This is it, he thought, clutching his M4A1 in protective
gauntlets. Drenched in sweat, fatigued to the point of
exhaustion, he was poised on the brink of the final push
to save New York City.

Nervously he looked around at the station – a sweep-
ing symphony in steel arches, like a giant white waterfall
or the skeleton of some exotic creature. It was beautiful.
Inspiring.

Please, God, thought Felix, *let it stay that way*.

With time of the essence, this initial expeditionary
force to locate the thermobaric device had been
scrambled from several different units; but since the
enemy had access to an array of military uniforms, everyone here was dressed in the same navy-blue bio-suits with

two thick strips of fluorescent tape worn diagonally across their overjackets for clear identification. More troops were on the way, but until they arrived it fell to Zane's improvised combat team to search the underground labyrinth of the city's third largest transit system.

Hot, sore and sweating in his protective suit, Felix chewed his lip. He longed to tear off the heavy garments and rest. But all hands were needed. While ATLAS might now suspect the general location of the hidden bomb, finding it was going to be one hell of a job.

Lucky we have a secret weapon.

Felix looked at the Girl. It was weird, seeing her delicate frame wrapped in body armour and the obligatory protective clothing, just like everyone else present. With her freaky talent for total recall, she had already memorized the entire tunnel network and so earned herself a place on the team.

Right now, she looked swamped in the suit and as scared as hell. She was supposed to lead the way, warning of points in the tunnel network that held potential for ambush. In addition, if they encountered hostiles and engaged in combat, she was to advise on best options for cover and retreat.

Felix felt for her. It was a ton of responsibility, and a few of the soldiers were less than happy about trusting their location to a young female of no true rank. A few gags about woman map-readers had done the rounds – at least until Hannah offered to tie the jokers' balls around their rifle grips.

The Girl saw Felix looking her way and gave a nervous

smile. He walked up to her. 'So . . . How're you doing?'

'How'd you think?' she said. 'I'm not used to being in the front line.'

'You're the most important person here,' he told her. 'You'll be well guarded.'

'Whereas us three are only here 'cos these gas masks hide our age from the regular troopers,' said Hannah.

Felix nodded gloomily. Since Zane had been given command, he was determined that as many Minos agents as possible would be seen to participate and perform in the mission. 'We're not here for real soldiering. It's just politics.'

'Like we haven't done enough for the cause already,' said Brad. 'Jeez, my retirement can't come soon enough.'

Felix was starting to feel that way himself. For a while after his helicopter heroics he'd felt unbeatable, eachaching muscle a testament to his prowess and ability. And when his little posse had figured out the location of the bombs and the truth of the remaining threat, well, that was another pretty damn cool coup for the Chapter. The biggest, most audacious terrorist plot of all time, and he and his mates were all over its ass. It had felt good.

But now here they were, tagging along like kids being indulged by their parents. It was the adults' show now, even with Zane calling the shots. A Hazardous Devices Technician from the New York Police Department – Martin someone-or-other – had been pulled in, his bergen full of counter-IED gear, all set to neutralize the device. Some Australian bomb-disposal operator fresh from a tour in Afghanistan was also on the way and due to arrive imminently. Felix had asked for his own bomb-disposal gear, but the request had not been acted on; with the adult specialist on board he'd effectively been made redundant.

'You can see why the bastards placed it under here,' Martin was telling someone. 'The explosion will split the slurry wall around the foundations which hold back the river . . .'

'So on top of everything else the Hudson will come crashing in like a miniature tsunami.' The guy shook his head. 'First pestilence, then fire and flood, Orpheus'll be springing a plague of locusts on us next . . .'

Felix shuddered, and moved away with mixed emotions. He knew Martin would be a pair of safe and experienced hands, and he was glad to have the man there. But a part of him felt he'd earned a crack at disposing of this bomb himself. He resented being made to feel less capable purely because of his age.

Guess if today doesn't work out, you won't be getting any older.

Zane gave the order to move out at a run, leading the squad onto the spacious white concourse. It was creepy: where usually thousands of New Yorkers would be bustling along, today an absolute silence pervaded the sunlit station. The soldiers shattered the unnatural silence, clanking down frozen escalators onto an empty platform, marching towards the gaping mouth of a tunnel. Felix stared into its depths, relieved to find that the maintenance lights mounted on the wall were on, casting sickly white light into the darkness.

'All right, listen up.' Zane halted the party, his dark eyes barely visible through the visor of his gas mask. 'I'm breaking you up into sections, A, B and C.'

He divided the squad into three teams of ten. Hannah was placed in A-Section, Brad and NYPD Martin in B-Section and Felix in C-Section.

Brad nudged Felix's arm. 'Isn't a C-section when they cut a pregnant chick's stomach open to get the baby out?'

'Thanks for giving me something nicer to think about,' Felix replied.

'Section leaders.' Zane picked out a man from each group. 'Once separated from the main unit you will maintain radio contact by giving me situation reports every sixty seconds.' He nodded to the Girl as if prompting her. 'Our search route has been carefully pre-determined . . .'

'Yes. As we progress,' she said haltingly, 'we will need to check tributary shafts leading off from the main tunnel system.'

'And remember, we don't know how much time we've got,' said Zane. 'Any clue could be vital, any evidence of recent habitation: tracks, litter, foodstuffs, human waste, whatever. Set your weapons to three-round bursts. Remember, any hostiles we encounter may be dressed in our own colours. If you see any soldier *not* displaying fluorescent tape across his or her torso you will shoot to kill. Understood?'

'Sir!' 'Yes, sir!' The responses came in a rasping chorus through thirty voicemitters.

Zane jumped down from the platform onto the dead

train track. He held a helping hand out to the Girl but she refused it and swung herself down onto the rails. Zane directed two men to flank her on her left, while he stood at her right with a Marine Sharpshooter. All three new-comers were combat veterans with mouths as big as their reputations.

Here's hoping they live up to them, thought Felix, as he hurried after Hannah and Brad into the tunnel.

The curved expanse of concrete stretched on seem-ingly for ever, a dome-roofed underworld that rang now with the dull thump of footsteps. They thudded through Felix's head over the rush and wheeze of his respirator like mortar shells. To his left marched Brad, gun gripped hard in both hands. On his other side was Hannah, looking constantly left to right and back again like a child crossing the road. Forward and behind, the tunnel ran on: grey, blank walls and miles of dark track, like colossal stitches in an endless wound.

Zane called a halt and conferred with the Girl. Felix tightened his hold on his gun. It had got darker. He saw several of the maintenance lights were out of order.

'Deliberate, d'you think?' Brad said quietly. 'If there *are* Orpheus agents still down here, they could be waiting to jump us.'

Felix said nothing, just held his gun tighter.

Turning from the Girl, Zane directed a detail of four men to move ahead and take a side tunnel. Then he signalled the remaining body of troops to keep moving on the darkening journey.

Thud, thud, thud. They pressed on quickly through the gloom.

'Why would they bust the lights?' Hannah muttered.

'To set an ambush,' Felix suggested.

With quick-fire efficiency, Zane was detailing troops from each section in turn to explore stores and side-vents; these were the most likely hiding places for the bomb. The big man's radio was squawking like a deranged parrot as contact was maintained with each group. Each time it went off, Felix felt his insides lurch; and as the troopers rejoined the main unit, their search fruitless, he found himself checking and double-checking the fluorescent strips across their chests. The tension in the air was rising like the temperature inside his suit.

As they tramped round the corner, Zane called a sudden halt to the march; an older tunnel, stained black with damp and algae, branched off from the cavernous concrete artery around them.

'A-Section, keep to the main tunnel,' Zane commanded. 'B and C, we're taking this one.'

'It's an old subway tunnel,' the Girl revealed, 'damaged in the nine-eleven incident and never pressed back into service.' She turned to A-Section's leader. 'You'll find a service shaft on your left approximately twelve hundred metres further on that connects to our tunnel.'

'If you encounter hostiles before that point, we will take that route to support you from the rear,' Zane instructed. 'If *we* make first contact, you will give us support in the same way. All right, move out.'

Hannah slapped a hand on Felix's shoulder. 'Laters,

boet.' She nodded to Brad as she broke away with A-Section.

Felix felt a sick feeling of dread creep through his aching frame as he followed his unit into the cracked and cobwebbed tunnel. He and Brad were bringing up the rear now. The Girl and her three escorts were at the front with Zane, NYPD Martin just behind them. *Is there really anyone else down here? What if we're wrong about the Chief and his call . . . or what if the Wall Street device goes up first . . . ?*

'Hold it.' Zane's command crackled over his voice-mitter. 'Is that what the hell I think it is?'

Felix pressed forward with all the others. Low mutterings crackled into the air. Chills went through him.

A massive steel cylinder lay in the tunnel, a crude missile that could never fly. The clues to its construction lay scattered over the area in full sight, everything from welding equipment to raw materials – sheets of metal, oil drums and crates, bolts and rivets . . .

But it was the sheer, gob-smacking size of this bomb that fixed Felix's attention. It was as big as a small car and some way longer.

Martin pushed past the Girl and her escorts to stand with Zane and check out the steel monster up close.

'A-Section, we have located the device.' Zane spoke into his radio, his voice low. 'Split your group – half to double back and trace our steps, the rest to rendezvous with us via that connecting vent-shaft. Proceed with caution. Out.' He signalled five men to join him, including one of the Girl's bodyguards. 'You five, fan out and check the immediate area for signs of hostiles. Now, search detail . . .' He patted five more men on the shoulder, pushing them onwards into the tunnel. 'Go through this debris. Compile a list of what we've got here.' Finally he turned to NYPD's finest. 'What do *you* make of this?'

'Looks to have been modelled on the Russian Aviation Thermobaric Bomb of Increased Power,' Martin said quietly.

Felix stepped forward. 'That's the Russian answer to America's MOAB, right? Massive Ordnance Air Blast bomb.'

Zane nodded. 'Or "Mother Of All Bombs".'

'This thing is more like the *Father*,' Martin said.

'The Russian design is better?' asked the Girl.

'Way better.' Martin unhitched his bergen. 'You're looking at maybe a 14,000-pound charge of liquid fuel – ethylene oxide, possibly – most likely mixed with an energetic nanoparticle, such as aluminium, surrounding a high explosive burster charge . . .'

As the guy ran through the basics of the bomb, Felix found himself recalling a stream of facts drummed into him during his training: *Most conventional explosives consist of a fuel-oxygen pre-mix, but thermobaric weapons rely on oxygen from the surrounding air to give them more destructive power. The result is that on a weight-for-weight basis they are more energetic – and deadly – than any other explosive known to man. Crude thermobaric and fuel-air explosives were used in the 1983 Beirut barracks bombing in Lebanon, the 1993 World*

Trade Center bombing, the 2002 Bali nightclub bombing . . .

'. . . I'd say the overall explosive mix in this weapon would be roughly equivalent to forty-four tons of TNT going off,' Martin concluded.

'Comparable to a nuclear blast,' the Girl murmured.

'But the ATBIP's an air-to-ground missile,' said Felix, 'and this thing's been modified for *ground* detonation, right?' He pointed to a shiny metal cover over one end of the obscenely big device. 'I mean, behind that we've most likely got an array of firing switches and an anti-handling device.'

'Very likely,' Martin agreed. 'But first things first. If the liquid fuel *is* ethylene oxide, it has a boiling point of just 13.5 degrees centigrade. This bomb has to be kept cool; if the temperature should rise even a little—'

'*Hostile sighted!*' the sharp-shooter's shout of warning almost distorted over the radio-speakers – and a moment later the violent chatter of gunfire erupted into the tunnel. One of the Girl's bodyguards jerked and staggered as bullets tore into their flesh. As he fell he revealed a figure in dark hazmat gear – no fluorescent tape in sight – thirty metres off, blazing away with an assault rifle.

'Take cover!' Zane roared, opening fire himself. '*Incoming!*'

...2...

First, dash for shelter. The protective drill was drummed
deep into Felix's memory; he grabbed the Girl's arm and
hauled her towards a wooden crate a few metres left of
the thermobaric. *Get down.* Felix threw himself on top of
her. Even through her visor he saw the terror in her eyes;
or was it his own fear reflecting back at him? *Crawl into
a position where you can observe the enemy.* He peered
above the crate and saw two more figures, minus reflec-
tive strips, flit through the shadows. *Check weapon sights
are correctly set and—*

'Return fire!' Zane ordered.

Felix felt the recoil judder through his shoulder as
round after round spat from his rifle. All around him,
others in his team had reached whatever cover they could
find and were firing too in wide arcs. Felix felt his heart
pounding to the cadence of the gunfire as enemy bullets
smacked off oil drums and ricocheted off the walls. His

cover took hits and he ducked back down. The Girl huddled close to him, body trembling.

There was a second's lull in the shooting, and a piercing scream rang out from the shadows ahead of him.

'Hold fire!' Zane bellowed. His radio was squawking. 'Repeat, hold your fire.'

Several further bursts of gunfire reverberated around the tunnel. Then silence.

Felix peeled himself away from the Girl and, weapon cradled, stared fearfully into the gloom. He pushed out a long-held breath to see figures marked with fluorescent tape come into sight.

'Three hostiles taken down, sir,' A-Section's leader reported.

'All dead,' called Hannah just behind him.

'How about our casualties?' Zane demanded.

'A-Section still standing.'

The Girl had stepped out from the crate, and crouched now beside the body of the guard who'd raised the alarm. 'This man, he . . . he never stood a chance.'

Zane swore. 'Bring all the bodies here. Brad, search the hostiles for any intel on this bomb. Martin, what were you saying about keeping the bomb cool? Would a bullet hitting that thing . . . ?' He turned, looking for the bomb-disposal expert. 'Where the hell is Martin?'

Felix found him first – lying on the ground with a bullet-hole drilled into the facepiece of his protective hood. He tugged the visor free and his stomach turned as he saw the gory mess beneath.

'Dead,' he said simply.

Zane paused for less than a second. 'Then it's down to you, Felix. You have to defeat that device.'

'Me?' Felix fought to stem the tide of fear swelling inside him. 'But I—'

'Martin just left you his disposal tools in his will. Do it.' Zane turned his back on Felix and went on giving commands, both to the troops around him and over his radio. 'I want a barricade constructed around this bomb,' he shouted. 'There may be other Orpheus agents dropping in unannounced . . .'

Felix carefully unpacked the dead man's tools, sweating hard now. An unearthly screech of metal on concrete jarred his attention away; it was Brad and some other guy dragging a heavy sheet of metal towards him. Hannah was rolling an oil drum on its side to give them something to prop it against.

'Too low,' Brad complained. 'We need to angle it higher.'

'Crates over there.' Hannah pointed. 'With me. Shift.'

He watched them go, protecting the bomb and trying to keep him safe while he went to work on it. Suddenly everything seemed to be focused on him. He'd wanted a crack at the bomb, but not in these circumstances. It felt like he was caught in some weird dream.

No more politics now. This is survival.

Felix took the Goldman X-ray generator and placed it gingerly on the edge of the bomb's casing. He could scarcely conceive the colossal power contained within the thermobaric device, or even begin to comprehend the true scale of devastation if that force were unleashed.

He waited for the generator to power up, limbs heavy with dread, thoughts racing. *You've been living on borrowed time too long. Better hope this Aussie bomb-expert they were expecting shows up, 'cos if he doesn't . . .*

'No,' he breathed. He wouldn't listen to the nagging doubts. As ever, there was only one thing he could do.

Just get to work.

Sort it. Fast.

Felix took Martin's hand-held radio scanner and turned it on. As it pinged into life, the green LCD screen came up with five digits: 433.92. *You bastard.* The bomb contained a dual-tone multi-frequency radio-controlled trigger – which meant it could be detonated remotely at any moment.

'Sir, I've got to jam all radio frequencies,' Felix told Zane. 'The remote trigger . . .'

'Rest of A-Section approaching, sir,' someone called. 'All accounted for.'

'Right! As of now, radio contact is out,' Zane thundered at top volume. 'Any sign of hostiles?'

'Evidence of a camp,' someone called. 'Sleeping bags and provisions in a side-shaft.'

Felix reached into his pack again and switched on his ECM set. He waited in agonized silence as he stared at the indicator on the device, praying the light would quickly turn red in confirmation that it was jamming the bomb's radio-controlled receiver unit. Unconsciously holding his breath, Felix counted each second tick by tick.

A sonorous clang made him jump, as another oil drum

joined the barricade behind him. He turned in annoyance, caught sight of the section leader crouched beside an Orpheus corpse. 'Satellite phone on this one, sir.'

'Perhaps he's the one who took the Chief's call,' the Girl said.

'Strip him. He may be carrying written instructions.' Zane raised his voice again. 'Newcomers, join in with the building of this barricade . . .'

More scrapes and clatter. Felix fought to keep his focus. As the FCM's light finally came on, he breathed out in relief and took the X-ray generator. Carefully he scanned the cold steel casing of the bomb, studying its contents via the device's tiny, high-def screen: a radio transmitter . . . a digital countdown timer . . . finally, a magnetic reed-switch. Each component was linked to a separate keypad. The timer was the primary trigger while the other two switches were obviously designed to cause the bomb to detonate in other ways – either by movement, or by a signal from a 'third eye' anywhere in the world. Cutting into those components by mistake would end this task before it had even begun, so Felix took three small plastic adhesive glow-sticks from the pile of gear beside the rucksack, snapped each one to activate it, then placed the luminous markers directly on the bomb's casing as a warning of where to avoid.

He glanced up, wiped sweat from his eyes. The soldiers' barricade was building up around him like a monster's shadow, shielding both approach and retreat. *Never mind that. Concentrate.*

He realized Zane was standing over him. 'Well, Felix?'

'I've got to stop the timer. I'm going to have to cut in. Everyone needs to evac.'

'Nice dream. But we don't know if we're alone down here,' Zane reminded him. 'If we clear out and you get negged . . .'

'So we stay?' the Girl said quietly.

'I'm going to take B-Section deeper into the tunnels,' Zane told her.

'But with no radio contact—?'

'We've no choice. If there are any more Orpheus fanatics hiding down here, we need to find them first. Taking the grid as a whole, what are their most likely positions . . . ?'

Felix shut out the conversation, trying to focus. He marked the location of the all-important countdown clock with another glow-stick, wishing he could see its display. For all its merits, the X-ray couldn't tell him how many hours, minutes – or even seconds – he had left.

Tiny rivulets of sweat were running down into his eyes as he removed a rotary cutting tool from its pack. He switched it on, its whine muffled through his mask. He was going to make the first incision – but just as he began inching its spinning blade towards the casing, a voice suddenly screamed inside his head. *What was it Martin said? The boiling point of ethylene oxide is 13.5 degrees* . . .

He felt his heart slam, found his facemask was starting to mist up despite the flow of cool air. *If I'd cut into the steel, the heat might have ignited the fuel and* . . . He yanked his mask away, took lungfuls of dank, stinking air and peeled off his protective gauntlets. 'What are you doing?' The Girl broke off from her discussion with Zane, staring at him in horror. 'If there's sarin down here—'

'I can't work like this,' he hissed, pulling off his overjacket, his muscles almost cramping with the effort. *Focus! No more slip-ups!*

'Leave him be,' Zane ordered. 'We need to brief B-Section . . .'

Felix pulled a sports bottle from Martin's pack, took a large swig from it to wet his parched mouth and check the water was still cold, then carefully let several drops fall onto the steel case. Starting up the rotary cutting tool again, he began slicing into the metal, adding drops of water every few seconds.

It was a delicate operation, and a painfully slow one. Around him, still, the barricade was building higher. Each rasp and clunk of metal was like a knife at his nerves.

Hannah's voice carried. 'We're running out of junk . . .'

And running out of time, thought Felix. He pressed on, purposefully hacking his way into the thick steel until he'd cut a small, ragged square.

Time to know what's what.

Keeping his composure, Felix unfolded Martin's toolroll and removed a set of forceps. Then, girding his nerves against any more sudden bangs from the building of the barricades, he carefully pulled clear the small square panel he'd cut, exposing the countdown clock.

The world seemed to tilt as he saw the display.

Five minutes and twelve seconds left.

Oh my God . . . Felix's pounding heart felt like it was about to rupture his chest. Bile burned in his throat with a simple, horrible realization – *There's nowhere anyone can run to that will save them.* The explosion would tear through the network of tunnels with the heat of a nuclear blast. In the space of a single second he saw the Girl and Hannah and Brad, nothing left of them but ash-shadows lost in the maelstrom. Chessa and Coral dying in un-imaginable agony, their bodies blackened and shrivelled like dried leaves on a raging bonfire. Soldiers and peace-keepers running in vain as the world crashed down around them, deafened as the blast-vacuum ruptured their eardrums, or drowned as the banks of the Hudson erupted . . .

Five minutes, and hell's going to be unleashed.

...1...

With supreme effort, Felix forced his thoughts away from the horror. He had to defeat the bomb, and that meant carrying out detailed diagnostics of the circuit to determine exactly which wires to sever. Again, the dispassionate words of his training officer echoed in his head. *Never, ever abandon methodical procedure. No shortcuts!*

With clammy fingers he pulled out a telescopic mirror tool, inserted it into the cavity and confirmed the presence of the magnetic reed-switch that was securing the cover he'd just cut into; the same sort of switch you got in burglar alarm systems – open the door, break the circuit, set off the alarm. If he'd tried to open the bomb cover manually instead of cutting his way inside, the bomb would certainly have detonated.

He grabbed a different-sized screwdriver, reached

back inside and started carefully unscrewing the keypad that was attached to the timer.

Zane's shadow fell over him. 'Well?'

Felix didn't look up, his voice low enough to keep word from the Girl. 'Less than five minutes.'

The big man was silent for a few seconds. 'You'll make it safe.'

The keypad came free. Felix braced himself for some booby trap he'd overlooked. Nothing. 'Safe,' he breathed. 'That an order, sir?'

'It's a God-damn commandment.' Zane raised his voice, speaking as if nothing had happened. 'B-Section, get ready to move out. The rest of you, improve this barricade. If I blew hard enough I'd knock the damn thing down myself.'

That's right, keep everyone occupied. Don't give them time to think. Felix located the four wires leading from the clock into a maze of resistors, chips and solder on a board beneath it – the timer's sheathed wiring circuit. He checked the timer.

Four minutes and twenty-two seconds.

There is *no time for thinking. Come on, come on. Got to work faster!*

Adrenaline pumping wildly through his veins, Felix snatched up his scalpel and forceps and reached in again through the ragged hole. He gripped the clock with the surgical tongs and edged the scalpel blade against the first wire . . .

Then the blast went off. Fierce white light seared his vision, an ear-splitting roar hammer-drilled at his head as the shockwave punched him backwards. Felix was slammed against the crates and oil drums behind him, the tools jarring from his hand. *The bomb . . . ?*

Felix held himself rigid in baffled horror, his senses straining to catch up with the situation. His hearing was shot; everything sounded as if he was underwater – screams, shouting, the crash of metal on metal, the deadly stammer of ARs spitting bullets. His sight cleared enough for him to find a gaping hole had been blown in the protective barricade. *Oh my God, oh my God . . .* Teetering wreckage was still collapsing on top of the bomb, bouncing off its steel hull.

We're under attack. What was that, an RPG? If another one of those hits the bomb . . .

His body jerked back into life and he threw himself forward, snatching up the fallen forceps and worming on his elbows towards the bomb. How much time could be left to him now? *Don't panic, don't panic.* How could he not? He heard Zane bellowing orders, trying to regain control over the situation. But the words themselves never reached him. He had only one focus now.

And it told him New York City had three minutes and forty-six seconds remaining.

'Felix . . .' He started at the Girl's voice. She was lying beside him, scrambling out from beneath a scorched sheet of corrugated metal. She clutched her facemask in her hand, her bobbed black hair scattered across her bloodied face. 'They came at us from nowhere . . . A half-dozen at least.'

'I need another scalpel!' he shouted. 'Look in the

tool-roll there.' He crawled over, reaching out a hand to hers.

She located one of the ceramic blades and pressed its handle into his bare fingers.

Felix turned back to the bomb, grasped the timer again with the forceps. 'If Orpheus have got another rocket-propelled grenade, and they hit this thing . . .' He gasped, screwed up his eyes as a hail of bullets ricocheted off the bomb's steel hull. 'No! *NO!*'

The Girl stared at him, wide-eyed. 'Can a bullet detonate the device?'

'If it penetrates the hull, the heat of impact could ignite the fuel-mix.' Hands slippery with sweat, he took the scalpel and set about scraping away at the wires' outer coating, chips of whittled plastic flaking away. 'Or if they hit the detonator that could do it too.'

Three minutes and thirteen seconds left.

'The barricade!' The Girl screamed to be heard above the rattle and shriek of the battle. 'We need to patch the barricade!'

Zane was crouched behind a pile of rusty scaffolding, returning fire in fierce orange bursts. Heavy echoes rolled around the tunnel like thunder, he couldn't hear her. More bullets smacked into the thermobaric device.

'The bomb's their target!' Felix bellowed. 'Block their fire!'

'Got all the good ideas, don't you.'

Felix started at the voice up close beside him. But it was only Brad, crouching now beside the same sheet of metal that had almost flattened the Girl. He'd removed his hood; one lens in his glasses was smashed, and his half-smile was smeared with blood.

'Mate . . .' Felix stared at him helplessly. 'I've got just three minutes to sort this before we all check out.'

'Some retirement party this turned out to be.' Brad turned, began manhandling the makeshift shield round in front of the bomb. 'I'm on it. Good luck, man.'

Immediately a hail of bullets peppered the unwieldy metal. Brad gasped, struggled to hold the shield upright.

'Somebody help him!' Felix screamed, still working at the strands of bare copper wiring inside the firing circuit. Finally all four were exposed. He dropped the scalpel, peered at the countdown timer, blinking the sweat from his eyes.

Two minutes, forty-eight seconds remaining.

Still holding onto the forceps, Felix looked to the Girl. She was struggling to drag a heavy hunk of rusted metal towards the device, bullets whistling all around her. *Trying to fetch me more cover,* he could've cried at her bravery. 'Leave that,' he told her. 'Pass me the circuit detector!'

She turned to him, so afraid, so determined. 'What, where . . . ?'

'Black plastic box, there on the ground by the bergen, eight wires sticking out of it.' He glanced back at Brad, who was darting out from behind his shield to grab for one of the battered oil drums. 'It'll tell me which connectors are carrying the charge.'

She found the magic box, crawled over, pressed it into his sweating hand. He saw the tears in her eyes, held her fingers for a second.

There were two minutes and thirty-one seconds remaining.

Felix forced the detector through the hole in the bomb wall, held it carefully to the exposed wires of the firing circuit and slid the single switch to 'run'. The internal processor went to work. *Come on, come on* . . . Any second now the schematic would show on the little screen, telling him which wires to cut and in which order. *If we can just hold out* . . . The screen presented its diagnosis in simple black and green. *Two to sever.* He squinted, sight swimming. Second wire first, it said. Then . . . He blinked furiously. Was that the third . . . ?

'They've got grenades!' Hannah's high voice carried through the chaos – and then another thunderclap exploded with hideous force somewhere close by; the foundations shook and dust and shrapnel billowed down from the ceiling. Another section of the barricade gave way, undoing all Brad's efforts. The long-forsaken tunnel had become the battleground from hell. Debris rained down around the thermobaric. Brad shouted out in pain, lost from Felix's sight beneath crates and boxes.

'Brad!' Felix yelled. He jumped up from behind the bomb, glimpsed a black-clad Orpheus man jump and twitch in a grotesque ballet as ATLAS bullets ripped into him.

'Drive them back!' Zane was up on his feet, blazing away with the assault rifle. 'Don't give them time to throw another. A-Section, continuous fire . . . !'

The blistering cacophony swelled in pitch and fury.

The Girl screamed Felix's name in warning – he looked up as a stack of upright scaffolding poles started to topple free from the ruins of the barricade. He jumped clear as the steel tubes bounced off the side of the bomb with a colossal clang before battering the ground beside him.

To his horror, one of them struck the Girl on the back of the head and sent her sprawling.

'No!' Felix scrambled up as the melee raged on around him. He checked her pulse with bloodied hands, caught a trace, caught *himself* – 'What are you doing?' he breathed. *She'll be dead for sure if you don't do something about that damn bloody bomb—*

He realized his hands were empty. He looked around wildly, saw the precious circuit detector on the ground.

It had been smashed open by the fallen scaffolding.

'This isn't happening!' He stared in horror, struggling to remember – what had the schematic said? *Think. Think.* Another bullet pinged off the gargantuan hulk of the thermobaric bomb. He squinted at the timer.

Just one minute, forty-nine seconds left.

Felix grabbed the dusty tool-roll, rummaged through, found some snips. Second wire first, the detector had said – hadn't it? He reached inside, positioned the snips around the wire, squeezed—

His leg buckled under him. Felix gasped as a pain like fire consumed his left shin. He looked down, disbelievingly, at the blood spewing through the hole in his bio-suit.

I'm hit. Stray bullet. Ricochet . . .

'Felix!' Brad slumped into view over the top of the bomb, his back to their attackers. A livid gash ran the length of his forehead. 'Get up, man.' His words were slurred but fierce as he reached out an arm. 'On your feet and finish this.'

Felix took Brad's hand and tried to stand. He wanted to howl with the pain of it. 'Are you crazy?' he hissed through clenched teeth. 'You're in the line of fire, your body armour won't—'

'My other arm's bust . . .' Felix saw the anguish in the boy's eyes. 'This is the only shield I can give you now.' Another round of deafening gunfire, and suddenly Brad toppled towards him, his body slamming into the side of the bomb under the force of the bullets.

Felix ducked his head, shook tears from his eyes.

Fifty-six seconds on the clock.

He stared dumbly at the circuit. Which was the wire to cut? His vision was blurring with tears. Brad screamed, convulsing in pain, fighting to stay upright, to keep Felix protected for as long as possible.

Pick a wire. Felix held the snips up to the bare metal with shaking hands. Lost blood from his shin was pooling in the leg of his protective suit.

Forty-four seconds.

The gunfire sounded closer than ever. Freeze-frame images flashed in his head like tracer fire. Chessa hugging him in Mexico. Him and Brad in bat shit, helpless with laughter. Hannah's smile.

Please, God. Please, let me be right.

As Felix squeezed the snips he remembered the Girl's fingers on his.

There was movement, then a flash burned with white brilliance and the world exploded around him.

COUNTDOWN: RESET

The peace felt unnatural, but it was so welcome.

Felix sat in a wheelchair on Central Park's Great Lawn, the only soul in a sea of well-manicured grass. A thick line of bushy trees guarded the tranquil gardens from the iconic skyscrapers at their fringes. Felix stared at the buildings' glass-and-steel faces, turned to these alien green acres with stoic indifference.

Soon the people, the lifeblood of the city, would be flooding back in. It had taken a week, but the majority of the bats and their deadly payloads had been accounted for. Many had been weakened badly by their enforced hibernation and died soon after their release. Hundreds more had been deliberately poisoned by pest control across the metropolis, along with a ton of innocent creatures.

So much for the legacy of the Crusaders for Animal Freedom, Felix reflected. *About as little justice for the beast as you can get.*

He stared out over the meadow.

What about justice for Brad Rivers?

'Howzit.'

Felix didn't turn round. 'Hey, Hannah. How'd you find me?'

'The medical centre told me you'd chartered your own ambulance out here. Enjoying what you saved, huh?' She sat down beside him. 'I'm flying back to Poland tonight . . . wanted to know you were OK before I left.'

'I'm OK.'

'You will be.'

He regarded her. Unlike him – and unlike most of the combat team in the aftermath of the underground fire-fight – there was barely a scratch on Hannah. He looked down at his injured leg, which hurt like wolves were gnawing on the bone, and wondered how much physio it would take to get him walking normally.

And how much counselling to get him sleeping nights again.

Lucky for him, the explosion that had finally cost him his consciousness in the tunnels had been mostly light and little content. The last Orpheus fanatic standing had opted to go out in a blaze of glory, sidling closer and closer to the ATBIP in a suicide vest, hoping to detonate it with the blast on target. But the vest had been faulty; only the argon flash detonator designed to trigger the IED and the detonating cord had gone off – just as Felix cut the crucial wire in the big bomb. Recoiling from the small but powerful blast, Felix had smashed his head against the wall and – lights out.

If the bomber had made it through even a second before the snips were closing on the last wire . . .

We were lucky, he knew. The old terrorist mantra sounded at the back of his mind. *'We only have to be lucky once. You have to be lucky always.'*

The bomber had died of his injuries shortly afterwards. But by then, Brad was already dead.

'Saving the world twice in three months,' said Hannah casually. 'Kind of showing off, isn't it?'

'It wasn't me,' said Felix. 'Brad gave his life to buy me the time to kill that device. And we'd never even have found it if Brad hadn't got us inside the Chief's laptop . . .'

'A laptop which is giving our analysts top intel on the double-dealing *skelm* who gave Orpheus access to New York in the first place,' Hannah told him. 'All the other bombs have been found and neutralized – proper grown-up bomb-disposal experts took care of them, along with the sarin stockpile intended for the Tri-State water supply. No dramas.'

'I know.' Felix nodded, still brooding. 'The Girl told me, in hospital.'

'Is she out yet?'

'Yeah. And back at work, helping co-ordinate New York's great move back.' He smiled blandly. 'Life goes on. And you can bet your life that the Orpheus agent in ATLAS is covering their tracks even as we sit here. I've got to bring them down, Hannah. I . . . I've got to.'

Hannah put a tentative hand on his. 'It's not your fault Brad died.'

'No?' Felix glared at her. 'Maybe if I'd overpowered Manton back at the caves—'

'Or if Zane's cavalry had stopped him and Deep escaping, or if Brad had been able to stop that Doc Stevens guy from supplying the CAF . . .' She cuffed him round the shoulder. 'Don't spend your life playing "what if", my bro. Spend it playing "why don't I?"'

'Like, why don't I just forget it ever happened, the way you do?' She met his angry glare with a raised eyebrow, and held it till he broke off. 'Sorry. That was out of line.'

'No biggie. You're built your way, and I'm built mine.' She paused. 'But you can't tell me that despite everything that happened . . . the deaths, the destruction, all of that . . . there isn't a part of you that's feeling good right now. That's feeling hard as hell. Maybe even missing the buzz already.'

Shut up, thought Felix. He didn't want to think about that.

Deep down in his wounds, in his aching muscles . . . he knew she was right.

What has this job turned me into? Hero or buzz-junkie?

Hannah laughed suddenly. 'OK, that's way too much analysis from me. I don't do analysis. But I do like the way you're built, Felix Smith. One of these days . . .' She paused, gave an exaggerated sigh. 'Shame I had to bring wet-blanket Chessa along with me, huh?'

Felix started. 'Chessa's here?'

'Zane thought it was a good idea you talked to her.

Now Minos is back on track with extra funding, he needs more recruits . . . and more results. If this traitor in ATLAS was dealing with terror groups direct, Chessa might be able to get us an in someplace else. Help us to get the bastard.'

'To turn Chessa to our side,' Felix murmured. 'That would be taking something good from all this, wouldn't it?'

Hannah shrugged. 'Zane must think so. He's ducked out of some seriously high-level debriefs and generally avoided hogging the glory from our underground capers to talk some sense into her.' She gestured behind him. 'They're waiting for you through the trees. Want me to push you?'

'No, thanks.' Felix swivelled round in the chair. 'I've always pushed myself . . .'

She walked beside him as he cut through the trees to a shady pathway studded with benches. Zane, dark and broad, his arm in a sling, sat on a bench beside Chessa. She watched as he wheeled himself forward.

Zane stood and smiled warmly at Felix. Then he turned and walked away silently into the trees. Checking behind, Felix saw Hannah had gone too.

It was just him and Chessa – the two of them with the whole of Central Park to themselves. The calm, un-troubled landscape sat uneasily with his mood and the look in her wide eyes.

Got to start somewhere, he supposed.

'So . . . a long way from Doctores, huh?'

'A very long way,' agreed Chessa.

An awkward minute passed in silence.

'This deal you told me you made with ATLAS,' she went on softly.

'Chess, I—'

'It was one you made long before you met me. Wasn't it?'

He nodded.

'It's fine. I understand. You had to lie to me. You needed a result as badly as the CAF did.' She looked down at her lap. 'Was it easy to lie to me?'

'No,' he said honestly.

'Thank you for not . . . encouraging me. For not making it worse.'

Felix looked at her. In Mexico, fear had most often shown on her face; now something colder festered there. Loss. Guilt. Anger.

He'd worn the same look himself for so long after Day Zero.

'Coral won't ever see again,' she said. 'She'll most likely wind up in a federal prison hospital for the rest of her life. Your friend – your *handler* – Zane says that the trial will go better with her if I help you people . . . if I trade on my sister's reputation to get in with other extremist groups. Like, spy on them. Keep observation, or whatever you call it.'

The words hung in the crisp air; she spoke them as though the notion was fanciful. To Felix, such things were everyday, and as she looked at him, he saw that she knew it.

'Are you happy,' she asked him, 'living this way? Living a lie?'

He looked past her, at the firs and saplings, the little bridge over the stream, the leafy branches overhead. The skyscrapers couldn't be seen so well from here.

You could see the wood for the trees.

Hero or buzz-junkie? Is it so wrong to make a difference being both?

'Well, are you?' she persisted.

'Yes,' he told her honestly. 'Most of the time, I am happy living this way. But I'll be a lot happier when I've done more.'

'More than saving the world?'

He half smiled. 'Saving it's one thing. Working out my place in it is another. Know what I mean?'

'Yeah.' She smiled a little. 'Oh, yeah.'

He wheeled himself back a little way, gave her a probing look. 'Then I'll be seeing you around?'

'I guess you might be.'

Felix's smile grew wider. Then he swivelled round, propelled himself briskly away along the path. He went on in solitude, in the opposite direction from the ambulance he knew was waiting. *Not just yet.*

As he emerged from the leafy canopy and into sunlight, he stopped the chair. His heart pulsed a little faster as he took out a mobile phone and dialled an unfamiliar number. A number he'd been given in hospital. A number that needed no passcodes or call logs.

The Girl picked up. Her voice was quiet and careful. 'Hello, Felix.'

'I'm glad you can talk,' he said.

'How was *your* talk – with Chessa?'

'You're in the know, as ever.'

'That's what I'm paid for.'

'It went well,' Felix told her, with a bittersweet feeling. 'She's going to help ATLAS. And she thanked me for not . . . you know. Encouraging her.'

The Girl was silent for a few seconds. 'I thank you, too.'

Felix released a breath he'd not known he was holding. 'I was just talking to her about how best to find your place in this world. Seeing as you know everything, and all . . . Any thoughts?'

'One or two,' she said lightly. 'For instance, it's easy to find *my* place. It's on the Upper West Side. I'll text you the address. I'm there right now.'

'Yeah?' Felix grinned. 'Well, I guess I could visit. I understand the traffic is quite clear.'

'Enjoy that while you can. Today the city comes back to life.'

He nodded. 'I'm with that. See you soon.'

Felix hung up, and pushed the phone back into his pocket. He surveyed the skyscrapers above the treeline and the Stars and Stripes flapping in the mellow brightness of the sky.

Back to life . . . It's so short. So precious.

'Here's to starting again,' he said.

GLOSSARY

Types of IED – Improvised Explosive Device

CWIED: A command wire IED that uses an electrical firing cable so that the person activating the device has complete control

RCIED: The trigger for this Radio-Controlled IED is controlled by a radio link so that it can be operated at a distance

Cell phone RCIED: A radio-controlled IED that uses a mobile phone connected to an electrical firing circuit. Often the phone receiving a signal is enough to initiate the firing circuit

Petrol bomb: A hand-thrown device that contains a flammable substance. It functions on impact

Pipe bomb: A crude IED that contains either a high or low explosive in a metal tube that is sealed at both ends. The device is normally activated by a timer

Secondary device: The purpose of these devices is to target those involved in responding to an IED incident

Suicide IED: Explosive devices that are delivered to the target and activated by a human. The bomber deliberately loses his life

VBIED: A Vehicle Born IED that has some kind of vehicle as part of its construction. The vehicle hides the parts of the IED and can make an explosion more dangerous

VOIED: Victim Operated – these function following contact with a victim and are also known as booby traps. They are operated by movement

AK47:	Selective fire assault rifle
AMS:	Acute Mountain Sickness
ARS:	Acute Radiation Syndrome
ATLAS:	Anti-Terrorist Logistics Assessment Service
Bergen:	Pack carried by British forces
Black Ops:	A covert operation
Coalition:	A unified group involved in a military operation
CS gas:	Tear gas
DZ:	Day Zero
ECM jammer:	Electronic counter-measure jammer blocks communication wavelengths to prevent signals getting through
Fast-roping:	Technique for descending a thick rope quickly
GI5:	Allied Secret Intelligence Service
GPS:	Global Positioning System
Guerrillas:	Small mobile groups of combatants using ambush techniques such as raids to combat a larger, less mobile force.
Handrail:	The orienteering technique of following long, narrow features without a compass
IED:	Improvised explosive device
LDR:	Light dependent resistor
LED:	Light emitting diode
MI6:	UK's Secret Intelligence Service
Minos Chapter:	Secret wing of ATLAS made up of teenage agents
MO:	Latin, *Modus Operandi* – meaning 'method of operation'

M3:	Submachine gun in service 1942-1992
M4 Carbine:	Shorter and lighter version of the M16 A2 – assault rifle
M16:	Primary infantry rifle of the US military
Navy SEAL:	Member of the US Navy, Sea, Air and Land Forces
PackBot:	A military robot
PE4:	British plastic explosive
Pelican case:	Airtight and watertight plastic container
Pentanex 8:	Chemical explosive more powerful than TNT
PIR:	Passive infrared sensor, detects movement or presence by infrared emissions
PKK:	Kurdistan Workers' Party, terrorist organization
PMN-2:	Type of anti-personnel mine
RPG:	Rocket-propelled grenade
S10:	Protective gas mask, respirator
SAS:	Special Air Service
SIG 229:	Automatic pistol
TA:	Territorial Army
TEDAC:	Technical Explosive Device Exploitation Centre
Tetryl:	A sensitive explosive compound
Thuraya:	Regional satellite phone provider
TNT:	Trinitrotoluene (standard military high explosive)
TPU:	Timing and power unit
XPAK:	Explosives detection device
747:	Boeing 747, large aircraft

ABOUT THE AUTHORS

STEVE COLE is the author of the huge, best-selling *Astrosaurs* and *Cows In Action* series and has now written forty-eight books published by RHCB.

Steve has also written many titles for other publishers, including several *Doctor Who* novels, which have become UK bestsellers. He has also been the editor of fiction and nonfiction book titles.

Steve lives in Buckinghamshire, with his wife and two children. You can find out more about him at www.stevecolebooks.co.uk

Major **CHRIS HUNTER** joined the British army in 1989 at the age of sixteen. He was commissioned from Sandhurst at twenty-one and later qualified as a counter-terrorist bomb-disposal operator, serving with many units in dangerous situations across the world. He was awarded the Queen's Gallantry Medal for his work in Iraq.

Chris now lives in London and works as an IED consultant. You can find out more about him at www.tripwirebooks.co.uk